Praise for *Fatal Forgery*

"I loved the sense of place, with some surprising revelations about jail and courthouse conditions and operations, and an interesting change of setting at one point, which I won't reveal for fear of spoiling the plot. There was great attention to detail woven skilfully into the writing, so I felt I learned a lot about the era by osmosis, rather than having it thrust upon me. All in all, a remarkable debut novel."
Debbie Young, author and book blogger

"From the start of this story I felt as if I had been transported back in time to Regency London. Walking in Sam's footsteps, I could hear the same cacophony of sound, shared the same sense of disbelief at Fauntleroy's modus operandi, and hung onto Constable Plank's coat tails as he entered the squalid house of correction at Coldbath Fields. I am reassured that this is not the last we shall see of Samuel Plank. His steadfastness is so congenial that to spend time in his company in future books is a treat worth savouring."
Jo at Jaffareadstoo

Praise for *The Man in the Canary Waistcoat*

"Having read the first Sam Plank novel and really enjoyed it I was so looking forward to the next, and 'The Man in the Canary Waistcoat' did not disappoint. Susan Grossey is an excellent storyteller. The descriptions of Regency London are vivid and create a real sense of time and place. Sam Plank, Martha and Wilson are great characters – well-drawn and totally individual in their creation. The dialogue is believable and the pace well fitted to this genre. The novel shows excellent research and writing ability – a recommended read."
Barbara Goldie, The Kindle Book Review

"Regency police constable Sam Plank, so well established in the first book, continues to develop here, with an interesting back story emerging about his boyhood, which shapes his attitude to crime as an adult. Like the first book, this is not so much a whodunit as a whydunit, and Grossey skilfully unfolds a complex tale of financial crime and corruption. There are fascinating details about daily life in the criminal world woven into the story, leaving the reader much more knowledgeable without feeling that he's had a history lesson."
Debbie Young, author and book blogger

Praise for *Worm in the Blossom*

"Ever since I was introduced to Constable Sam Plank and his intrepid wife Martha, I have followed his exploits with great interest. There is something so entirely dependable about Sam: to walk in his footsteps through nineteenth century London is rather like being in possession of a superior time travelling machine... The writing is, as ever, crisp and clear, no superfluous waffle, just good old fashioned storytelling, with a tantalising beginning, an adventurous middle, and a wonderfully dramatic ending."
Jo at Jaffareadstoo

"Susan Grossey not only paints a meticulous portrait of London in this era, she also makes the reader see it on its own terms, for example recognising which style of carriage is the equivalent to a 21st century sports-car, and what possessing one would say about its owner... In short, a very satisfying and agreeable read in an addictive series that would make a terrific Sunday evening television drama series."
Debbie Young, author and book blogger

Praise for *Portraits of Pretence*

"There is no doubt that the author has created a plausible and comprehensive Regency world and with each successive novel I feel as if I am returning into the bosom of a well-loved family. Sam and Martha's thoughtful care and supervision of the ever-vulnerable Constable Wilson, and of course, Martha's marvellous ability, in moments of extreme worry, to be her husband's still small voice of calm is, as always, written with such thoughtful attention to detail. As one book finishes I am heartened to know that, like buses, another one will be along soon; after all, the author did say that there would be seven Sam Plank stories and I am holding her to that promise."
Jo at Jaffareadstoo

"Do you want to know what a puff guts is or a square toes or how you would feel if you were jug-bitten? Well, you'll find out in this beautifully researched and written Regency crime novel. And best of all you will be in the good company of Constable Sam Plank, his wife Martha and his assistant Constable Wilson. These books have immense charm and it comes from the tenderness of the depiction of Sam's marriage and his own decency. The plot revolves around revolution, murders and the trade in miniatures and there are some fascinating descriptions of Custom House."
Victoria Blake, author

Praise for *Faith, Hope and Trickery*

"What I like about the delightful law enforcement characters in this series – notably Constables Plank and Wilson – is their ordinariness. They are not superheroes, they do not crack the case in a matter of a quick fortnight, but weeks, months, pass with the crime in hand on-going with other, everyday things, happening in the background. This inclusion of reality easily takes the reader to trudge alongside Constable Plank as he threads his way through the London streets of the 1820s during summer heat through to winter rain, his steady tread always on the trail of bringing the lawbreakers to justice."
Helen Hollick of Discovering Diamonds book reviews

"The mystery at the heart of the novel, is as ever, beautifully explained and so meticulously detailed that nothing is ever left to chance and everything flows like the wheels of a well-oiled machine. And such is the great partnership which exists between Sam and Wilson that it's an absolute joy to see them continue to work so well with each other. There's an inherent dependability about Constable Plank which shines through in every novel and yet, I think that in *Faith, Hope and Trickery* we see an altogether more vulnerable Sam which is centred on Martha's unusual susceptibility and on his unerring need to protect her."
Jo at Jaffareadstoo

HEIR
APPARENT

Susan Grossey

Susan Grossey
Publisher

With grateful thanks to Dr Gerhard Prenner, Dr Gwilym Lewis and Dr Mark Nesbitt of the Royal Botanic Gardens at Kew – for their expertise, so generously (and unquestioningly…) shared.

And I hope that Graham Thomas approves of how I have used his chosen character name of Thomas Burling – the perfect name, as it turns out, for a fellow who is very much in the nice category.

This novel is a work of fiction. The events and characters in it, while based on real historical events and characters, are the work of the author's imagination.

Book layout ©2019 BookDesignTemplates.com

Heir Apparent / Susan Grossey -- 1st edition
ISBN 978-1-9160019-5-4

For Roy –
when it comes to beta readers, there is no better

The worst of all deceptions is self-deception.

—PLATO

CHAPTER ONE

A fine, upright, handsome man

TUESDAY 20TH JANUARY 1829

Despite my thick overcoat and Martha's large bowl of porridge at breakfast – which she had insisted I eat almost while it was still hot enough to burn my tongue – the cold of the morning was ferocious. By the time I reached Oxford Street there were crystals of ice clinging to my whiskers. Around me, people looked down at the ground as they trudged through the settling snow, while the wheels of the carts were muffled as they were hauled eastwards by snorting horses, clouded in steamy breath. So far, this year had brought us nothing but snow and ice, and the yellow hue of the sky suggested more to come. I hunched my shoulders and ducked my head, thanking whoever had decreed that the magistrate's constable must be shod in the sturdiest boots. But if I had hoped to spend an hour or two in the cosy back room of the Great Marlborough Street police office, I was out of luck. As soon as I climbed the steps and pushed open the door, office keeper Thomas Neale beckoned me over. I went across to his counter and, glancing down, raised an eyebrow at the floor covering that had appeared overnight.

"Yes, it is a pile of grain sacks," said Tom, plainly not for the first time that morning. "And no, it is not a mistake. If you had had to mop this floor as often as I have since this blasted snow arrived, you'd understand. The filth that you constables tread in on your boots – it has to be seen, and smelt, to be believed."

I looked down at my own boots and he was right. "A fine idea, Tom," I said, "and one I shall recommend to Mrs Plank, who makes a similar complaint." I took off my gloves, placed them on the counter and rubbed my hands together to warm them. "Now, what do you have for me?"

Tom looked over my shoulder as the door opened again. "You!" he said, pointing to the young constable who had just come in. "Stand over there – yes, on those sacks. That's it. Wait there until I'm ready for you. Don't you move an inch."

We constables might wear the uniform but we all knew that Tom was master in the front office, and I sent a conspiratorial wink to the young fellow standing stock still on a second pile of sacks.

"You wanted me for something, Mr Neale?" I asked.

"Not me, Sam – upstairs," said Tom, jerking his chin upwards to signify the rooms on the first floor occupied by John Conant, our chief magistrate.

I slipped my gloves into my pocket and made my way back outside. As the door closed behind me I heard Tom turning his attention to the other constable. "Now you – step over here onto these sacks. And don't you dare drip on my floor as you do it.".

♦

I knocked on the door at the foot of the stairs leading to Mr Conant's rooms and it was opened almost immediately; the footman must have been waiting for me.

"Good morning, Billy," I said. His proper name was Williams, but with his spare frame the nickname Thin Billy was inevitable, and to his face no-one downstairs at Great Marlborough Street could ever remember to call him anything more formal than Billy.

"Constable Plank," he said in reply, closing the door and indicating that I should go up. "An unexpected death," he added in a quieter tone.

At the top of the stairs I knocked on the door of the dining room.

"Come in," called the magistrate. He was standing by the fireplace, stabbing at the logs with a poker, and looked over at me as I went in. He was as lean as ever, with fine-boned features and the good posture that gave away his naval background. "Ghastly weather, is it not, Sam?" he observed. "Come: stand near the fire to keep the chill at bay." He put the poker down on the hearth. "Help yourself to coffee." He waved a hand at the pot standing ready on the table.

I poured myself a cup and felt its welcome warmth on my hands. After taking a sip I turned to Mr Conant. "Tom said you wished to see me, sir," I said. "A death, I understand. Not someone in the family, I hope?"

The magistrate held his hands out to the flames. "Not my family, no, but in the household of someone I have known for many years. A sad business." He shook his head and went to sit in one of the two chairs that he had drawn close to the fireplace, indicating that I should take the other. "Have I ever talked to you of my friend Captain Henderson? We sailed together on the *Beaulieu*, oh, thirty years ago now – in the Mediterranean. Fine chap – if a bit too fond of the grog." Conant smiled and shook his head at the memory. "I dined with him a fortnight ago; he was on good form and had quite a tale to tell. But today I have received further news from him that, well, it makes me uneasy."

"Young Edwards is downstairs attending to the early warrants, sir," I said casually. "I am in no rush."

John Conant was a widower and – with only his daughter Lily at home to keep him company – I think he sometimes felt the lack of a trusted ear into which he could pour his concerns. Knowing how often I relied upon Martha to listen to me and make sense of my worries, I tried to be sensitive to any signals that he might wish to talk. I sipped again at my coffee and looked into the flames.

After a few moments, the magistrate began. "Captain Henderson had a cousin, George Foster. They were close as boys – before I knew Henderson – and went to sea together. I met Foster just once; he died young, from fever in the East Indies. Many did, of course – I myself was lucky." He paused, perhaps thinking of those long-ago days spent in warmer climes. He continued. "George Foster had an older brother, Hugh – ten years older than us. His wife was kind when my own dear wife was dying and Lily spent some time at their home; we hoped that being in lively company with other children and their dogs and horses would distract her from the sadness of the sickroom. But Hugh and I had little in common, to be honest. He's about sixty now, a widower, and in failing health. He has a house here in town, and, out of regard for his long-ago friendship with his brother, Captain Henderson visits Hugh Foster a couple of times a year. On his most recent visit – about a month ago, perhaps six weeks – he found the whole household in turmoil after the arrival of an unexpected visitor. Hugh had two sons: the elder one died a few years ago in a fall from a horse, and the younger one – James – perished last year in the Cayman Islands."

"The Cayman Islands?" I asked.

"Pass me the Cary's," said Conant, pointing at his bookshelf. I knew the volume well; like many an old sea dog, the magistrate enjoyed telling tales of his voyages and the places he had seen, and often we would trace his progress in the pages of his atlas. I passed the book to the magistrate and he stood and took it to the table, leafing through the colourful pages until he found the one he wanted. "There," he said, pointing, as I stood at his shoulder. "Just south of the island of Cuba – you see that empty space?" I nodded. "The Cayman Islands are there. Administered by Jamaica." He pointed to the island to the south.

"What was Mr Foster's son doing out there?" I asked.

"The family has a plantation – cotton," he explained. "Hugh Foster worked there as a younger man, and I suppose the younger boy went to seek his own fortune. He was his mother's favourite, and when word came last year that he had died, she took to her own sickbed and died not long after. The grief has weakened Mr Foster, and for the past year he has been dying by degrees, nursed by his daughter – now his only child. Or so we thought." Conant closed the atlas and we returned to our fireside seats. I will admit that I was intrigued.

"Has a bye-blow scented an inheritance?" I asked.

Conant shook his head. "Hugh Foster has always been something of a Puritan, according to Henderson," he said. "A man most unlikely to stray from the marital bed. No: the unexpected arrival is his son James Foster. Back from the Caribbean."

"Back from the dead," I added. "But you mentioned a death: has he died again?"

The magistrate shook his head. "No: the family members are fine. The dead man is Hugh Foster's butler."

◆

Wilson reluctantly shrugged on his coat and then drained the last drops of warming tea from his cup.

"Perishing it is, out there," he observed unnecessarily as he opened the door of the back office and walked out ahead of me.

"Look lively, young Wilson," said Tom as we passed his counter. "It's starting to snow." He winked at me as Wilson muttered something under his breath and shoved open the door with ill grace. At the foot of the steps he looked back at me and I pointed eastwards. As Tom had warned, flakes of snow were once again falling from the leaden sky and my junior constable and I hunched our shoulders as we trudged down Poland Street. He remained silent – although, as I had learned from Martha, such a silence can speak volumes – until we turned into Haymarket.

"What I don't understand," he said then, as though we had been in the middle of a discussion, "is why we're needed." He put out his arm to indicate to a fellow pulling a barrow that we wished to cross in front of him and we passed in front of the Theatre Royal to gain a few moments' respite from the snow under its pillared entrance. We negotiated the slippery cobbles by the College of Physicians at the junction with Pall Mall, and then continued into Cockspur Street. "After all," he added with indignation, "an old man has died at home. What need could there be for constables?"

"Less of the 'old man', if you don't mind," I said. From the scant details passed to Mr Conant by his friend Henderson, I understood that the butler had been about my own age. "Have you heard of intuition?" I asked. Wilson shook his head. "It is a skill you will need," I continued, "but not all constables can learn it." I knew that this would catch his interest; despite his occasional childlike sulks, Wilson always wanted to show that he was the equal of any constable.

"What is it then, this intuition?" he asked.

I smiled to myself. "It's hard to put your finger on it," I explained. "You remember a few weeks ago when we had that tussle with those two cracksmen in Albemarle Street?" Wilson nodded. "And when we walked home to Norton Street, Mrs Plank was waiting with a bowl of warm water, ready to clean us up?" He nodded again. "Well, that was intuition: she knew that something had happened and that we would need her ministrations."

"I thought Mr Neale had sent a message from the police office," Wilson said.

I shook my head. "How could he have known anything about it? We went straight home and I didn't write up my report until the next morning." I stopped for a moment to get my bearings. "It's one of these streets on the right – Villiers Street." We walked on. "Some people think that it is only women who have intuition, but I think that's because it is the women who take care to listen out for it. We can all have intuition if we open our minds to it – and Mr Conant certainly believes in it. A feeling in your bones. And he has that now, concerning his friend's household – two feelings, in fact. Ah, here it is." We turned into the street. "Firstly, the son everyone thought was dead has returned, if not from beyond the grave, well, certainly from the family plantation thousands of miles away across the sea. And secondly, the butler – a man in his prime who apparently had never known a day's illness – has been found dead in his bed. Number fourteen; here we are."

♦

Wilson walked towards the steps leading up to the front door but I put a hand on his arm to stop him.

"We're to go downstairs," I said. "We need to see the housekeeper, Mrs Godwin."

We doubled back to the gate in the railings and walked down the steps to the tradesman's entrance. I rang the bell and was surprised to see a mature woman who could only be Mrs Godwin answer the door herself, rather than sending a maid. She beckoned us in and quickly ushered us into her room, which I could see had a good view of the basement steps and the feet of those passing in the street. She indicated an armchair and I sat down; Wilson, as is his habit, stood by the door and took his notebook from his pocket. The housekeeper, a neat little thing but no beauty, sat down, fidgeting, on the chair in front of the desk, on which were open two large books – at a guess, the household accounts and the log of guests and meals.

"Forgive me, sir," she said. "I was waiting for you and did not want the other servants to know why you are here – I am sure you know what servants' halls are for idle chatter and speculation. It was good of you to come so promptly. When I sent my note to Mr Henderson, I was concerned that he might think, well, to be honest I was not sure what he would think. But I know him for a compassionate man, and for Samuel's sake, I had to do something. And then he sent word that he had notified the constables." She put a hand to her throat as if for reassurance.

"Mr Henderson obviously knows you for a sensible woman, Mrs Godwin – not given to flights of fancy," I said. "Now, I am Constable Plank and this is Constable Wilson. And Mr Conant the magistrate has asked me to find out a little more from you about Mr Harding – Samuel, you said?" The housekeeper nodded. "Had Mr Harding been with the family for a long time?"

"Oh yes, sir, all his life, I should say," she replied. "He worked for Mr Foster's father as a stable boy, and when he grew into a handsome young man they brought him indoors as a footman. He became butler, oh, fifteen years ago now, I should think."

"When did you join the household, Mrs Godwin?" I asked.

"Four years ago this March," she said.

"Was Mr Harding a sickly man?" I asked. "In recent months, had he complained of illness or infirmity? Or had you seen any signs yourself?"

The housekeeper shook her head decisively. "Far from it, sir. Samuel – Mr Harding – was in good health.

He was still a fine, upright, handsome man." She blushed slightly as she said it and put a hand to her cheek. "By which I mean, sir, that he was more than equal to his duties."

"I understand, Mrs Godwin," I said carefully, "that the household has seen some changes recently – and not just in the past few days, with the death of Mr Harding."

"You mean the return of Mr James?" asked the housekeeper.

"And when was that, Mrs Godwin?" I asked.

"November last," she said. "The day before Stir Up Sunday. Not that the pudding was made in the end, as we were all at sixes and sevens with his unexpected arrival."

"Unexpected?" I repeated. "He gave no notice of his return – no letter, no message sent with a friend coming on ahead?"

The housekeeper shook her head. "Nothing that we heard in the servants' hall," she replied, "and according to Mr Harding they were just as surprised upstairs. But delighted, of course – a miracle, Mrs Moncrieff called it."

"Mrs Moncrieff?" I asked.

"Miss Foster as was," explained the housekeeper. "Sister to Mr James. There were five children in all, Mr Harding told me." She held up a hand and counted on her fingers. "Two little ones died before their first birthday – a boy and a girl. Then Mr Gordon – he fell from his horse just before I arrived, out hunting. Then we heard about

Mr James dying on the plantation last year – it broke his parents' hearts to lose their last son. Mrs Foster never recovered and we lost her soon afterwards. We all thought Mr Foster would follow her to the grave, but then Mr James came home. Maybe Mrs Moncrieff is right, and it is a miracle." Mrs Godwin's hand strayed to the crucifix hanging from a chain at her neck.

I smiled. "Perhaps it is," I said and waited for a moment before continuing. "Was Mr Harding pleased to see Mr James return?"

"Of course," she said swiftly, and then a frown passed quickly across her face. "We all were. Especially Mr Foster and Mrs Moncrieff. At first, that is. But a few days after Mr James arrived, well, it may be something and nothing." She stopped and looked down at her hands, clasped in her lap.

I leaned forward. "Mrs Godwin," I said gently, "I know that it is not easy for you to talk like this, but if we are to help you – if we are to help the family – we need to understand what has happened. Mr Harding would want that, I am sure."

At the mention of the butler's name, Mrs Godwin sat a little more upright in her chair. She closed her eyes for a moment, swallowed once and then spoke. "About a week after Mr James had come home, I went to say good-night to Mr Harding before I went upstairs – it was our routine, at the end of each day. And I found his room in chaos – the butler's pantry, behind the servants' hall." She pointed towards the back of the house. "Usually it was spotless – a butler is of necessity a fastidious man. And he kept the door locked so that no-one could disturb his arrangements. But that evening there were papers everywhere, all the drawers and cupboards opened, and Mr Harding was sitting on the floor – the floor! – rummaging through them as though he had lost something. I asked whether I could help, and he looked at me with such despair that I made up my own mind and closed the door and sat on the chair that he keeps for visitors. After a minute or two, he said that he would tell me what was troubling him as long as I promised to keep it to myself, and I did. I didn't say a word to anyone. But now with him gone, and so unexpectedly, I don't think I can keep that promise." I nodded but said nothing; once someone has resolved to speak, interrupting them serves no purpose at all. "He said that he thought that Mr James was not Mr James at all, but an impostor."

◆

"You'd hope a father would know his own son," said Martha as I sat back in my chair. She looked at my empty plate and then at the two potatoes remaining on her own, and wordlessly speared one with her fork to pass it over. I stuffed it into my mouth all at once, to make her laugh, and she rolled her eyes. "If you're hoping for this one as well, you can think again," she said, and then quickly ate the last of her meal. "But then," she continued, "you say that he had been away for, what, more than five years? A man can change a great deal in that time – a young man especially."

"And Mr Foster is in failing health," I added, "with poor eyesight. Maybe his mind is wandering."

"But still," said Martha, pushing back her chair and standing to clear the table, "a child. You'd remember your child."

"I'd hope so, my love," I replied, "although of course we're in no position..." I left the thought unexpressed; it was not the first time we had felt our lack of experience in this area and it would not be the last.

But Martha was having none of it. "I'd know Alice anywhere," she said stoutly, "even if I hadn't seen her for years. And little George too – I first saw him when he was a few weeks old and I'll know him when he's as old and grizzled as you."

I ran a hand across my chin – she was right about the state of my beard. And about the love we both felt for Alice, who was like a daughter to us, and the plump little baby who had come into our lives a few months earlier. "And the sister – Mrs Moncrieff," I added. "She seems to have no reservations. The housekeeper says that she's overjoyed to have her brother restored to her, as indeed she might be after her recent losses. She's a widow, with a young son, and in quick succession she lost – as she thought – both brothers and her mother."

Martha shook her head in sympathy. "That's a deal of sadness for one person; the return of her brother will be a great comfort to her."

"Aye," I said. "But if a person very badly wants something to be true, might they overlook anything that suggests otherwise?"

Martha was silent for a few moments, and I knew she was thinking about her own brush some months earlier with the fabrications of that charlatan John Buxton. "You're right, Sam," she said eventually. "And for the sake of that poor woman, I hope you'll do your best to make sure that no-one makes a fool of her. After all, she has no husband to protect her." And she squeezed my shoulder as she walked behind my chair.

CHAPTER TWO

Thoughts of mortality

FRIDAY 23RD JANUARY 1829

Wilson and I walked carefully along St Martin's Lane as the cobbles glistened with ice and a frozen stream of water gathered in the gutter running down the middle of the narrow street. A few hardy souls were out, looking into the windows and making their way gingerly from shop to shop, but the biting cold and the threat of more snow meant a lean day for most proprietors. Near the end of the lane Wilson glanced up at the number painted above the door and grunted.

"Number 148," he said, standing back to let me go in. I knocked the snow from my boots on the side of the step and pushed open the door. It was mercifully warm inside, but with the powdery, almost dusty smell common to apothecaries' premises everywhere. Standing behind the wooden counter was a lad of about fourteen, with pocked skin and rather lank, dark hair plastered to his head – an apprentice, I guessed. And behind him were wooden shelves and drawers reaching from floor to ceiling, with the familiar big-bellied jars lined up neatly, each with a label naming its contents.

"Do you dispense, then?" I asked the lad, pointing at the display.

He shook his head. "They're just for show," he said. "Some of our older patients like to see them, but to be honest they're old-fashioned. Your modern apothecary, now," he stood up a little straighter as he said this, and smoothed down the pristine apron that he wore, "your modern apothecary dispenses advice only, not remedies."

The door to the back of the premises opened and an older man – tall and spare, bald but for tufts of white hair behind his ears – emerged in time to catch this final remark. "Just so, Hawes, just so. I am sure these gentlemen are well aware of all that – the sign on the window does not say druggist, after all." He slid in behind the counter and young Hawes moved along to give him room, passing him a book as he did so. The older man opened the book to a marked page and ran his finger down it before looking up at me questioningly.

"You are obviously not my next patient – a lady of advanced years – and so perhaps you are here to make an appointment?" he said, reaching for a pen.

I shook my head. "We are not here because of your profession, Mr McNab, but because of ours. I am Constable Samuel Plank from Great Marlborough Street, and this is Constable Wilson."

"Ah," said the apothecary, closing his appointment book. "Hawes, the parlour needs tidying, if you please." He waited until the apprentice had squeezed out from behind the counter and closed the connecting door behind him and then turned to me again. "Now, constable, what is it you wish to know?"

"I understand that last week you were asked to inspect a body – Mr Samuel Harding, butler to a household in Villiers Street." I paused.

"That is correct, yes," replied McNab. "It was – may I?" He indicated his appointment book again and I nodded. He opened it and turned back a few pages. "Ah yes, here we are. Wednesday 14th January, first thing in the morning."

"Why were you summoned, Mr McNab?" I asked. "You are not a coroner, and I assume that Mr Foster has his own doctor for the family."

"Quite so, constable, quite so. But I provide care for those below stairs," said the apothecary with some dignity, "and Mr Harding was well known to me."

"Was he a sickly man?" I asked.

"Oh no, not Mr Harding," said McNab. "But as butler he had responsibility for all the servants in the house, and whenever I was called to see them, I saw Mr Harding as well, to inform him of the advised treatment and to settle my account."

"So he had not been unwell before he died?" I asked.

The apothecary shook his head. "The usual aches and pains of ageing – familiar to us all, I am afraid – but nothing serious. Nothing, as far as I was aware, that would have caused his death, if that is what you are asking."

"Indeed it is, Mr McNab," I replied. "Did you examine the body closely?"

"I did, constable, and I made notes." He reached below the counter and brought out a second book, smaller than the first. "My own notebook," he explained, leafing through it. "Ah yes, here we are. 'Male, aged fifty-nine, bachelor. Generally fit, with good muscle tone and upright form. Death sudden and silent.' The footman who slept in the room next door says that he heard nothing – no fall, no choking, no cries for help." He looked again at his notes. "There were no injuries. I palpitated the abdomen, feeling for growths or swellings, and looked inside the mouth for signs of poisoning, and checked the eyes for discolouration, but there was nothing."

"And so your conclusion, Mr McNab?" I asked.

"Heart seizure," he said. "Sudden and catastrophic."
He closed the cover of his book with a snap, for emphasis.
"In all, not a bad way to go."

♦

Wilson was quiet on our walk back to Great Marlborough Street and I guessed that he was mulling over what
the apothecary had said. Young men – quite rightly –
rarely think of how they will meet their end, but Mr
McNab and I, being of a similar age, know enough to
hope for a quick and painless death.

"What do you think we should do next?" I asked as we
proceeded into Wardour Street and passed the looming
red brick front of St Anne's Church. My plan was to distract Wilson and it succeeded admirably.

He looked across at me, a half-smile on his face, and
asked, "You want to know my opinion?"

"Of course," I said gruffly. "You know the facts of the
situation, do you not?"

"I do, yes," he replied. "A man who has been from
home for several years, suspected deceased, has returned.
His family welcomes him with delight, apart from an old
servant," Wilson cleared his throat, "I mean, a man of mature years, who thinks that the new arrival is an impostor.

That servant dies unexpectedly, but not in suspicious circumstances, some weeks later." We crossed into Portland Street. "Have I missed anything?"

"I think not," I replied. "And so I ask again: what should we do next?"

"It seems to me," said Wilson slowly, "that there is little for us to do. The apothecary said that the butler died of heart failure, which is sad but not suspicious. As for the son, his own father and sister say that they know him, and surely they are the ones most closely affected by his arrival."

"Affected?" I repeated. "In what way?"

Wilson shrugged. "I assume that the son will inherit his father's estate – and the old man is ill, you said, so these matters will be on his mind. And if the son had not returned, the money would have gone to his sister, and so the same matters will be on her mind. If they are both content for everything to be passed to this man, that must mean that they are satisfied of his identity. The butler must have been mistaken."

CHAPTER THREE

Every one a child of God

FRIDAY 30TH JANUARY 1829

I had only just stepped into the small banking hall of the house at the corner of Cheapside and Milk Street when the door leading to the partners' parlour and rooms beyond opened and Edward Freame appeared. He was as neatly dressed as ever and with the same open, welcoming countenance, although his hair had become speckled with grey over the years of our acquaintance – as indeed had mine. The senior clerk looked up from his ledger but Freame waved his hand at him and he bent once more to his task. The junior clerk – already on his feet – walked over quickly and took my hat.

"Constable Plank," he said with great dignity, "welcome to Freame and Company. Inclement weather, is it not?"

"Inclement indeed," I agreed, trying not to catch Freame's eye as I took off my coat and handed it over. "It is a pleasure to see you again, Stevenson. You are progressing well, I see."

In the manner of all lads he seemed to have grown about a foot since I had last seen him, but his clothes still hung loose on him and the best that could be said of his whiskers is that they showed ambition.

"Thank you, sir," said the clerk, much on his dignity and with a slight bow. "Application and dedication, that's the key."

"So I am told," I said.

"Come, Sam," said Freame, seizing his chance. "Tea in the parlour, if you'd be so kind, Stevenson – and a cup each for yourself and Mr Harris on this chilly morning. And if I am not mistaken..." the banker glanced at the parcel that I was holding and I nodded, "we find ourselves in grateful receipt of one of Mrs Plank's delicious loaves."

"Walnut," I said, handing the loaf to Stevenson, whose dignity was forgotten as he put the parcel to his nose, took a good sniff and grinned.

◆

The banker looked like a little boy himself as he licked the tip of his finger and dabbed it on his plate to collect the last crumbs from his slice of loaf.

"Martha will be pleased to know that it went down well," I observed, smiling.

"You are the luckiest of fellows in your choice of help-meet," said Freame, "as we both know." He inspected his plate and reluctantly returned it to the table. "But now to business."

I wiped my own fingers on my handkerchief and took out my notebook. "Your message said that you wanted to talk about Hugh Foster," I said.

Freame nodded. "I heard about the death of Mr Harding and so I went to call on Hugh, as I knew he would be deeply affected. Harding had been with him for thirty years or more."

"If I may start at the beginning," I said, "for my own understanding." The banker nodded. "How is it that you know Hugh Foster? You are his banker?"

"I am, yes, but first I was his friend. We met six, nearly seven, years ago, when he returned to England from his family's plantation in the Cayman Islands. You know about the plantation?"

"I know where it is," I replied. "Mr Conant showed me in the atlas."

"And you know of my interest in the work of the Anti-Slavery Society?"

I looked across at Freame. "Slavery? You mean Jamaica?"

"The progress in all our colonies is unbearably slow." The banker shook his head sadly. "When I remember how optimistic we were – how jubilant – when the Slave Trade Act was passed. But that was more than two decades ago, and still human beings are treated like cattle. Worse, because every farmer knows that to ensure the best work by his cattle, or to gain the best price for the meat, those cattle must be cared for and treated with compassion. Across the globe, human beings are treated ten times worse than cattle."

"But if the trade is forbidden…" I started.

The banker leaned forward in his chair and interrupted me. "Aye, the *trade* is forbidden, Sam, but not the *ownership*. And those families who have made their fortunes from owning slaves can see no reason why they should hand over what they consider to be their rightful property. Property!" He said the word with great bitterness. "Half a million slaves toil still in Jamaica and Barbados, Sam. Every one of them a child of God. It is insupportable."

"I will confess," I said after a moment, "that I am surprised you should befriend a man like Hugh Foster, knowing about his plantation. Knowing him to be a slave owner."

"Ah, but that is precisely why I value him so highly," said Freame. "He is the prodigal son, as it were. The repentant." He leaned back again. "Hugh Foster travelled out to the plantation as a young married man, leaving behind his wife and three children. The Caribbean, with its jungles and its fevers, is no place for English women and children – indeed, Hugh went out there to replace his father who had died of some ghastly disease or other. When he first arrived he carried on his father's work, and inherited twenty-three slaves." He paused to allow me to catch up as I wrote my notes. "Inherited, Sam – as you might inherit a horse, or a silver dish."

"How did Mr Foster's father acquire the slaves?" I asked.

"As I understand it," said the banker, speaking slowly as he tried to recall, "in the last years of the last century, we signed an agreement with Spain which obliged us to hand over and quit our settlements in the Mosquito Shore territory. Some planters resettled in the region, taking their slaves with them, while others returned to England and sold their slaves. Hugh's father – looking for cheap labour for his cotton plantation – bought a gang of slaves who were put up for sale in the Caymans. By the time Hugh took over, they had given up on the cotton trade, and instead were cutting mahogany."

"Not sugar?" I asked. "I thought the trade with the Caribbean was mainly sugar."

"The Cayman Islands are small and the land is poor – they cannot compete with the huge cane fields in Jamaica," explained Freame. "Instead they send mahogany to Jamaica and get goods in return – including sugar."

"I had no idea," I admitted. "I had heard of these islands – the Caymans – but I did not know that they supported slavery."

"I am not sure that they do, any more," said the banker. "I don't suppose you have heard of James Horne?" I shook my head and Freame continued. "Not many have, although he is a hero to abolitionists. He is a Methodist missionary working in the Caribbean; he calls Jamaica home but travels to all the islands, preaching against slavery, and with a deal of success. Hugh Foster heard him speak on a visit to Grand Cayman and was entirely won over to his way of thinking. Hugh was so determined that when ill health forced him to return to London – which was when I met him – he was resolved to sell the plantation and give the slaves their freedom. He left the property in the charge of an overseer, intending to put it up for sale, but he came home to a crisis."

"Involving his son James?" I asked.

"Involving his son James," confirmed the banker. "The older son – I forget his name – had died."

"A fall from his horse," I said.

"Yes, that was it," said Freame, nodding. "He had been a steady sort, according to Hugh, but the younger brother

James always fancied himself a man of the town – gambling, women, drinking. And when Hugh arrived in London he found the house in an uproar. James was in disgrace, with his mother insisting that he be shipped off to the Caymans, out of harm's way. And before you ask, I know nothing of the nature of the disgrace: I have never asked and Hugh has never told me."

"How old was James Foster when this happened?" I asked.

The banker paused. "Twenty, I should say."

"And this was six years ago – maybe seven?" I asked.

"That's right," confirmed Freame. "There is a sister as well. Catherine. She is a year younger than James."

I leafed back through my notebook. "Mrs Moncrieff," I said.

"By the time Hugh came home," said the banker, "she was living with a cousin in Suffolk. Her mother had sent her away, such was the malign influence of her brother. In the circumstances, Hugh felt he could not sell the plantation, but instead he sent James out there to take charge, with strict instructions to treat the slaves with compassion and dignity until such time as replacement labour could be found and they could be given their freedom. The poor parents hoped that a stint of hard work would put him back on the straight and narrow."

"And did James do as he was told?" I asked.

"He claims that he did," replied Freame.

I knew the banker well enough to detect a deeper meaning behind his words. I stopped writing in my notebook and looked up at him. "But you do not believe him."

The banker shrugged. "His father believes him. But I fear that Hugh's understandable joy at having his son returned to him – a son he had believed dead – is blinding him to all but that. I do not have the heart to suggest to him that his son may be lying, or worse..." He looked at me. "But perhaps a constable, charged with confirming the cause of death of a household servant and knowing nothing of the family history, might be able to ask a question or two."

CHAPTER FOUR

The old soldier

WEDNESDAY 4TH FEBRUARY 1829

On my second visit to the house in Villiers Street I walked up to the front door instead of using the tradesman's entrance. As I climbed the steps a movement caught my eye and I glanced down to see Mrs Godwin looking up at me from the window of the housekeeper's room. I nodded to acknowledge her and knocked on the door.

The footman took my hat and coat. "Mr Foster asks you to wait for him in his study," he said, and led me into a most singular chamber, shutting the door behind him as he left. It was a good-sized room, with light coming in from a tall window at the front of the house, and would once have made a very pleasant space in which to sit and read. But now every surface, every shelf and even most of the floor was covered in piles of books and papers, with ornaments balanced precariously wherever they could find the smallest foothold. Somewhere beneath the jumble I discerned a large oak desk with a chair pushed up against it, stacked high with ledgers, and near the window there was an upholstered armchair serving as a resting place for several more large volumes. I could not indulge my usual habit of scanning the bookshelves – which always reveal so much about the interests and aspirations of the owner – as it was impossible to move more than a yard from the door without risking dislodging a pile of papers or a stack of books. I waited.

After ten minutes or so, the door behind me opened and I turned on the spot and stepped back carefully to avoid being knocked. I saw first one walking stick poke its way into the room and then a second, and finally their master appeared.

"Hugh Foster," he said. "Forgive me for not shaking your hand, constable – I have to manage these blasted things."

I tried to squeeze myself into an even smaller space to give Mr Foster room to manoeuvre. He had once been a tall man but now his back was bent as he dragged himself forwards.

"Be a good fellow, would you, and clear the armchair," he said. "Move it all onto the floor. That's it. Is it clear, and just to the left of the window?"

"It is, sir, yes," I said.

With stiff-legged steps he jerked his way to the chair until he was standing in front of it. He dropped one of his sticks, felt for the arm of the chair and then pivoted into the seat, throwing down the second stick to join the first. "Hah!" he said with satisfaction. "My children tell me to confine myself to my bedroom but here," he gestured around the room, "here is where I need to be. I need those dratted things," he kicked out at the sticks, "but at least they let me move around my own house. It was easier when Harding was here, of course – he knew how to manage it all. My legs, my eyes, he dealt with all of it. Splendid fellow." Foster stopped and blinked rapidly then looked away.

"I understand that he is a great loss to your household, sir," I said. "Mr Conant and Mrs Godwin both said so."

The old man continued looking out of the window but nodded. "A great loss, constable. But he was not a young man. Much younger than me, of course, but still – a mature man." He turned and looked at me with eyes that I could now see were clouded with age. "But your request to see me, constable – it puzzles me. Surely there is nothing to trouble the coroner?"

"I do not act for the coroner, sir," I explained. "I have been asked to visit you by Mr Conant."

"And does he send you in his capacity as magistrate?" asked Foster. "Or to convey his condolences?"

I shifted where I stood. "A little of both, sir," I said.

The old man put his head to one side and smiled. "At least you're an honest fellow," he said, "but I can't have you looming in the doorway. Make your way over there," he waved a hand towards the desk, "and take that seat. Just move the papers wherever you can. My wife, I am afraid, was the clerk in this family, and I have been in a sorry mess these past few months. Now that James has returned, thank the Lord, I shall put him to work sorting it out."

I managed to clear enough space to perch on the edge of the chair near the desk. "Mr Conant mentioned that your son had returned," I said, trying to keep my tone light, as though I were not really interested.

"A miracle, constable," said Foster, putting a hand over his heart, "although I know that many would scoff to hear me say it."

"A miracle, as I understand it, sir, is an event that cannot be explained by facts and is therefore attributed to a divine agency," I said.

The old man steepled his hands and looked over them in my direction. "You know your theology, constable."

I shook my head. "I know my dictionary, sir," I replied apologetically. "Do you consider your son's return to be inexplicable?"

The old man was silent for perhaps a minute. "No, not inexplicable," he said at last. "If only his mother... She died of a broken heart, I am convinced of that." He paused again and I waited, not wishing to disturb him as he examined his memories. "She had a special fondness for James. She often said that she regretted allowing me to send him to the plantation."

"In the Cayman Islands?" I asked.

Foster nodded. "Indeed. When I came home in, when was it, October of 1822, I had made up my mind that James should replace me and oversee the liberation of our workers. I meant to do it myself, you see, but increasing blasted decrepitude forced me back here, and on the journey home I decided that my son would go out and complete this important work. All young men need an adventure, constable, but I had anticipated a battle with my wife over my plans – no mother wants the sea to separate her from her son."

"But there was no battle?" I asked.

"There was not," said the old man. "I wondered about it at the time – I suspect that James had been rather wild in my absence and Maria feared a scandal – but she agreed readily enough. Of course, when we heard that James had died last year, she blamed me and then God – but for the most part she blamed herself for not keeping him safely at home. She refused to eat, she would stay awake for days on end and then sleep around the clock. Nothing I could do or say, nothing our daughter Catherine could do or say, brought her any comfort. My dear wife died two months later, on the last day of August."

"It is certainly a great sadness for you all that she did not live to see her son returned to you," I said. "I understand that he arrived in London last November."

"The twenty-ninth of November," confirmed his father. "It was a cold and dismal day and Catherine and I were here at home, talking about Stir Up Sunday. We wanted little Arthur – my grand-nephew by marriage but more like a grandson to me now – to enjoy the celebrations, but neither of us could face the thought of trying to be cheerful with most of our family missing. And then, as though God had heard us, there was James, returned to us."

"And this was six years after he first set sail?" I asked.

"Just over six years, yes," replied Foster, nodding.

"And was he in good health?" I asked.

"He has grown into a fine man, constable," said Foster proudly. "A little taller, a little broader – and much wiser. Not the reckless boy who left home, not by any measure. I wish you could meet him, but he and Catherine are inseparable and they are from home for a few days, visiting cousins."

There was a snuffling at the door, then a scrabbling.

"Could I trouble you to open the door, constable?" asked the old man. "Orthez is nearly as blind as I am these days, and he frets if he cannot find me."

"Of course," I said, picking my way across the room and opening the door. In padded a large dog with long legs, entirely black apart from three white paws and one white ear, and a greying muzzle to give away his age. He swayed his broad head, scenting the room, and then walked unerringly to his master and sat heavily at Foster's feet. The old man scratched the dog behind one of his ears and the hound yawned widely.

"He must be pleased to have your son home," I said from my station at the door.

"To be honest, constable," said Foster, turning his head towards me, "I think Orthez finds it hard to forgive James for leaving him behind all those years ago – he's giving him the cold shoulder. Not that I mind; I have grown used to being followed about by this old soldier."

♦

I sat at the table in the kitchen, turning pages in my notebook and using my pencil to underscore important words and phrases from my discussions with Edward Freame and Hugh Foster. I sighed deeply and Martha looked round from the stove, wiping her hands on her apron.

"You've been huffing since you sat down, Sam," she said. "Far be it from me to interfere, but would you like to tell me what is troubling you?"

"Far be it from you, eh, Mar?" I said, pushing my chair away from the table and patting my knee. My wife rolled her eyes with mock impatience but came over and sat on my lap. She held her chin in one hand, her elbow on the table, and with the other hand she leafed through my notebook.

"Your penmanship, Samuel Plank," she said, "is shocking."

"That's not penmanship," I protested. "It's just my notebook – not an official report." I poked her lightly in the ribs and she squirmed.

"You've spoken to Mr Conant, and to Mr Freame, and now to Mr Foster," she said, turning pages. "Do they all tell the same story?"

"Are you questioning the honesty of a magistrate, a Quaker banker and a respected plantation owner?" I asked.

Martha carried on reading. "I didn't say that they are lying," she said, "but sometimes people see the same thing and remember it differently. Like here." She pointed at something Freame had said. "He thought that James Foster was sent off to the plantation in disgrace – that's the word he used?" I nodded. "But here, the father suggests that it's all part of a scheme to give the boy an adventure."

I shrugged. "But that's natural, surely, for a father to see the best in his son and to overlook the more unpleasant details."

Martha looked over her shoulder at me. "Of course it is, Sam, but you're not the lad's father and you can't overlook any details. You have to sift through what people remember and what they say, and what they forget and what they don't say, to work out what actually happened."

"So tell me then, Martha Plank," I said, leaning up to kiss her on the cheek, "if this is you not interfering, just what might actual interfering look like?"

CHAPTER FIVE

A pie at midnight

SUNDAY 15TH FEBRUARY 1829

"Sam! Wake up, Sam!" I was pulled from a warm sleep by Martha shaking my shoulder and hissing into my ear. "There's someone at the back door." With that, she gave me a push and then pulled the covers more tightly around herself. A constable's wife learns quickly that bad news comes to the front door, while work goes to the back. I picked up my dressing gown from where I had flung it over the bed the previous evening and shrugged it on as I went downstairs, cursing as I caught the point of my elbow on the doorframe. I felt my way through the dark kitchen to the back door where indeed there was someone tapping on it.

"Who is it?" I called quietly.

"Dawson," came the reply. "Mr Conant's coachman. And Miss Lily."

I quickly pulled open the door and standing in the back yard, lit dimly by the lamp-post in the street, were Fred Dawson and Miss Lily Conant, the former hunched in his greatcoat, his hat gripped in his hands, and the latter with her cloak clutched about her. I ushered them into the kitchen and lit the lamp before going to the foot of the stairs and calling up to my wife. When I returned, Miss Lily was perched on one of our chairs while Dawson was hovering near the door.

"Come on, Fred," I said. "Stand closer to the stove – there's some warmth left in it. Martha will be down in a moment and she'll know what to do." I could see his shoulders sag a little. A lifelong bachelor with a good heart, he was out of his depth dealing with a young woman who – I could now see – was distressed and had been crying. Usually poised and beautiful, with her late mother's fine appearance and her proud father's quick intellect, tonight Miss Lily looked like a frightened child. Martha appeared, her hair hastily gathered up under a cap and a woollen shawl thrown around her shoulders, and took in the scene with a single glance.

"Good evening, Fred," she said, as though finding the coachman in our kitchen at midnight were the most normal thing in the world. "You look chilled through. Hang up your hat and coat and put a couple of logs into the stove, would you, and we'll heat some water for a hot drink." As Fred did as he was told, grateful to hand over control to my wife, Martha turned now to Miss Lily. "And you, young lady, are dressed for a ballroom and not for a winter night in my kitchen. Come with me and we'll tidy you up a little."

The two women left us and after a moment we heard them walking overhead in the bedroom. I pulled out a chair and pointed to it, and the coachman all but collapsed into it.

"Well, now, Fred," I said.

"Well, now, Sam," he echoed. "What a to do this is." He looked at me and I nodded. "It's – well, it was – St Valentine's Day, and Miss Lily was invited to a rout hosted by Mrs Moncrieff, at Villiers Street. It seems she was keen to reintroduce her brother James Foster – the young fellow just back from the Caribbean." Something in the way the coachman said the man's name made me feel uneasy. "Mr Conant told me to take Miss Lily and to wait to bring her home; he was looking forward to a quiet night with his books." Everyone in the Conant household knew that the magistrate doted on his high-spirited daughter and took great solace in her intelligent company, but was grateful for the occasional peaceful evening alone by his fireside. The coachman stopped and seemed not to know how to continue.

"Was Miss Lily looking forward to the rout?" I asked.

"Oh yes," said Fred, with a tone of regret. "She was full of smiles when we pulled up at the house. Told me to come back three hours later – always thinking of others, Miss Lily. She didn't want me waiting in the cold and knew I could get a bite to eat and a hot drink nearby." He shook his head sadly.

"And when you returned?" I prompted.

"It had just gone eleven and a few were already leaving," said the coachman. "I had been waiting for a little while – ten minutes, no more – when Miss Lily appeared, but not at the front door. She came up the steps from the tradesman's entrance, looked around – like a rabbit peeping out of its burrow – and when she saw me she dashed over and all but threw herself into the coach. I looked in to ask if she was ill and she was crying. When she put her hand to her reticule to find a handkerchief I could see that she was trembling. I asked if she wanted to come here and she said yes. It was the only place I could think of, with you having a wife. I couldn't have the master seeing her like that and there's no mother..." Fred's voice trailed off miserably.

"Were there any signs of injury?" I asked, keeping my voice as neutral as I could. "Or interference?"

The coachman looked levelly at me. He was of my own age and I knew that he had been part of the Conant household since before Miss Lily was born. She may have lost her mother, but there was no shortage of people who cared for her. "The same thought crossed my own mind," he replied after a moment. "I looked at her skirts as I tucked a blanket around her and could see no dirt or... anything else. Her gloves were clean but her hair was a bit..." Fred put a hand to his own head and twirled the fingers to suggest untidiness.

Just then I heard the two women coming down the stairs and I put a warning finger to my lips. Miss Lily, walking into the kitchen behind Martha, looked more like her usual self; her head was held high and she looked over at me with a smile. It was a rather weak one, if I am honest, but a smile is a smile. Her face had been washed, taking away the traces of her tears, and her hair was pinned up neatly again. I patted the chair next to me.

"Come and sit beside me, Miss Lily," I said. "The stove is warming well and I daresay Mrs Plank intends to fill us all to the brim with tea."

"And what is wrong with that, Samuel?" asked Martha in a jovial tone that I knew was for the benefit of our young guest. "I have yet to hear you complain at being handed a cup of tea and a piece of apple pie."

"Apple pie!" I said, sitting up a little straighter. "We didn't know there was apple pie in the house, did we, Fred, otherwise we'd have pinched it."

The coachman followed my lead and nodded. "Indeed, Sam – pinched the lot."

Martha busied herself at the stove, heating the water for the pot. She collected the pie from the larder, wrapped in a cloth, and put it on the table, handing me the knife. "Four decent slices, Sam, but leave some for Constable Wilson and Alice – they're calling round tomorrow with little George," she said, picking up four plates from the dresser and handing them to Fred.

"How old is George now, Mrs Plank?" asked Miss Lily, sipping her tea but leaving her pie untouched when Fred put it in front of her.

"Five months, and there never was a more contented fellow," said Martha proudly. "You'd never know that Alice isn't his real mother – they couldn't dote on each other more." She reached across the table, picked up Miss Lily's fork and handed it to her. "Just a bite, there's a good girl."

Miss Lily broke off a small piece of pie with the fork and put it into her mouth, and then smiled. "Mrs Plank, this pie is delicious. Quite the match of any I have tasted."

"It's just an apple pie, miss," said Martha, but I could tell she was pleased.

We talked of this and that and nothing much until I looked at Miss Lily's plate and the pie had gone. The watchman went past, calling one, and I looked at Martha, and she nodded.

"Now then, Miss Lily," I said, "it's high time you were in your bed. Your father will be waiting up for you, although he will pretend to be reading when you come in."

Miss Lily laughed. "That's true, constable – it's the same every time. He'll be asleep in his chair, snoring away, and wake only when I shake him." She stood and stretched and yawned, clapping a hand over her mouth when she realised that we were looking at her. "Oh, I am sorry, Mrs Plank – how rude of me. But Constable Plank is right: I am very tired."

"Then home we shall head, Miss Lily," said Fred, putting on his coat and taking hold of his hat.

"Thank you again, Mrs Plank," said our young visitor, putting her hand on Martha's arm. "You have been so kind."

♦

Ten minutes later Martha and I were back in our own bed. I flinched as she pressed her chilled feet to me – although such is the lot, I fear, of husbands through the centuries.

"I could grow used to a slice of apple pie in the middle of the night, to keep me going," I said.

Martha poked me gently in the gut. "You don't need any more pie, Sam, but I knew Miss Lily wouldn't eat unless we did."

"Did she tell you what had happened, Mar?" I asked.

My wife moved a little away from me and we looked at each other in the dim light.

"Nothing too dreadful, Sam," she said. "Miss Lily might not have a mother to explain things to her – to tell her what to expect from marriage – but she has spent long enough in her father's rooms at Great Marlborough Street to know something of the ways of the world."

"Aye," I said. "Mr Conant tries to shield her from it, but she's a bright and curious girl." I paused for a moment. "Fred thought she was upset and perhaps a little frightened, but nothing more."

"And he was right," said Martha. "It seems that a fellow at the rout – a Mr Foster – is a guzzle guts, and forgot his manners. He cornered Miss Lily in a parlour and tried to kiss her but she stamped on his foot and made good her escape."

"He's lucky that's all she did," I said. "There are softer targets on a man than his feet."

"You can stop growling, Sam," said Martha. "Miss Lily was chilled from waiting downstairs at Villiers Street, and a bit cross at herself for not being more canny, but there's no lasting harm. And it will have done Mr Foster good to learn that no young lady of consequence will be swayed by his boasts about the fortune he intends to inherit. Miss Lily didn't want to embarrass her hostess by reappearing in company with her hair awry, and so she crept down into the servants' hall and gave a maid a penny to retrieve her cloak from upstairs."

"That explains why Fred saw her at the tradesman's steps," I said. "Foster said he would be inheriting a fortune, did he?"

"Mmm," said Martha, turning from me and pulling my arm across her. "If a man in his cups can be believed. Sleep now, Sam."

CHAPTER SIX

Dull religion and exciting adventures

MONDAY 2ND MARCH 1829

I put my head outside the back door and sniffed. "No need for my gloves today," I said. "That's spring I can smell."

Martha took the gloves from me and smiled. "You've lived in London all your life, and your father before you – what do you know about the smell of spring?" she asked.

I stepped back indoors and slipped my arm around my wife's waist, pulling her to me. "I know that it's not half as sweet as the smell right here," I said, bending to kiss her neck.

"For heaven's sake, Sam," she said, pushing me away, "what will William think?"

"Wilson?" I said, puzzled. "What is it to do with him?"

"Behind you," she said, pointing. And indeed my junior constable was standing in the doorframe, twisting his hat in his hands and looking anywhere but at us.

I cleared my throat. "He will think that I am a lucky man to be married to such a beauty," I said – rather smoothly, I thought.

"You do talk some nonsense, Samuel Plank," said Martha, handing me my own hat, but I could tell from the flush in her cheeks that she was pleased.

♦

Wilson and I set off down the road on our usual route to Great Marlborough Street. He was as quiet as ever but he did whistle to himself, almost under his breath – a sure sign that he was uneasy about something. We were almost at the market and only a few minutes from our destination when he spoke.

"I think I would like to be a lucky man too," he said. "Like you. Married."

"Ah," I said, pausing to let a coach roll past on its way into the city. "I suppose you are of an age to be thinking of it."

"Twenty-four, sir," said Wilson, "and Alice is nearly eighteen now."

That surprised me – I still thought of her as a young girl of perhaps fifteen. Martha had been eighteen when we married.

"I told you of my plans last year," Wilson continued stoutly, perhaps mistaking my silence for disapproval.

We crossed the road together and ducked into Blenheim Street. "I think a little more air would be beneficial before we face the morning's business," I said, deliberately turning away from the police office. There is little point in expecting a man to work well when his mind is on other matters. We turned down Poland Street, past the lodge of the workhouse, and after a few minutes we found ourselves in Golden Square. The gate to the garden was open and I went in, Wilson following me without comment. We sat on a bench, the sound of a piano being tuned floating down to us from the open windows of Stodart's at number one.

We both gazed around the small garden and Wilson started to speak. "When I told you of my plans, in November last, you asked me whether I was sure that Alice would make me a good wife. And I am. I've been watching her, how she is with little George, and how she is with you and Mrs Plank, and she's nothing but kind and loving and gentle."

"There's no doubt about that, lad," I said. "My concern was only that Alice is, well, perhaps not very robust. She will need a strong husband – strong in his body and strong in his heart – to lean on. And that husband will need to not mind being leaned on."

Wilson shifted on the bench beside me and sat more upright. "I am used to that, sir," he said. "I've been the man of the house since I was fifteen." He reached into a pocket and pulled out a rather tattered piece of paper, which he unfolded and handed to me. "These are my reckonings. I had that pay rise in January, and I've taken those rooms I told you about – in the same building as my mother. Janey has started sewing at the same place as Sally so they're both bringing money home, and I'll add five shillings a week to that. This is my wages coming in, then that's the rent and the money for my mother," with each he pointed at a figure on the paper I was holding, "which leaves this for living on – for me, Alice and George. It won't be a life of luxury, but we'll manage. And if I work hard and steady, I'll get more pay rises. They were talking in the office about this new police force." He looked at me as he said this.

"Indeed," I said. "A new police force for the metropolis."

"Will you be signing up?" Wilson asked.

I shook my head. "Too set in my ways for that. They won't want a square toes like me."

"I think you're wrong, sir, if you'll permit me," said Wilson. "They will need experienced men to look after all the new recruits: the force is new, but the work is what we've been doing for years, you and me."

I glanced at him; thoughts of marriage had certainly made him more opinionated.

"We shall see," I said, "but for now we are discussing the end of your bachelor days." I folded up his page of calculations and handed it back to him. "Have you asked Alice?"

Wilson shook his head. "She knows that I am very fond of her, and of little George, and I think that she has hopes for us being a proper family one day. But," and here he straightened his shoulders, swallowed hard and turned to face me, "you're the closest thing to a father that Alice has, and it is only right that I ask your permission to marry her."

I made sure not to smile; I could remember only too clearly the prickling of sweat I had felt down my own collar when I had asked Martha's father for her hand – and he was just a worthless toper who would have given his permission to any fellow who sweetened the request with a few coins to spend on booze. I stood and held out my hand; Wilson likewise stood and shook it.

"You are a good-hearted man, Wilson, and I know that you will care for Alice and for George. If she makes you half as happy as Mrs Plank has made me, you can count yourself the luckiest of men."

♦

"What's the joke?" asked Tom Neale, jerking his head at Wilson. My junior constable had smiled all the way to Great Marlborough Street and was still grinning as he headed down the corridor towards the privy.

"He is going to be married," I explained.

"Marriage is no laughing matter," said the office keeper grimly. None of us had met the fearsome Mrs Neale but Tom's tales of her temper were legendary. "Is his intended a fiery woman, a woman who knows her own mind and is not afraid to tell him about it, whether he asks or no?" Tom shuddered.

I shook my head. "It is young Alice – you remember her. Most certainly not fiery. And if she does know her own mind, she's keeping it to herself."

"An excellent choice, in that case," said Tom. He leaned under his counter and retrieved a note which he handed to me. "This was delivered for you, about an hour ago."

I thanked him and walked down the corridor to the back office, hanging up my coat and hat before breaking the seal on the folded note – the black wax prepared me for the worst. It was from Mrs Godwin, the housekeeper at Villiers Street. Her handwriting was neat and precise, but some smudging betrayed the haste with which the missive had been written and sent.

"Constable Plank," it said, "I hope you will forgive this request direct to you. The master – Mr Foster – died last night and I fear that all is not as it seems. If you can find a reason to come to the house, I can explain further. Yours respectfully, Elizabeth Godwin (Mrs)."

I sighed and put my hat and coat back on.

♦

As on my first visit to the house in Villiers Street, I used the tradesman's entrance and knocked on the door to the servants' hall. A silent maid with a tear-stained face let me in and showed me to the housekeeper's room; Mrs Godwin herself was sitting in her armchair, a handkerchief to her eyes.

"Constable Plank," she said, getting to her feet. "Tea, Mary, if you please," she said to the maid, who sniffed loudly. Mrs Godwin felt in her own pocket and drew out another handkerchief which she handed to Mary. "Don't sniff, girl – blow and wipe," she said, but with kindness. The maid nodded and returned to the kitchen. The housekeeper gestured to a chair and I sat down.

"I am sorry for your loss, Mrs Godwin," I said. "I can see that you were all fond of Mr Foster."

"He was a good master, constable," she said, returning to her own seat. "For the years that I knew him, at least. He returned from the Caribbean a changed man, I'm told

– gentler, and more patient. I never spoke to him of it, of course, and it was before my time, but Mr Harding said that the master saw terrible things on the plantation that made him change his own ways." She dabbed her eyes again. "He had a temper – if you moved something and he couldn't find it when he needed it, goodness, he could shout – but I can understand that. Imagine being all but blind, sir." The housekeeper shook her head. "But he was generous to a fault."

There was a knock at the door and the maid nudged it open with her elbow, balancing a tray of tea things. She put them onto the table and left. The housekeeper went over to the teapot and put her hand against it. Satisfied, she poured two cups, handing one of them to me and returning to her chair with her own.

"Generous?" I asked. "Do you mean he gave you money?"

Mrs Godwin looked at me with a half-smile and I could see the pretty young woman she had once been. "Not in the way you imagine, constable," she said. "Mr Foster was a true husband, and he was still in mourning for his wife." She put her cup onto a low table at her side. "My own mother died two years ago but before she died she was ill for nearly a year. When he heard of it, Mr Foster insisted that his own physician should visit her, and then he paid for the medicines she needed. He did the same when the coachman's young lad broke his arm."

"Did he use the same physician until the end?" I asked, taking out my notebook.

"He did," said Mrs Godwin. "Doctor Branscombe has served the family for many years, I am told. Although the master hasn't... hadn't had cause to consult him for many months." She shook her head sadly. "Gentlemen are often reluctant to think of their own health, I have found. Even when his wife died he did not take to his bed. Mrs Moncrieff moved back from the country to offer companionship and the little lad she brought with her – her poor cousin's son Arthur – well, you'd think Mr Foster was his grandpa, the way he doted on the boy." The housekeeper put a hand to her mouth. "Poor Arthur: it's his birthday on Friday and the master had been planning a special day out. He even went to Noah's Ark in Holborn last week and bought a kite – a great big thing taller than Arthur." Mrs Godwin shook her head. "He was so looking forward to giving it to the boy. He was in such high spirits, which is partly what makes me, well, uneasy." She stopped and looked down at her hands.

"Partly, Mrs Godwin?" I prompted. "What else has made you uneasy?"

"When the master died," she said slowly, "he was almost alone in the house. Mrs Moncrieff and Arthur were spending the day in St James's Park. On Sunday afternoons most of the servants go to visit family. I myself went to see my sister in Vauxhall. Daniel – the young footman – was supposed to be here, in case the master needed anything, but Mr James," she looked at me, "Mr James sent him on an errand, to deliver a message to a friend clear across town. When Daniel arrived back, the master was dead and Mr James sent him straight back out to fetch Doctor Branscombe."

"Is this footman here now?" I asked.

"I'll find him for you," said the housekeeper, and she left the room. A few minutes later she returned with a young man of about twenty – it was easy to see from his height and handsome face how he had found his employment. The housekeeper returned to her seat and Daniel stood before us, neat in his uniform but pale and – to judge from the way he tugged at his cuffs – nervous.

"You are a footman, Daniel?" I asked.

He nodded but said nothing.

"You are to speak freely to the constable, Daniel," said Mrs Godwin. "You have my permission. My instruction."

"Yes, Mrs Godwin," said the footman. He squared his shoulders and looked directly at me. "Yes, sir. I am one of two footmen here."

"And your surname, Daniel?" I asked.

"Finch, sir," he said. "Like the bird," as he watched me write it in my book.

"Thank you, Daniel," I said. "I understand from Mrs Godwin that you were the only servant on duty yesterday afternoon." The footman nodded. "And with you, here in the house, were Mr Foster and his son, Mr James – is that right?"

"Yes, sir," said Daniel. "Mrs Moncrieff and Master Arthur had gone out with Miss Napier."

"The governess," added Mrs Godwin.

"Do you know where they went?" I asked.

"Yes, sir," said Daniel. "Jeffreys – the coachman," he added quickly, before Mrs Godwin could speak, "took them to St James's Park after church. Master Arthur wanted to see the Life Guard and their horses, and Mrs Moncrieff thought that some fresh air would be good for him. Cook packed a cold luncheon for them."

"So this was a planned day out?" I asked. "Not a sudden idea?"

Mrs Godwin stood and went to her little desk and consulted her ledger. "Miss Napier asked for the cold luncheon on Thursday last." She watched me note this in my book and then returned to her chair.

"Once the coach had set off," I continued, "who was left here in the house?"

"Just me downstairs," said Daniel, "and the master and Mr James upstairs."

"And what did you do?" I asked.

"At noon I served luncheon in the dining room for the two gentlemen," said the footman. "Cook had left a tureen of soup on the stove, to be followed by a plate of cold meats and cheese, and a lemon posset for afterwards."

"And did Mr Foster seem well during the meal?" I asked. "Did he have a good appetite?"

Daniel nodded. "He had two bowls of soup and a good plateful of meat, along with some bread."

"And did he and his son seem to be easy in each other's company?" I asked.

The footman nodded again. "They talked of a new horse Mr James had been to see," he said. "The master asked Mr James to accompany him on his next visit to Gracechurch Street – to the Quaker meeting house," he clarified, "and Mr James said that he would think about it." He glanced at Mrs Godwin and she nodded. "He always said that, Mr James – he would think about it. But we all knew that he never would – the life of a Quaker, well, that's not for Mr James. We all knew."

"Except Mr Foster," I suggested. The footman raised his eyebrows but said nothing. "And what did the two gentlemen do after their meal?" I asked.

"The master went to his study and asked me to come to him in an hour's time to help with some reading," Daniel replied.

"Why did he not ask his son?" I asked.

The footman stayed silent. The housekeeper leaned forward. "Mr James has not the patience for it," she said. "It was always Mr Harding's job," she paused for a moment, "and after he died the master thought it would help Daniel – improve him – to read to him."

"And has it improved you, Daniel?" I asked.

Daniel smiled shyly. "Some of what I read I didn't really understand – if it was about law, or religion. But I enjoyed the stories about history and far-away places – adventures. The master would ask me to bring him the globe and describe the shapes of the countries to him – he could always tell me their names."

"And what did you read about yesterday?" I asked. "Dull religion or exciting adventures?"

The footman's face fell. "We didn't do any reading in the end. Before the hour was up, Mr James rang for me and asked me to deliver an important message to a gentleman in Nelson Square. He said he would read to his father."

"Nelson Square?" I said, looking up at him. "South of the river?"

"That's right," said Daniel. "Off Great Surrey Street. Nearly two hours, it took me, there and back, even though I paid the jarvey to wait for me."

"Which means that you reached home at what time?" I asked.

"I let myself in just as the kitchen clock was striking four," he said.

"And that's a good clock," added the housekeeper.

"And what did you do then?" I asked.

"I knew that the master would be wanting some tea," said Daniel, "so I was about to fill the kettle and put it on the stove. But then I heard Orthez."

"The dog?" I asked.

"That's right," he replied. "He's a big brute, but gentle as they come, and usually very quiet. I knew something was wrong, because he was howling – and the noise was coming from the larder."

"Behind the kitchen," explained Mrs Godwin. "Next to the coal cellar. Someone had shut the poor beast in there."

"Could it have been an accident?" I asked. "The dog was looking for food and the larder door closed behind him?"

The footman shook his head. "Another dog, perhaps – but not Orthez. He never leaves the master's side except, well, when he needs to relieve himself." I nodded and Daniel continued. "We tried feeding him in the yard down here, but it distressed him so much that Mr Harding said we should put the bowls in the corner of the master's study. He even sleeps in the master's room at night, on a rug at the foot of his bed. He would never have wandered off leaving the master like that."

"And the larder door is not left open, constable," said the housekeeper with some dignity. "I am responsible for its contents and everyone knows to close the door securely."

"What did you do next, Daniel?" I asked.

"I opened the larder door and Orthez pushed past me and galloped up the stairs. I chased after him and caught up with him at the door of the master's study, pawing at it and barking." The footman stopped. "I knew then that something had happened. I knocked on the door, then called out – and all the while Orthez was barking and barking."

"Did Mr James come to see the cause of all the noise?" I asked.

Daniel shook his head. "Mr James was not at home." I nodded and he continued. "I opened the door a little and Orthez pushed it with his head, barging into the room. The master was sitting in his armchair, his eyes closed, for all the world as if he was asleep – but I knew. And the dog knew. He laid his head on the master's knee and licked his hand, then he sat back on his haunches and he howled. It broke your heart to hear it, sir. Well, it broke mine." The footman blinked and quickly wiped his eye with the back of his hand. "I went out into the street, whistled for a lad and sent for Doctor Branscombe."

"You did well, Daniel," I said. "It is very helpful for me to hear this from you." I paged back through my notebook. "Just one more thing, Daniel. The message that you delivered for Mr James, to the address in Nelson Square. Can you remember who the message was for?"

"I can, sir, yes. It was for a Mr Alexander Greene, at number fourteen."

"And was Mr Greene at home?" I asked. "Did he send a reply?"

The footman shook his head. "It seems that Mr James was mistaken with the address," he said. "There was no Mr Greene at number fourteen, and the footman there could not think of any neighbour with that name."

◆

"A wild goose chase, you think?" asked Wilson. "To keep the footman out of the house?"

"It's possible," I said. "It's certainly a coincidence that no-one was home that afternoon, in a household that is usually busy with people."

"But maybe…" Wilson started and then stopped and shook his head.

"But maybe what?" I prompted him.

"When my grandmother died when I was a lad," he said, "she waited until we were all out at church – it was like she wanted to be on her own. Ma said that old people often do that: they don't want to upset anyone and so they slip away quietly, trying not make a fuss." He stopped and rubbed his chin. "Probably nonsense," he said gruffly.

"Probably," I agreed, smiling, "but perhaps not." I reached behind me, putting my hand into the pocket of the coat hanging on the hook. "I had a look around Mr Foster's study and I found this on his desk. The footman said that it had been delivered earlier in the week. The housekeeper allowed me to have it on strict instructions to return it tomorrow."

I put the small wooden box on the table and opened the lid. Inside were six rings. I took one out and handed it to Wilson.

"Mourning rings?" he asked.

I nodded. "A half-dozen of them." I reached into the box again. "According to the receipt, Mr Foster ordered them from Thomas Ayres in Fenchurch Street, and paid for them in advance."

I picked up one of the rings myself and looked at it. It was rather old-fashioned to my eye but perhaps it suited the taste of a gentleman of Mr Foster's generation.

"It's just like a dog collar," said Wilson.

And indeed it was. The gold ring was encircled by a black enamel hoop engraved in gold with the words 'Sacred to the memory of'. Inside the band was engraved the name 'Hugh Foster Esq'.

"Dogs represent faithfulness," I explained, "so perhaps Mr Foster was hoping to remind people to be faithful to his memory."

Wilson put the ring he was holding back into the box. "Does this mean that he knew he was dying? If he ordered the rings, to be given to people when he died. That there is nothing suspicious about his death after all?"

"No-one reaches that age without considering his death," I said, "and with his son recently returned, perhaps his mind turned to leaving his affairs in order." I put the lid back on the box. "But I am still uneasy about that dog."

CHAPTER SEVEN

A speck of soot in the eye

SUNDAY 8TH MARCH 1829

Martha waved her hand to indicate that I should turn around – I tutted but did so.

"Very smart, Sam," she said approvingly.

"I am always smartly dressed," I said, affronted.

"In your uniform, yes," said my wife as she glanced around the kitchen before pushing me out of the door ahead of her. "But it is months – perhaps years – since you went to church, and I don't want Alice to be ashamed of us." She put a hand to her head, tucking a curl away under her bonnet, and looked up at me. "Will I do, Sam?"

"You look..." I chose my words carefully, knowing how important the day was for Martha. "You look charming, my love."

She smiled and then tugged at my arm. "We can't stand here all day while you flatter me, Samuel Plank," she said briskly. "It's a fair step to Holborn."

♦

And indeed it was. We neither of us wanted to arrive red-faced and out of breath so we walked at a comfortable pace, enjoying the spring sunshine, and arrived at Queen Square an hour later. Wilson and Alice were waiting by one of the two doorways and no-one, seeing her gazing up at him and the tenderness with which he smiled down at her, could have doubted their love for each other. Martha obviously thought the same, as she squeezed my arm and sighed. Wilson glanced over and caught sight of us, raising his hand in greeting.

"You look perfect, my dear," said Martha to Alice, who ducked her head modestly and flushed, as she always did when attention was drawn to her. "And you have not brought George, after all."

"William was worried what people might think," said Alice. "You know, that he was, well, that we hadn't..."

"People can think what they like, Alice," I said, "and they will. All we can do is live our lives in the right way, and those who know the two of you would not think that for a moment."

Hurried along by the rather dissonant peals of bells from the new tower, we went into the church. The interior was pleasingly plain, with slender columns holding a square ceiling high above the rows of pews. At Alice's suggestion we made our way up a steep flight of steps to take seats in the gallery, giving an excellent view of both the pulpit and the congregation.

"I like sitting up here," she whispered to me as we settled ourselves, "because I can see everything in the church and then look out through that window", she pointed to the magnificent arched window across from us, "at the sky outside. It reminds me that God is everywhere – in here and out there."

I am no churchgoer myself. I do not think that God needs special buildings to remind us of His glory: the sky that Alice admires is His work, as is the smile of a mother looking at her child, and the hand of a man reaching to help another. I often think we would do better to remember God in our daily lives rather than spending our Sundays in great structures designed more often than not to show off our own skills and wealth. But Wilson had been so grave and so serious when he asked us to hear their banns being read that I had not the heart to refuse. I pointed out that they could have paid ten shillings for a common licence instead but Martha agreed with Alice that a young couple starting out should save every penny they could and that hearing the banns would be romantic.

A dig in my ribs reminded me that I was daydreaming and that I should start to pay attention. The vicar – a rather tall fellow with a scrawny neck poking out of his collar – turned to the back of the Bible propped on his lectern and took out a piece of paper, smoothing it with the side of his hand before reading from it. "I publish the banns of marriage between William Wilson of the parish of St Pancras and Alice Godfrey of the parish of St Andrew's. If any of you know cause or just impediment why these two persons should not be joined together in Holy matrimony, ye are to declare it. This is the first time of asking." He paused for a few seconds and then went on with other church business. Beside me, Alice let out the breath she had been holding and looked at me, her eyes shining.

"Next week we shall go to William's church to hear them read again," she whispered to me. "The Seymour Street Chapel is very new, I am told. And then back here for the third reading. After that, we can be married." And she smiled with such sweetness that even my old heart felt the joy of the moment.

"I shall look forward to hearing all about it," I whispered back. "I go to church only three times a year, and if you want me to attend your wedding we cannot waste another of those visits on the banns." I winked at her. On my other side Martha elbowed me again and I returned to contemplation of the window and the sky until the end of the service.

We filed out of the church and stood, blinking in the bright light. I knew that Alice would be keen to return to the Blue Boar; George was fretful while he was teething and although Louisa Atkins was a skilled mother and a kind woman, the little lad really only settled with Alice. But despite this, she seemed reluctant to leave, and after a few minutes of awkward conversation she seemed to make a decision. She looked at Wilson, who nodded, and then she turned to me.

"Constable Plank," she said, and then repeated it with more certainty. "Constable Plank, William and I would like to ask you something. As I know nothing of my own father, and as you have looked out for me these past three years, I was hoping that you would agree to give me away at our wedding. I know that you dislike going to church and wearing fancy clothes when you're not on duty," she indicated my suit, "but I cannot bear the idea of walking all that way through the church, with people watching me, on my own. And of course William cannot..."

Wilson smiled at her and added, "I would like Alice to feel safe on her wedding day. We would be so grateful, sir."

I cleared my throat. "For the privilege of walking alongside the second most lovely woman in all of London on her wedding day, Alice," I said, "I would wear the fanciest of clothes and go to any church you could name."

"Oh, thank you," said Alice, reaching across and squeezing my arm. "Thank you." And the young couple headed off.

"I see you have a speck of soot in your eye, Sam" said Martha as we turned our step westwards. "We shall have to make sure to keep a handkerchief ready on the day itself, in case of more soot."

CHAPTER EIGHT

Indigo and imperfection

TUESDAY 10TH MARCH 1829

The fine rain gave the approaching crowd a soft, almost dream-like appearance as they passed through the gates into the Bunhill Fields burial ground. It was perhaps five years since I had attended the burial of the banker Fauntleroy in the same place, but that had been a desolate occasion, with only his mother and two siblings to bid him farewell; by contrast, Hugh Foster was leaving this world mourned by many. Martha stood neat and quiet at my side; ordinarily, of course, she could not have attended a funeral but the Quakers – holding men and women to be equal – do not bar their wives and mothers from such ceremonies. A man detached himself from the group and as he came over to us I recognised Edward Freame.

"Samuel," he said sombrely, tipping his hat. "Mrs Plank." I shook his hand and Martha curtseyed.

"You have been to the meeting house?" I asked.

The banker nodded. "Aye," he said. "It was very affecting. Mr Foster was well-regarded and we shall miss his energy for the cause, and his good humour."

"The cause?" asked Martha.

"Anti-slavery," said Freame. "Mr Foster was a passionate writer of pamphlets and attender of meetings on the subject."

"But is not the slave trade already outlawed?" she asked.

"The trade, yes," I replied, "but not slavery itself. It is still permissible to own slaves, but not to buy or sell them."

"And many of us – Quakers and others – believe that the very idea of owning another human being is unconscionable," added Freame.

"Indeed it is," said Martha promptly. "And these people here today: are they all Quakers?"

Freame looked over at the crowd, which had stopped by a freshly-dug grave. "For the most part, yes. We gathered at the meeting house in Coleman Street an hour ago and held the memorial service. You will note that many of them wear undyed cloth." He looked at Martha and she nodded. "Indigo comes from plants grown on plantations that use slave labour and many Quakers refuse to support its use. Sadly I am too vain to forgo a smart coat and hat. I am an imperfect man." He smiled ruefully as he indicated his own attire.

"I like this place," observed Martha after a few moments of silence. "It is restful."

"Indeed it is," I said. "The final resting place for many."

My wife tutted at me. "This is no time for your little jokes, Sam. What I mean is that I find it very calming. There is no fuss."

Freame looked across at Martha appraisingly. "Perhaps you are a Quaker at heart, Mrs Plank," he said. "We believe that there is no use for fancy gravestones or memorials, as God already knows everything about us, and our loved ones will remember us in their hearts. We have no need of consecrated ground for our eternal rest as all ground is consecrated by God. See, now they will place Foster into his grave."

We all looked across as the plain coffin was lowered into the ground. The mourners stood in silence around the grave, heads lowered. There was no priest reciting words from the Bible, no prayers or rites – as Martha had said, it was restful. As the people turned from the grave, many of them were smiling.

Perhaps anticipating my question, Freame spoke. "We do not believe that a burial is a time of sadness, but rather a time to honour and remember the brother or sister who has gone from us. We gather to celebrate their life and to give thanks for the friendship and joy it has brought us."

Martha took hold of my arm as we moved towards the grave with Freame, to pay our own respects. "I like that sentiment," she said, "although I should be sorry if you did not shed a few tears at my graveside, Sam."

Freame nudged me and indicated two of the mourners, a man and a woman, who were walking away from the graveside arm-in-arm, smiling at each other. "James Foster and his sister Mrs Moncrieff," he said in a low tone, raising an eyebrow at me. "And now, if you will excuse me Mrs Plank, I must return to my banking house."

Martha and I had just walked out of the gates and turned our step for home when someone tapped me on the shoulder. I turned to see Mrs Godwin, dressed in sombre black and with the reddening around the eyes that suggests the shedding of many tears.

"I thought it was you, Constable Plank," she said. "I am sure that Mr Foster would have been flattered that you would give up your time to attend his funeral."

"Mr Conant asked me to express his condolences," I said, hoping that I would not be caught out in my lie. "This is my wife, Mrs Plank. And this is Mrs Godwin, my dear – Mr Foster's housekeeper."

The two women nodded at each other. "I understand that Mr Foster was a good and kind man," said Martha. "Will you stay in the household?"

"I have not yet decided," replied Mrs Godwin after a pause. "I was very fond of Mr Foster and of his late wife, but Mr James Foster is a single gentleman and I think I prefer to serve a mistress."

Martha looked at the housekeeper for a long moment and then made up her mind. "Mrs Godwin," she said, "my husband and I had just decided to stop for refreshments before our walk home. He promised to buy me some cheesecake from Birch's in Cornhill. Could we tempt you to join us? Please." She reached over and put her hand on the housekeeper's wrist. Mrs Godwin gave a small sob and nodded wordlessly.

♦

Twenty minutes later the three of us were sitting at a small table in the tiny dining area of the celebrated confectionery shop. It was true that I had once rashly promised to bring my wife here – Martha had overheard two ladies of consequence in Oxford Street talking of the "incomparable cheesecake" they had sampled and had since longed to know how a cake can be made of cheese – but I had not envisaged putting my hand in my pocket for two dining companions. But I need not have worried: a combination of grief and unfettered access to her own larder meant that Mrs Godwin's appetite was small, and she asked only for a pot of tea. Martha requested the longed-for cheesecake, and for myself I chose a sugared bun. I will confess that it was not the first Birch's bun I had tried – the former mayor of London who gave his name to the premises had been an excellent pastry cook and his recipes lived on. Our refreshments arrived quickly and Martha made sure that our guest had been furnished with tea before turning to her and again placing a calming hand on her arm.

"Mrs Godwin," she said gently. "I think there is something you would like to tell my husband, and that is why you came across to us at Bunhill Fields. You will both forgive me, I hope, if I tell you that Sam – Constable Plank – has already told me what the butler said to you about Mr James Foster." The housekeeper's eyes widened but she said nothing. "Sam is a good man, Mrs Godwin," continued my wife. "He has not forgotten what you said and is doing his best to uncover the truth of the matter. If there is something more troubling you, there is no-one better you could tell. You must trust me in this."

The housekeeper reached across with her other hand and placed it over Martha's. She took a deep breath and then squared her shoulders with resolve. "Constable Plank," she said. "Oh, Constable Plank – such a time of it!" She closed her eyes and shook her head sadly. "I have not known where to turn. First Mr Harding dies, and now this. And Mr James running wild with grief. Such a time of it."

"Running wild?" asked Martha. "He looked calm enough to me, Mrs Godwin."

The housekeeper looked over her shoulder as though we might be overheard and then touched a hand to her face. "Did you not notice his eye?" she asked. We both shook our heads. "Then they did a good job on it." She sighed. "Four nights ago, Mr James went out as usual and came home..." she leaned forward and all but mouthed the word, "drunk. Grief takes us in different ways, Mrs Plank, I know. He made such a racket coming in that I went to see what was wrong and he had been beaten. He insisted that he was fine but I thought him in no state to know one way or the other. Finch and I put him to bed and first thing in the morning I sent for the doctor. Bad bruising to the chest, he said, suggesting Mr James had been kicked – one broken rib, he thought. And then the black eye. Mrs Moncrieff helped him cover it for the funeral, with powder."

"What a worry for you, Mrs Godwin," said Martha, refilling the housekeeper's cup. "When drink controls a man, he is either not himself at all, or too much himself." I knew she was remembering the days when her drunken father had terrorised her. Both women shook their heads sadly.

"Mrs Godwin," I said in a tone that I hoped suggested sympathy and reliability, "I think it best that you start at the beginning. What is it that concerns you about the death of Mr Harding?"

"Apart from the shock of it, of course, and your grief at losing your friend," added Martha, giving me a look.

"It is not his death that is troubling me," said Mrs Godwin, "beyond the normal feelings of grief, as Mrs Plank says, and the worry about Mr James since he said what he said. I know that in some households the housekeeper and the butler form an understanding," she looked down at her hands as she said this and I saw a little colour rise on her neck, "but I promise you that Mr Harding and I had no more than a friendship, and a mutual respect for each other. If it had been more than that, I would tell you, Mrs Plank."

"I know you would," said Martha. "Tell us, then, Mrs Godwin, what is troubling you?"

"Mr Harding was a man who liked order," began the housekeeper. "He liked things to be just so – you remember I told you that, constable."

"You did, yes," I confirmed.

"And as he was not a young man and did not want to leave anything to chance, or to cause inconvenience for his friends, he paid regularly into a burial club. He was a dignified man, Mrs Plank, and had a horror of being put into a pauper's grave. No funeral, no headstone..." Mrs Godwin shuddered. "A terrible prospect, and for those of us with no family, a very real one."

"Indeed," I said, extracting my notebook from the pocket of my coat. "Do you mind if I take notes? It will help me to decide what to do to help you."

"Of course," replied Mrs Godwin. "Every other Thursday evening a man from the burial club would call at the servants' hall and collect the contributions."

"More than one contribution?" I asked, looking up.

"Oh yes: four of us subscribed, on the advice of Mr Harding. There was Mr Harding, of course, and then I signed up, along with Jeffreys – he's the coachman. And only a few months ago young Daniel Finch joined up." She shook her head and looked even more miserable. "Poor Daniel – such a good lad, and now his money is lost."

"Isn't it unusual for a young bachelor to join such a club?" asked Martha. "A man with a family, yes, or some-one of more mature years... but a lad like that?"

"I asked the same thing, Mrs Plank," said the house-keeper, "but Daniel was not saving for his own funeral: he has a widowed mother and wanted to put her mind at rest concerning her own burial. A good son."

"And you fear that all is not well with the burial club?" I asked.

Mrs Godwin shook her head fiercely. "When the undertakers came to collect Mr Harding, I mentioned the club to them. They gave each other a look, like they knew something. And when I sent a message to the address we had been given, the lad came back and said there was no such person at that address."

"And what about the man collecting the contributions?" I asked, looking back through my notes. "Every other Thursday evening."

"Well, we never saw him again," she said.

♦

Martha sighed deeply as she sat in her armchair. She held out her foot towards me and I unlaced the boot and eased it from her foot and then reached for her other foot to do the same.

"Well, that was quite a day," she said. "When you first told me that you were a constable I knew that life with you would be interesting, and so it has proved."

"And when you first told me that you did not want to share your life with a constable, I knew you were fibbing – and so it has proved," I replied, bending to remove my own boots.

"A lady can't appear too keen," she said, smiling. "Although when I see an old girl like Mrs Godwin, it's a warning against not being keen enough."

"There was no Mr Godwin, then?" I asked.

Martha shook her head. "A spinster, that one. You heard what she said about having no family." She sighed. "These burial clubs, Sam. I know how they work, of course: you pay a few pennies each week or fortnight against a named person – yourself, or a parent, or child – and when the time comes the club pays out for the funeral. But I thought they were all run by churches – or at least the ones I've heard about have been."

"Some of them are, yes," I replied, "but others are organised by friendly societies, some by undertakers – and some simply by groups of friends and neighbours, to take care of their own." I stretched out my legs and wiggled my toes – we had walked several miles that day and I was glad to be sitting down. "There have been scandals, of course."

"Scandals?" repeated Martha.

"Aye. There are those who pay into more than one club for the same person and then claim several lots of money when they die. Or – more serious, this one – there have been cases where people have been murdered so that the money can be claimed."

Martha shook her head. "The things people do for money, Sam." She sat silently for a couple of minutes. "What do you think has happened to Mr Harding's money?"

"Oh, they've just pinched it," I said. "I shall ask Mrs Godwin for the address of the club and Wilson and I will take a walk over there and have a word with the neighbours – see what we can find out. And now, Mrs Plank, where is that soup you promised me on the way home?"

Martha sighed theatrically and pushed herself up out of her chair. "Yes, oh lord and master, at once, you have only to ask," she said, bowing and then backing out of the room. "Sam," she called from the kitchen. "The fellow who collected the money from Mrs Godwin and the others every other Thursday: how did he know not to go back? And why did he not go back: did he already know that Mr Harding had died and that there would be a claim against the club?"

CHAPTER NINE

Rings of mourning and regard

WEDNESDAY 18TH MARCH 1829

"I did not realise I had married a fashion plate," I said as I caught Martha looking sideways at herself in a window. "All these years you pretend to be sensible and now I find that you are just as silly as Miss Lily and her friends."

"And all these years you pretend to be a gentleman, and now I find that you are a rude fellow," she replied, quick as a flash. "And a foolish one: you cannot expect me to accompany you to a fashionable jewellery shop looking like I've been scrubbing the floors."

I chose not to remind her that accompanying me to the premises of Thomas Ayres in Fenchurch Street had been Martha's idea, not mine, because I enjoyed her company and – if I am honest – I liked to see her dressed in her finery. She was no longer a young woman but Martha's curves suited her, and with her curls escaping from her bonnet as they always did, and her eyes shining with the excitement of her adventure, she had drawn one or two admiring glances from other fellows. I patted her hand where it lay in the crook of my arm and drew her closer to me.

"Indeed I cannot," I agreed.

We walked for ten minutes more, with me pointing out sights as we passed them: I will admit that I liked to show off to my wife, and if she had heard the same stories from me before, she was kind enough to keep it to herself. She shivered theatrically as we passed first the Fleet prison and then Newgate, declining my offer to call in at the latter to see our friend John Wontner. "We should not disturb him at his place of work," she gave as her excuse, but I knew that she disliked the chill and despair of his surroundings.

St Paul's Cathedral reared up ahead of us and – as I always did – I stopped to admire its size and elegance. "Those are Corinthian columns," I said to Martha, pointing. "And on top of them – the triangle – that's called the pediment. I read about it in a book that Mr Conant bought recently. And that's St Paul standing on the top of the pediment." We both craned our necks to look up at the saint. "It was designed by Sir Christopher Wren," I continued, "and took nearly forty years to complete – he was an old man by the time it was finished."

Martha sighed. "Can you imagine looking at something like this and being able to say, I made that?"

"I daresay he had a little help, my dear," I replied. "A stonemason or two, perhaps, just to do the fancy bits."

She squeezed my arm. "To make up for teasing me, husband, you will need to put your hand into your pocket and buy me some refreshment."

"And I know just the place, my dear," I said as we set off once more.

♦

"Mrs Plank," said Edward Freame delightedly as he walked towards us across the floor of his banking hall, his hands held out in welcome. "It is as well you have Sam with you, otherwise I would not have recognised you in that fine outfit. I fear my parlour is far too shabby to do you justice but it is all I have."

"It is a pleasure to see you again, Mr Freame," said Martha, "and your parlour sounds very tempting after our walk."

"Take your wife through, Sam," the banker said to me, "and I will see what Stevenson can do about some tea and biscuits."

A few minutes later we were both settled into chairs in the parlour, with Freame pouring the tea and his junior clerk making sure that we had at least three biscuits each before bowing quite elegantly to my wife and leaving us.

"He's come on leaps and bounds," said Freame, as Stevenson shut the door behind him. "You recall what a gawky lad he was – hah!" I nodded and smiled as I thought back. "His arms and legs seemed to confuse him terribly – forever tripping over himself and knocking into things. But he's grown into them now, and my spies tell me that a young lady from the silk mercer's next door has caught his eye, which may account for his somewhat smarter appearance. The things we men will do for love, Sam." He shook his head ruefully. "But talking of smart appearances, Mrs Plank – well, you are a picture today. And much as I would like to, I cannot believe that you have put on this finery simply to call on me. After all, we saw each other only yesterday, and you were not wearing that magnificent hat."

For the past two years, Martha had been spending a day a week, and sometimes more, at the school in Harrison Street that Mr Freame and some fellow Quakers had founded for young unmarried women who fell pregnant and would otherwise have been thrown onto the street. The young women lived at the school until their babies arrived and then for six months afterwards, learning to read and write – this from Martha – and to cook and sew, equipping them to earn a living. Martha's years as the wife of a constable had exposed her to the cruelties of life without hardening her; this made me love her even more, and it had also convinced Freame that she would be an ideal teacher.

"And it is as well I wasn't," said Martha. "Just after you left, Abigail – the little red-haired one – went into labour. Easy as you please; three hours later we had a pretty baby girl with big blue eyes. Hannah, she's called, after Abigail's grandmother. And there's some more good news, Mr Freame: the grandmother has agreed that Abigail and Hannah can live with her, in Bermondsey."

The banker smiled broadly. "I knew that Abigail was a clever little thing: no old lady can resist a new baby, and particularly not one named after her." He raised his cup. "To little Hannah: may life be kind to her."

♦

Fortified by our tea and biscuits, Martha and I walked past Mansion House, where she pointed out some pillars and pediments to me, and along Lombard Street into Fenchurch Street. We quickly spotted the shop we were looking for. With the bulk of St Dionis Backchurch behind it and the road running right in front of it, the premises of the goldsmith had an excellent location and took advantage of that with one of the largest windows I had seen: the main one must have been a dozen panes wide and three high, with another almost as large forming the corner with Lime Street. Painted above the window in large, clear letters – visible from any passing coach – was the name of the owner and his trade: T Ayres Goldsmith & Jeweller.

"Now remember, Martha," I said, as she pulled me towards the windows and their glittering displays, "we are here for information, not for jewellery."

"Then you'd better keep tight hold of your budget, Sam," said my wife with a smile.

Inside the shop there was even more to catch the eye, with cabinets and display cases filled with jewellery, ornaments and curios. Martha tapped me on the arm and whispered into my ear, "There – I could have chosen a hat like that," indicating with her eyes (and her raised eyebrows) the purple feathered confection perched on the head of a matronly woman who was peering through a lorgnette at a glass cabinet of jewels. She was attended by a handsome young fellow in a ridiculously high collar who sighed deeply once or twice but seemed resigned to his lot. I looked around for someone to speak to and just then a man of about my own age appeared at one of the counters; I realised that he had been crouching down behind it. We walked over to him.

"Good afternoon sir, madam," he said, inclining his head. "How may I help you?"

"Are you Mr Ayres?" I asked.

"Alas, no," he replied. "Mr Ayres is advanced in years and does not come into the shop very often. I am his partner, John Bennett – trained at the master's knee, you might say."

"I wanted to ask about mourning rings, Mr Bennett," I said.

The goldsmith's face rearranged itself into an expression of regretful concern. "Ah, well – a prudent man plans ahead, to leave his loved ones with a token of his affection by which they can remember him. We have a fine selection of traditional rings, sir, which can be engraved when the time comes." He paused for a respectful moment as we all pondered our mortality. "Or you can commission something particular, for a modest fee."

"I was particularly interested in dog-collar rings," I said.

"Ah yes, an enduring favourite," said Bennett. "I have a tray that I can show you, Mr..."

"Constable Samuel Plank," I said. "Working under the instruction of John Conant Esquire of Great Marlborough Street. Do you keep records, Mr Bennett, of those who purchase your items? A ledger of receipts?"

"Of course," said the goldsmith with some dignity. "When one is in the business of value, it is important to know how much value one has, and how much value one has sold, and for what... value."

"In that case, Mr Bennett," I said, taking my notebook from my coat pocket, "please could you consult your records to find out when a Mr Foster ordered six dog-collar mourning rings from you. Black enamel."

"Our ledgers are kept in the office upstairs," said Bennett. "If you will excuse me, sir, madam." He disappeared through a door at the back of the shop. Martha turned her attention to an arrangement of five gold bracelets on a background of black velvet; I caught the eye of the companion to the purple hat and he sighed wearily once again.

"Did you say Mr Hugh Foster or Mr James Foster?" asked the goldsmith, returning with an open ledger in his arms. "I have them both."

"Hugh," I said. "And then James."

The goldsmith raised an eyebrow. "Mr Hugh Foster ordered a dozen dog-collar mourning rings on the 16th of January this year. They were engraved and delivered..." he ran a finger across the ledger, "a fortnight later. Paid in full."

I wrote the details in my notebook. "And James Foster?" I asked.

"Mr James Foster came in on the 4th of this month and sold to us six mourning rings, one sterling silver pocket watch and one gold, enamel and pearl musical snuff box."

"And how much did you pay him?" I asked.

The goldsmith sniffed and looked at me for a long moment. "The mourning rings are worth very little second-hand, as they are engraved," he said eventually, "but the watch was good quality and the snuff box is a beauty. If it were mine, I would not sell it. Let me show you."

He beckoned and we followed him across the shop to a corner cabinet with a glass front. He pointed. "There: the one with a blue enamel frame and Diana painted on the lid – is it not fine?" The tiny object – about the size of my palm – was pretty enough, but I struggle to see why a man would want to take his snuff from a painted box that plays a tune. Bennett stepped closer to me and spoke in an undertone. "We paid him fifty-five guineas for it. Plus another twelve for the watch and rings."

♦

"Well, it didn't take him long to start selling the family heirlooms," said Martha indignantly as we set off. "His poor father not even buried. He probably thought he might have to give away some of the rings and decided to sell them instead. It just shows: those with more money aren't always better off."

I tucked her hand into my arm and smiled at her. "Go on then, Mrs Plank: if we had all the money in the world and I took you back to that fine shop, what would you choose? A gold bracelet, perhaps – I saw you looking at them. Earrings with diamonds and sapphires?"

Martha retrieved her hand and pulled off her glove to reveal the regard ring that I had given her two years earlier to mark – to celebrate – our twenty-fifth wedding anniversary. She held her hand out in front of her and moved it so that we could both see the stones winking in the late afternoon sunshine. "There is nothing that Mr Thomas Avery or Mr John Bennett could conjure out of the finest gold and the rarest gems that would come close to this. I have all I want right here." She glanced around and then reached up to kiss me. "Now let's go home – there's a pigeon pie keeping warm for us."

CHAPTER TEN

The worldly Miss Lily

THURSDAY 19TH MARCH 1829

The next day I occupied myself until the end of the morning's hearings at Great Marlborough Street and then went upstairs to call on Mr Conant in his rooms above the police office. I knocked on the door and he called to me to enter. Thin Billy was setting out the magistrate's midday meal on the table.

"Come, Sam, join me," said Conant, indicating the plate of cold meats, the dish of pasties, the bottle of wine and the jug of barley water. "There is more than enough for both of us; I thought that Lily might be calling in but she has not appeared."

"Thank you," I said, taking a seat at the table. "I am a little peckish, as it happens, and a pasty would be most welcome." Thin Billy put a plate in front of me and then left the room – he knew that the magistrate preferred to serve himself at table. Conant pointed at the drinks; I chose the barley water and he poured himself a tumbler of wine. "And how is Miss Lily?" I asked, taking a bite from a pasty and brushing the crumbs from my lips.

The magistrate raised his eyebrows. "My daughter baffles and delights me in equal measure, constable. Although she is my child, I sometimes think that she is already wiser to the world than I will ever be. I confess that I never miss my dear wife more than when I am trying to guide Lily." He shook his head wonderingly and swallowed a mouthful of wine. "I catch her looking at me sometimes, Sam, as though she puts up with my advice simply to please me but doesn't need it at all."

"Wise beyond her years, eh?" I said. "It may be nothing to do with age, of course. I sometimes see the same look on Mrs Plank's face, almost as though she is humouring me."

Conant pointed his knife at me. "That's it precisely: she is humouring me. Wives or daughters – we men are at their mercy." He speared a piece of cold beef. "And I hear that Constable Wilson is soon to join our bewildered ranks."

I nodded. "He is indeed. He and Alice are to marry at the end of the month. He has taken rooms in the same building as his mother so that he and Alice can care for her when the time comes and also keep an eye on Wilson's sisters. As you know, Alice acts as mother to a young child – George – and Wilson loves them both. They imagine that marriage will be all hearts and flowers, of course, but we most of us start out that way."

Conant smiled. "We do, Sam – we do. Will you ask Mrs Plank what would be best for Lily and me to send the newlyweds – a gift or some money."

I nodded and turned my attention to the bowl of pears, selecting one that looked ripe and juicy and biting into it. It was delicious and I had to use my napkin to catch the juice on my chin.

The magistrate stood and walked over to the sideboard where Thin Billy had set out the coffee pot and cups. "Coffee?" he said but I shook my head and he poured just one for himself. We moved to the more comfortable chairs by the fireplace. "Now, Sam," he said, "much as I enjoy your company as I eat, I imagine that you came to see me with a purpose in mind."

I shifted in my seat. John Conant and I had known each other for a long time and we were used to each other's ways – ways of doing and ways of thinking. I was fortunate to work under him as he was more imaginative than most of his kind, willing to look at things from a different perspective, and moreover he trusted me to do my job in the way I saw fit. But I valued his good opinion of me and I did not want him to think that I had taken leave of my senses.

"It is concerning James Foster," I said after some hesitation. At that moment the door opened and Miss Lily bustled into the room, discarding her hat and cloak and leaning over her father to kiss him on the cheek. She flapped her hand at me as I stood.

"Please sit down, Constable Plank," she said. She walked over to the dining table. "I shall help myself to some food; please do carry on. I shall be as quiet as a mouse."

I paused, remembering the last time I had seen Miss Conant, on the evening of the party she had attended at the Foster house.

"You were saying something about James Foster," prompted the magistrate. Glancing over, I could see his daughter stiffen, and I knew she was listening carefully. "Hugh Foster's son, you mean? You know the fellow, do you not, Lily?"

"Yes, papa – a little," said Miss Lily, busying herself at the table.

"That's the one," I said, drawing the magistrate's attention back to me. "Did you know that his father died this month – Mr Hugh Foster?"

"Captain Henderson mentioned it, yes," said Conant. "Not unexpected, I understand; the fellow had been declining for some years."

"He was hit hard by the deaths of his loved ones," I said. "I sent word to his doctor, to ask if there was anything that should concern us, but he was satisfied: death following heart failure related to age." I looked across at Miss Lily and leaned towards her father. "But there is something else." Conant looked questioningly at me. "It is possible that James Foster is not his father's son."

Miss Lily abandoned her plate of food and walked over to us, perching on the footstool by her father's chair. "Is James Foster illegitimate – is that the suggestion?" she asked.

"Lily!" said her father.

She smiled at his outrage. "Papa, if you are going to welcome me into your place of work and introduce me to your constables, you must expect me to learn a little of the ways of the world. I am perfectly aware that children may arrive outside marriage."

Conant shook his head and sighed. "When your mother and I are reunited in Heaven," he said, "I am sure she will have plenty to say to me about the exposure of young minds to unsavoury facts. In any case, it is highly unlikely: by all accounts Hugh Foster was not the sort of husband to stray, unless you mean before he was married…" He looked enquiringly at me.

I shook my head. "The suggestion is not that James Foster is the illegitimate son of Hugh Foster; rather, that he is not his son at all. An impostor. The housekeeper told me that the late butler – Mr Harding – had his suspicions."

"An impostor?" repeated the magistrate, and I nodded. "Do you know whether the butler discussed his concerns with anyone else?" He was sharp, Mr Conant – as I had done, he was wondering whether the butler had been killed to silence him.

"It's possible," I admitted.

"Quite a coincidence, to die so soon after mentioning his worries to the housekeeper..." said the magistrate, almost to himself.

"I wondered the same myself," I said, "and Constable Wilson and I visited the apothecary who was called to see the butler's body on the morning after he died. And he said that it was a heart seizure."

"So nothing suspicious," said Conant. "A natural death?"

"Quick and painless, the apothecary said," I confirmed. "A good way to go."

"Indeed," said the magistrate.

"Papa!" said Miss Conant. "What a thing to say!" She shuddered. "The poor man." She leaned against her father's knee and he stroked her hair. Suddenly she sat up. "Was Orthez still there, Constable Plank?"

"You mean that enormous dog?" I asked.

She nodded. "He looks frightening but he's as gentle as a lamb. Heavens, he must be quite an age now."

"At least fifteen," said the magistrate, "if he was named in honour of the Battle of Orthez. That was in 1814."

"Men and wars," said Miss Conant, shaking her head. "How you do like to remember them. Imagine seeing a sweet little puppy and deciding to give it the name of a battle." She smiled sadly. "I should imagine Orthez was heartbroken when James went away to the plantation – he was always James's dog really. If only that dog could speak: I'm sure he could tell you whether it really is James or not."

As I had said to Wilson, I was still uneasy about that dog.

CHAPTER ELEVEN

Angry and careless

FRIDAY 27TH MARCH 1829 – MORNING

Martha's question about the burial club had stayed with me: how did payment collections stop so promptly after Harding's death? I sent a letter to Mrs Godwin and her reply was waiting for me at the police office. Tom Neale held it to his nose before passing it to me.

"Perfumed, Sam," he said with a wink, "and most definitely a lady's handwriting. You'll be giving our young constables something to chat about, if you've a sweetheart hidden away."

I rolled my eyes at him. "Stop your nonsense, Tom – some of them are just daft enough to believe you."

The office keeper laughed before turning his attention to a constable struggling up the steps to the office with a drunkard leaning on him. "Don't bring him in here, lad," he cried, rushing out from behind his counter. "If he casts up his accounts on my floor, it'll be you busy with the bucket and mop, not me."

I left them to it and took my letter into the back office. "Dear Constable Plank," it began, in clear and careful script, "In answer to your questions I can confirm that Mr Harding and I, along with several others here at Villiers Street, were due to make payments to our burial club on Thursday 22nd January last. The payments were collected every other Thursday, usually in the late morning, but no-one called that day and no-one has called since. According to the receipt they issued when I first subscribed, the address of the club's office is the Fountain public house in Wych Street. I remain, sir, your servant. Elizabeth Godwin (Mrs)."

I read the letter again, noting the name of the public house in my book, and heard footsteps in the corridor. Wilson came into the office but before he could take off his coat I waved Mrs Godwin's letter at him.

"Burial club," I said. "Wych Street – a public house."

His face brightened at the prospect of a tankard and we set off for Aldwych.

◆

Half an hour later we turned off Drury Lane into the narrow shade of Wych Street, the buildings crowding in on us and a stench rising from the overfilled gutters. The great fire had spared this part of London, but the overhanging upper floors of the old buildings were not suited to modern life. The door of one dwelling flew open as we passed and two dogs came tumbling out, fighting over a scrap of food. A ragged child of no more than four watched them hungrily from her perch on a neighbouring doorstep but wisely kept her distance; I crossed over to her and pressed a coin into her hand, putting a finger to my lips. She stared up at me and quickly hid both hand and coin in her apron pocket.

The Fountain was easy to spot, with its creaking wooden board hanging outside. Rearing up behind it was the lovely tower of St Clement Danes, and at that moment the bells began to peal the hour.

"Oranges and lemons, say the bells of St Clements," said Wilson, a shy smile on his face. "Alice sings that rhyme to George."

"You will have to tell her that you heard them today," I said. We went in to the Fountain, Wilson ducking his head to fit through the low doorframe, and paused for a moment for our eyes to adjust to the gloom within. The room was about half full, with some customers in the overalls of market porters – we were not far from Covent Garden – and others in the sombre outfits of clerks from the nearby Inns of Court. Wilson spied a small table and led the way to it, catching the eye of the pot boy as he

passed and ordering two tankards. I thought of protest-
ing – Martha would soon detect the beer on me – but I
was thirsty after our walk.

"He's a lovely little lad, your George," I said as we
waited for our drinks.

"He is that," agreed Wilson. The pot boy put down
two brimming tankards and Wilson took a long draught
of his, wiping his mouth with the back of his hand. He
looked at me and seemed to make a decision. "Alice says
that we're not to tell him about his real parents until he's
grown. He's to think we're his mother and father." Wilson took another swig from his tankard. "It's not a lie exactly, but then it's not telling him the truth either." He
paused. "What would you do in my shoes?"

I pretended to think for a moment. I didn't need to
consider my answer, but if someone asks you an important question it's polite to take your time. "There's
more to being a parent than the act of procreation, you
know," I said eventually. "Begetting a child is the easiest
thing in the world, for most people. But staying put and
raising that child, now that's the hard part. And there's
no doubt in my mind – none at all – that you will stay put
for George, and for the other little ones that will come
along soon enough. If that's not being a father, I don't
know what is." Wilson looked down at the table but I
could tell from the reddening of his cheeks that he had

heard me. I cleared my throat. "Now, what do we know about burial clubs?"

"I know that my mother subscribes to one," he replied, "run by the church. I don't know how we would have managed, otherwise, when we lost Peter and Ellen. Two funerals, even for little ones, well, that's not cheap." Wilson blinked hard and looked down at the table; he rarely talked of the two siblings who had died in a fire some five years earlier, but I suspected they were often on his mind.

"And it's the same burial club that she uses now?" I asked.

Wilson nodded. "We're lucky, I do know that. Ma's friend was in another club, and when her husband died they refused to pay out, saying that she'd fallen behind on her payments – and we know she paid regular as clockwork. But they said she didn't have all the receipts to prove it. Disgusting, that was: cheating a grieving widow. We had a collection for her and she managed in the end."

"Well, it seems that Mr Harding's burial club might be up to the same tricks," I said.

"The Fosters' butler?" asked Wilson. I reached into my pocket for the housekeeper's letter and held it out to him; he took it and read it. "So they are all paying in," he said, handing the letter back. "That soon adds up – and they won't be the only household involved." He looked over his shoulder to the bar, where the tavern keeper was standing, arms folded over his stomach, surveying his customers. "D'you think he's running the burial club?" he asked, indicating the fellow with a jerk of his head.

"Perhaps," I said, "although it's more likely – if it is a racket – that they just use this address, knowing full well that no-one will come looking for them until it goes wrong. Only a cork-brained fellow would run a rig from his own premises. That said, I doubt they chose this place at random, and our fine host may be able to tell us something."

As I approached the tavern keeper he idly scratched his whiskers, but I saw him hesitate for a second as he caught sight of my uniform. He shoved his hands into the deep pockets of his apron, which bore the stains and scars of many a wrestle with a barrel.

"Constable," he said, managing to make it sound like an insult.

"Aye," I said. "And your name, sir?" I took out my notebook; in truth I had not intended to write anything but his manner irritated me. I waited, my pencil poised above the page.

"Scott," he said reluctantly. "James Scott."

I wrote it down. "And you are the proprietor of this public house?" I asked.

"The victualler, yes," Scott replied.

"And are you aware, Mr Scott, of a fraudulent burial club being run from your premises?" I asked, and had the satisfaction of seeing the fellow lose a little of his swagger.

"Hold on, now, constable," he said, taking his hands from his pockets and spreading them before him on the bar, perhaps to indicate that he had nothing to hide. I said nothing; it is a rare man who can stand a silence for long, and indeed Scott soon started to talk again. "There's Jem Fanshawe and his pals – they run a burial club. They meet here every week to count the takings and make up their books. But Jem's no deep file: I've known him a decade or more, and he's an honest fellow – you can take my word for that."

I raised an eyebrow. "A man might give his word to all sorts of things, to keep his licence."

Scott's eyes darted around the room before he leaned forward and spoke in a low tone. "Jem started out years ago running a clothing club – there's plenty round here wearing every last rag they own and glad to put a penny aside when they can against the day when they need a pair of boots or a heavy coat. Back then he was a pious man, Jem, and I was happy to help by letting him keep the takings here." His glance flicked to the curtain leading to the private room behind the bar; I guessed he kept his strongbox under his bed, like many of his kind.

"Did people make claims against the club?" I asked.

"From time to time, aye," said Scott, "and Jem paid out what was due, if that's your next question."

"And what happened to Jem's piety?" I asked.

"Last year he lost his wife and their three little ones within a week – measles took them all." The tavern keeper shook his head sadly. "Jem was spared, but he was a changed man – angry, careless."

"Angry and careless enough to turn to a life of crime?" I asked.

"Not on his own, no," said Scott, "but a while back – perhaps six months – he started coming in here with some rough fellows. Three or four of them."

"Did you know them?" I asked.

Scott shook his head. "They're not from round here, I can tell you that. South of the river, if I had to guess."

"Rough in what way?" I asked. "Causing trouble for you?"

"As you can see, constable," said the tavern keeper, indicating his own substantial girth, "I am not an easy fellow to push around, and my boy is the same, only twenty years younger and about a foot taller. Rather like your friend over there," he indicated Wilson with a jerk of his head, "he's a handy fellow to have around. So no trouble, no, but I could tell they had it in them. Once or twice I tried to talk to Jem, to warn him…"

"But he wouldn't listen?" I suggested.

"Like I said: he's careless these days."

"Aye, you did," I said, closing my notebook. "That will do for now, Mr Scott. It would be best – given your license and all – if you didn't tell Mr Fanshawe that we were asking about him." I looked at the tavern keeper and he gave a nod. "And if you or your son remember anything about these rough fellows from south of the river, you can send word to me at Great Marlborough Street – Constable Plank."

I could almost see the thoughts crossing Scott's mind as he considered his options. I took my time over putting away my notebook and brushing imaginary dust from my coat, and he made a decision. He leaned forward and spoke quietly.

"One of them," he said, "boasted about being one of your lot."

"A constable?" I asked. "From a police office?"

He shook his head. "Not a constable, no. One of the fancier lot – a runner. George, I think they called him."

◆

Wilson was indignant. "A runner?" he said as we turned our step towards Piccadilly. "And they lord it over us, claiming to be the... the...". He struggled to find the word. We stopped to let a coach barrel past us before we stepped out into Drury Lane.

"The top of the heap?" I suggested. "The elite?"

"That's it," he said vigorously, stabbing the air with his finger. "The elite."

"I was a Redbreast once," I said casually.

Wilson stopped dead. "You?" he said. "You were a runner?"

"A Principal Officer, if you don't mind," I said, carrying on walking. "'Bow Street Runners' makes it sound like a gang of footmen, but the public seems to like it."

Wilson was still looking at me with amazement as he scurried to catch up with me. "You were a runner? When?"

"Before you were born, lad," I said with a smile. "I was only a nipper myself – sixteen years old – and I liked the look of the uniform. A handsome red waistcoat and a gilt-topped cane – I fancied myself swaggering around with that and catching the eye of the girls. And the money's good, if you have the right clients: the Bank of England pays forty guineas a year to the Redbreasts who stand guard when the quarterly dividends are paid. And I hear tell that a pair of them goes with the King whenever he travels out of London."

"What happened?" asked Wilson. "Why did you leave?"

We were walking past the Tavistock Chapel on Broad Court and I stopped. "This is a pretty little place," I said. "Well-situated for the resting of feet." I pushed open the door and went inside, Wilson following me. We chose a pew towards the back of the chapel and sat down; we were alone apart from an old woman sitting and praying – or more likely snoozing – in the corner of the first pew.

"In his life," I began, looking straight ahead at the altar, "a man will make many decisions. And everything has consequences, and a price. To marry or not, for instance. This time next week, you'll be a married man yourself. You'll pay the price of your bachelorhood, and in exchange you will receive a good woman and children. For the rest of your lives together, you will bring in money to support Alice and your family, and in exchange she will love and care for you."

Wilson shifted in his seat. "Do you mean to say that it is not worth the price – that I should not marry?" he asked.

"Goodness me, no," I said hurriedly, imagining vividly the price Martha would make me pay if I caused a rift between Wilson and Alice only days before their wedding. "I mean it only as an example: nothing in life is without consequences – some good and some bad." I tried again. "You asked me why I gave up the Redbreast life. In all honesty, I enjoyed it to begin with. I was apprenticed to an experienced runner and wherever he went, I followed – and it was exciting. We could be called anywhere in London and had no idea what we would find when we arrived. He went further afield too – runners can be summoned anywhere in the country – but no justices would have granted arrest authority to a youngster like me, so I stayed home at Bow Street when he went away. I watched and I listened, and the more I saw and heard, the less I liked it."

Wilson had turned towards me with wide eyes. "What did you see and hear?" he asked.

"Do you know how runners are paid?" I asked in return. Wilson shook his head. "They are given a very small annual allowance – not enough to live on. And the rest depends on how well they do their job." I stopped and corrected myself. "On how they do their job. If you want a runner's assistance, for example, you will have to pay him a guinea a day plus fourteen shillings for expenses." Wilson blew out through his lips in admiration. "And then there is the Parliamentary reward."

"I've heard tell of that," said Wilson.

"Aye," I said, "you will have done. If a serious felon is convicted, forty pounds is shared out between those who contributed to the conviction – witnesses, say, and the runner who arrested him."

"But I've never had a share of any forty pounds," said Wilson indignantly, "and we've sent all sorts of rogues before the court."

"And there's a good reason for that," I said. "The temptation of a share of forty pounds has proved too much for many – including many runners. Money becomes the reason for doing the job; they won't waste their time on offenders who don't yet weigh forty pounds, as they have it. And then you know the story of George Vaughan, maybe a dozen years ago now." Wilson shook his head. "He was a member of the Horse Patrol," I continued. "Very smart, they were, in their day: blue coat and scarlet waistcoat, of course, and then a leather stock, white leather gloves, black leather hat and steel spurs. And a pistol and a truncheon." Wilson raised his eyebrows. "Indeed," I said. "Well, this George Vaughan realised that waiting for criminals to commit crimes so that he could arrest them and claim his bounty might take some time, and so he decided to hurry things along. He planned a robbery in Hoxton, recruited a handful of birdwits and nibblers to do the dirty work, and then arrested them in the act to claim the forty pounds per head. Five years' hard labour they gave him for that." I sighed. "That's why we magistrates' constables are organised differently: we're paid our salary, whether we arrest anyone or no – we take no share of any bounty or reward, and we turn our backs on inducements." Wilson looked confused. "Sops," I said. "Bribes. Keeps us honest." I smiled. "Well, keeps most of us honest."

"Do you still have friends amongst the runners?" asked Wilson. "Someone you could ask about what Scott said?"

I shook my head. "That was more than thirty years ago; I daresay most of the men I knew have long gone." I stood to leave, and then a thought struck me. "The keeper at Coldbath Fields – is it still John Vickery?"

Wilson nodded. "That was our first job together, wasn't it – a run out to Coldbath to deliver a prisoner."

"That's right," I said. "The Fauntleroy case in twenty-four. I don't get there much these days – I leave the escorting of prisoners to you young fellows. But Vickery is still there?"

"Aye," said Wilson. "I was there only last week. Why?"

"He was a runner," I said. "I don't think he'd been long at Coldbath when we took Fauntleroy to him, so he's sure to have friends still at Bow Street."

"D'you think he'd tell you anything?" asked Wilson. "He might still be loyal to his old pals."

"Well, we'll see, shall we?" I said. "Coldbath can't be more than a half-hour from here."

CHAPTER TWELVE

A cruel master

FRIDAY 27TH MARCH 1829 – AFTERNOON

Coldbath Fields loomed in the distance as we turned onto Grays Inn Lane and then ducked down an alleyway towards Mount Pleasant – which had been named with the usual London irony when it was used as a dump for cinders and other refuse. Although smaller than its plans had allowed, not least because the money had run out during construction, the house of correction was still an imposing place, with its red-brick buildings squatting behind a high wall. We approached the entrance gateway on Dorrington Street; the pale grey stone arch was decorated with fetters, as a nod to the function of the building it guarded, and across the top was carved "House of Correction for the County of Middlesex 1794". I knocked loudly using the brass ring and after a moment the bolt was scraped back and one of the turnkeys stuck his head round the door, looking us up and down appraisingly.

"Yes, constables?" he asked. "What is your business?" He stuck out a hand, anticipating a warrant.

"We have no warrant today," I said, "but it is a matter of some importance. We would speak with Mr Vickery, if he is here."

"O' course the guvnor's here," said the turnkey with a snort. "Where else would 'e be? Sharing a pastry with the King at Windsor?" The fellow chuckled with appreciation of his own wit. He paused and then thrust out his hand again. "It's a fair step to the guvnor's house," he said craftily, "if you're wanting a guide."

I knew full well that the keeper's house was just inside the gate but I did not want to waste time arguing with the turnkey for the sake of a small coin. I pulled one from my coat pocket and held it out to him; he took it and inspected it carefully, turning it to the light and then biting it. He seemed satisfied and hauled open the door for us to step into the prison. As we stood for a moment, waiting for him to close the gate again, we could hear the rhythmic cranking and grinding of the treadwheels for which Coldbath Fields was notorious. I had seen them in use once, a few years earlier, and had no wish to view them again, for they symbolise to me the very worst approach to punishment: the imposition of cruel, painful and pointless labour without any hope or intent of improvement. Each treadwheel – and Coldbath Fields had more than a dozen of them – is an enormous wooden drum with a range of steps about it, at a distance of about a foot and half from each other. About thirty prisoners at a time work the wheel by walking on it, which rotates it towards them; their weight keeps the wheel in motion and they must keep climbing, as though going uphill, but the treadwheel sinks down to meet them and they go nowhere.

"There's no need to trouble yourself with the guided tour," I said with exaggerated politeness. "We will find our own way." The turnkey shrugged his indifference and went back into the gatehouse.

♦

The keeper's house was, as I knew, just to our right. It formed part of the high wall surrounding Coldbath, giving it a curious dual aspect: the bulk of the house, including its front door, was inside the prison, while two of its windows – a large bay window downstairs and a smaller one above – looked outwards over a small neat garden to the world beyond the prison. I knocked on the door, noticing that the knocker was polished to a high shine and that the doorstep had been recently scrubbed; Vickery was no bachelor.

Wilson followed my eye. "Maybe one of the female prisoners…" he said. But the words died on his lips as the door was opened by an elegant woman in a stylish green dress, her red hair caught up in an artless fashion that I knew, from Martha's daily battle with her own curls, took a great deal of time and a several handfuls of pins.

"Constables," she said. It was not a question but a statement, and told me that she was used to life at Coldbath Fields.

"Madam," I said, "we would like to see Mr Vickery, if he is at home. I am Constable Plank of Great Marlborough Street, and this is Constable Wilson."

"My father is about the prison," she said, "but," she lifted a finger to indicate that we should listen and then smiled as the bells of a nearby church started to toll, "I expect him home at any moment. He is not a man to keep a meal waiting."

"None of us is, Miss Vickery," I said.

"You will join us, I am sure, constables," she said. "Ah, here he is." I turned to see John Vickery striding towards us. "Papa, Constable Plank and Constable Wilson have come for lunch."

"Sensible fellows," said Vickery, holding out his hand and greeting us in turn. "Come, come – I am famished."

Wilson looked nonplussed as the keeper ushered us into the house and his daughter preceded us into the dining room. She disappeared through a door which I guessed led to the kitchen, to warn the cook that there were two extra mouths, and Vickery waved us into chairs while he opened a sideboard and extracted plates, cutlery and tumblers for us.

"Mr Vickery," I said, "we cannot impose on you like this. It was our mistake to arrive at this time."

"And what would you be eating if you were not here?" asked the keeper. "A greasy pie and a glass of ale in a tavern? A hot pork roll on the corner of a dirty street? You cannot expect to do good work on such meagre rations. I live above the shop, gentlemen, as you can see, and a day without visitors is a rare one. Phoebe – my girl – knows enough to expect hungry fellows and keeps extra rations to hand. But I take my dues, you can be sure. One day I shall arrive at your place of work and demand a hearty meal and you will be in my debt. You are from Great Marlborough Street, yes? I recognise you." And he put a meaty hand on Wilson's shoulder.

"We are, yes," I confirmed. "And you and I have met too, about five years ago, soon after you moved here to Coldbath. Fauntleroy – the banker."

The keeper finished setting the table and sat down. "Oh, I remember him. Quiet as a mouse – very neat, very polite. And now I remember you, constable." He smiled ruefully. "I'm afraid that I often remember the prisoners better than the officers who accompany them. This fellow," he indicated Wilson again, "I know better – still young enough to be doing the Coldbath run."

Wilson nodded. "Aye, sir – once or twice a month."

There was a bang on the kitchen door and the keeper jumped up to open it; his daughter appeared carrying an enormous tureen, with cloths over her hands to protect them from the heat. She put the tureen on the table and went back into the kitchen twice more, fetching first a whole loaf of bread on a wooden platter and then a large jug of barley water. At a glance from her father, she rolled her eyes but went out once more and returned with a slightly smaller jug of ale. She put it on the table and then checked that everything was in place before taking the lid off the tureen and serving us each with a generous bowl of mutton stew.

"Slice your own bread, lad," the keeper said to Wilson, pouring each of us a generous tumbler of ale. "There's another loaf in the kitchen. But save room: my Phoebe's apple tart is the best in London. It's what I shall miss most about her."

His daughter tutted in an affectionate way; this was plainly not the first time he had made this observation.

"Are you going away, Miss Vickery?" I asked.

"I am to be married, constable," she said. "Later this year, to a gentleman from Edinburgh."

"That fiery hair of hers was bound to catch the eye of a Scotsman," said her father. "If only I had had the foresight to paint it with boot blacking while she slept."

"And shall you move to Edinburgh, Miss Vickery?" I asked.

The young woman nodded. "My husband-to-be – Mr Steventon – is proprietor of the Black Bull Hotel and coach office in Princes Street, and I am to help him. There are plans to start a direct coach from there to London, so we shall see plenty of each other, papa." She reached over and patted her father's hand.

"Apple tart, my girl – can't you see Constable Wilson casting desperate eyes towards the kitchen?" said her father gruffly, while Wilson flushed at having been caught.

After the meal, Miss Vickery took her leave of us and went upstairs. Vickery sat back in his chair and patted his belly. "And now, gentlemen," he said, "to business." He looked at me. I glanced at the kitchen door; the clattering within told me that we were not alone. Vickery smiled. "That's Bertha," he said. "No need to concern yourselves about her – she's deaf as an adder."

I leaned forward. "It's your time before Coldbath that I wanted to talk about," I said.

"Bow Street, you mean?" asked Vickery.

"Aye," I said. "Wilson and I are looking into some… irregularities in a burial club." Vickery's face gave away nothing except mild interest. "People have paid into the club and the money has disappeared. A familiar story, I am afraid." I cleared my throat. "But there is something a little peculiar about this case. We are told that one of the men running the racket is a runner."

"And you want to know whether I know the fellow, and whether I think it likely that he is an old file," said Vickery, with a slight tone of amusement.

"Would you tell us if you did?" I asked.

"Constable Plank," he said, "I was a runner for more than twenty years, but I am no longer a runner – I am the keeper of a house of correction. And as such, I devote my time to the punishment of crime. If I suspected a man of fraud, whatever his profession, I would do what I could to bring him to justice. So who is this man?"

"We don't have a name – yet," I said. "But he is one of a gang of three or four men, possibly from south of the river, and their front man for the burial club is called Jem Fanshawe. They meet him in the Fountain tavern, off Drury Lane."

"Fanshawe?" repeated Vickery. I nodded. "I knew a runner called George Fanshawe." I made sure not to react to the name and hoped that Wilson was doing the same. "Brothers, perhaps," mused Vickery.

"Is George Fanshawe still a runner?" I asked.

Vickery thought for a moment. "As far as I know. He's younger than I am – ten years perhaps. Plenty of years left to serve."

I spoke carefully. "If a runner was abusing his power to feather his own nest, would his fellow runners know about it, do you think?"

The keeper looked at me appraisingly. "We are not children, constable, you and I. We know that the world is a complicated and contradictory place. It can be tempting for a man to take perhaps too much advantage of the opportunities he encounters." I said nothing. Wilson's pencil paused above his notebook. "The financial rewards can be significant for those who make that their priority." He waved a hand around the perfectly pleasant but entirely ordinary dining room. "As you can plainly see, I did not."

"Did George Fanshawe?" I asked.

There was a long pause. "Perhaps," said Vickery eventually. He raised a hand as though stopping a runaway horse. "I am not saying that he did; I am saying simply that he is the type of man who might."

"I understand, sir," I said. I indicated to Wilson and he closed his notebook and stood. "Thank you for your hospitality," I said, "and for the plain answers to my blunt questions."

Vickery walked us to the front door and opened it. As we stepped out, he spoke again. "Did you know that I gave evidence to the Committee on the State of the Police in London, back in 1816?" I shook my head. "By then I had been a runner for seventeen years. They asked about our remuneration – whether runners were cheating the system of Parliamentary rewards. I said that we were not. Some runners do make a fortune from rewards offered by private parties, yes, but that is not cheating the system – it is taking full advantage of the system. The system could perhaps be improved. Personally, I am happy with my regular keeper's salary: no-one can accuse me of favouring one prisoner or doing another down for the sake of money." He held out his hand to each of us and we shook it. "Good day to you, constables – and remember, you owe me a meal." He smiled and went inside, shutting the door behind him.

Wilson and I were just about to knock on the turnkey's door to ask him to open the gate when we heard footsteps behind us. I turned to see Miss Vickery. She glanced over her shoulder and then beckoned us into the shadow of the wall, out of sight of her father's house.

"Constable Plank," she said in a low tone. "George Fanshawe." I looked at her enquiringly. "I came back downstairs for my shawl and heard you mention him to papa. And then I listened at the door. Papa does not know much about Mr Fanshawe, but I do. He is a wicked man, constable – a harsh man, and a bully. Our cook, Bertha – she used to work for him."

"The deaf woman?" I said.

"That's thanks to George Fanshawe," said Miss Vickery. "He was a cruel master. One day he struck her so hard that she lost her balance and hit her head on the corner of a bench and then the floor. She was lucky to live, constable, but the blows to her head damaged her hearing."

"Did she not report it?" asked Wilson.

"Report a runner? To whom?" she replied. "Fanshawe said he would kill her if he had to. She decided instead to escape. She knew our cook at the time, who wanted to go and live with her daughter in Kent, and so Bertha came to work for us."

"And she has never mentioned any of this to your father?" I asked.

"Not a word," said Miss Vickery. "And she only told me when I found her sobbing in the kitchen one day; she'd seen Fanshawe in the street and was terrified. She made me promise not to say anything, and it seemed safest. And now I must go: my father will be returning to work and will wonder where I am." She reached out and gripped my arm. "Whatever you suspect George Fanshawe of doing, constable, I am sure you are right."

CHAPTER THIRTEEN

Liberal with the brandy

TUESDAY 31ST MARCH 1829

I had thought I was allowing plenty of time, arriving at the church a half-hour before Martha had told me to, but when I turned into Queen Square Wilson was already there and raised a hand to greet me.

"A fine day," I said as I approached.

He nodded wordlessly.

I gestured at his uniform. "I see you have followed Mrs Plank's advice. As have I," I added, pointing to my own outfit. Knowing how little money the newlyweds would have, and how far it would need to stretch, Martha had suggested that if I wore my uniform to the wedding, then Wilson would be able to do the same and would not have to buy a smart coat. I had not objected: my blue frock coat suits me, and Martha had polished all eight buttons to a high shine.

"Aye," said Wilson, "although the collar feels a little...". He ran a nervous finger around the inside of his collar, stretching his neck this way and that, before shrugging and rolling his shoulders and glancing down Gloucester Street.

I made a decision. "Come on," I said. "We have at least half an hour before the others arrive, and I'm parched. Shall we head for the Red Lion?"

Wilson hesitated, looking again down Gloucester Street. "I promised I would be here first," he said. "If Alice arrives early and I'm not waiting for her..."

"Hah!" I said. "That shows me you're still a bachelor. You will soon learn that a woman can be on time, if it suits her, or late, if it suits her, but never early. Besides, it's traditional for a fellow to have a drink with his father on his wedding day, but you'll have to make do with me instead."

♦

"Samuel Plank, have you been drinking?" whispered my wife as she leaned forward to remove a stray hair from my coat.

"Wilson needed to calm his nerves," I replied. "Would you have me refuse a fellow on his wedding day?" Martha gave me a level look. "One small tankard of ale apiece," I added. "And I daresay you ladies had a little something before leaving home."

She smiled at me. "A thimbleful of wine, if you must know."

"I knew it," I said. "One night away from your husband, gallivanting in a public house with the innkeeper's wife and a reckless bride-to-be, and you throw yourself into a life of pleasure and abandon."

Martha stood next to me and squeezed my arm. "What nonsense you do talk," she said. "But it was fun, Sam, to spend the evening with Alice and Louisa. And all dressing together this morning in Alice's room at the Blue Boar – it made me feel young again."

"Then it was worth every minute of the lonely night I spent missing you," I said. "And I must say that it was a treat to wake up this morning with a fair share of the blanket still on my side of the bed."

Martha had to bite back her retort when Wilson came up to us accompanied by a tall woman of about my age and two smiling young women who looked very like her. "Mrs Plank, sir," he said, "this is my mother, and these are my sisters, Sally and Janey."

"Mrs Wilson," said Martha immediately, "I am so very pleased to meet you at last, after hearing so much about you. William is such a good lad – always so polite and helpful – and I know we have you to thank for that. You must tell me what he was like as a little boy." Wilson shot me a pleading look but there was nothing I could do: the two women had linked arms and were walking off towards the church. Sally and Janey looked at their brother, burst out laughing and followed their mother.

"You had better go in yourself," I said to Wilson. "It's nearly eleven o'clock." I held out my hand and he shook it before putting his shoulders back, taking a deep breath and turning towards the church.

I heard someone call "Good morning, Sam," and looked round to see George Atkins walking towards me with Alice at his side. When they reached me, Alice handed baby George to the innkeeper and leaned up to kiss each of them on the cheek.

George Atkins smiled, reaching up to take hold of the chubby fist the baby was waving around. "With Alice looking so beautiful today I couldn't risk letting the ladies walk here alone," he said. "A gentleman in a passing carriage might have snatched her up." I looked at Alice and she blushed but said nothing; I daresay she had grown used to his teasing ways. "But now, as you see, I am to be nursemaid and take this little rascal," he tickled George's belly and the baby laughed delightedly, "home with me so that we can prepare the bridal feast. I would say I drew the short straw but no straws were even offered: Louisa made it perfectly plain that she was not going to miss this wedding." He was suddenly serious. "He's a fine fellow, isn't he, Sam – your William? He'll be good to Alice."

Alice looked up at the innkeeper with shining eyes. "He will, Mr Atkins," she said with absolute certainty. She turned to me. "Are you ready, Constable Plank?" she asked. And just then the bells started chiming the hour.

Alice's dress, my wife later told me, had been made by the sister of Louisa Atkins – a talented seamstress – from cloth bought as a wedding present by all those who work at the Blue Boar. It was a pretty pale yellow in colour, and Alice had tucked a dainty posy of matching flowers into the band of her bonnet. As we stood together at the church door and readied ourselves to walk up the aisle, I patted the hand that Alice had tucked into my elbow and told her how well she looked. I could see Wilson waiting near the altar, his head turned towards us, and when we drew closer I felt Alice's grip loosen until, once we were standing alongside her future husband, she let go entirely and my arm felt chilled where her warmth had been.

The ceremony was unremarkable, with the vicar reading the familiar words from the prayer book and us bobbing up and down and answering as required. The young couple both confirmed that they wished to marry and then I stepped forward again to take hold of Alice's hand

and pass it to Wilson. As they said their vows – first Wilson in his steady, deep tone and then Alice, quieter but equally unfaltering – I looked across at Martha. She was watching the ceremony but felt my gaze on her and turned to smile at me with such sweetness and happiness that I was instantly cast back a quarter-century to the day on which we had said the self-same words to each other. And I will confess that I remember little of the rest of the ceremony, although it was touching to see Wilson slip the simple gold ring – which he had shown me with such pride the day before – onto the slim hand held out so trustingly by his bride.

The vicar led Wilson and his new wife into the vestry, with the parish clerk accompanying Martha and Wilson's mother, who had been asked to sign the marriage lines as they were written in the register, to confirm that they had witnessed the ceremony. Martha had been practising her name for days, to make it as neat as possible for posterity. When the party came back into the church, I could see Alice clutching her copy of the lines; clergy are careful always to hand the document to the woman, whose ability to prove her married state might one day be vital.

We followed the newlyweds back to the Blue Boar, where George Atkins and his cook had laid out a wonderful luncheon of bread, hot rolls, buttered toast, hard-boiled eggs and baked ham. As a nod to the occasion, there were pots of chocolate at one end of the table, and the wedding cake in the middle. The almond icing covering the cake had been browned in the oven, and my first forkful told me that George had been most liberal with the brandy.

"You be careful," I said to Martha, indicating the cake. "If you eat a whole slice of that, you'll be as soaked as the fruit."

When we had all eaten our fill, the table was pushed back and George Atkins picked up his fiddle. Wilson held out his hands to Alice and the two of them started to dance, the rest of us clapping and stamping our feet, and after only a few minutes we found ourselves unable to resist joining them. I daresay we made quite a spectacle, with baby George and the little Atkins children being passed from dancer to dancer, and everyone laughing and growing merrier. And that evening, as Martha and I finally climbed into bed, it was as though that quarter-century had fallen away and I was once again holding my own bride in my arms.

CHAPTER FOURTEEN

An imaginary coachman

THURSDAY 2ND APRIL 1829

I f I had any doubts on the matter, I could tell from the tightness of Martha's lips and the abruptness of her movements as she laid my breakfast before me that she was displeased.

"The Fountain is a tavern," I explained once again. "I shall be there at six o'clock – it will be full of people. The landlord knows who I am and knows my business; he's the one who told me when Fanshawe and his cronies would be making their weekly visit to count up their takings. It would be madness for Mr Fanshawe to cut up rough in such a place, and even if he does, he will be outnumbered."

"Humph," said Martha, turning her back on me and wiping the table with unnecessary energy.

"Do you think I am such a poltroon that I cannot do my job properly anymore?" I asked.

She turned to look at me. "Could you not wait until William can go with you? If it's that important, you could fetch him: they're only in Southwark."

"Good heavens, wife," I said in exasperation. "Do you not remember how I managed perfectly well before Wilson came along? I am not heading off to war with Boney – I am going to Drury Lane to talk to a scoundrel." I held out my hand and after a moment or two Martha reluctantly put hers into it. I pulled her onto my lap and she leaned against me. "Come on now, Mar," I said to the top of her head. "Mr and Mrs Wilson are enjoying their honeymoon at the Talbot Inn – you would not have me disturb them. Would you?" A little shake of her head. "And my work cannot stop just because Wilson is off duty, can it?" Another little shake. "And you don't want me setting off into the teeth of danger without a kiss from my wife, do you?" Martha pulled away at the mention of danger and saw me smiling.

"Samuel Plank," she said, pretending outrage, "you could talk the birds down from the trees." But she kissed me in a way that told me all was forgiven.

♦

I pushed open the door of the Fountain and, as I had expected, it was busy. Clerks from the nearby Inns of Court and from the naval and other public offices in Somerset House mixed with those readying themselves for an evening at the theatre, along with the usual complement of ladies of easy virtue and their bawds. I elbowed my way through to the counter. Scott was there, along with a sturdy woman I took to be his wife – both were so occupied pouring drinks, shouting orders through to the kitchen and dealing with the money that it took him a few minutes to notice me and make his way across to me.

"Your order, sir," he said and then looked again more closely. "Ah," he said.

"A tankard of ale," I said, "and a nod in the right direction."

Scott busied himself with my drink and, as he passed it to me with one hand and held out the other for my coins, said quietly, "Corner table, far right at the back. Four men – your fellow's in the blue neckerchief."

I picked up my tankard and held it high in front of me to protect it from jarring elbows and careless shoulders as I made my way towards the rear of the tavern. A curtain hung across a narrow doorway and from the frequency with which men disappeared behind it and then reappeared moments later I guessed it led through to the privy. I stopped to sip my ale and took the opportunity to observe Jem Fanshawe and his companions. With his blue neckerchief Jem was easy to pick out; he sat looking into the tavern, with the sunken face of a man who rarely eats a proper meal and the reddened nose of one who drinks too much and too often. Two of the others at the table were youngsters – no more than sixteen – but the fourth man was a different proposition. I suspected he was one of the rough types that Scott had mentioned. He was a strapping fellow, the cloth of his coat stretched across the width of his shoulders as he perched on a chair that seemed too small for him. Evidently his business with Fanshawe had just finished, as he stood, turned and walked out of the tavern, people moving smartly to let him pass. Glancing at the table through the gap he had left, I saw Fanshawe scoop a pile of coins from the table into a cloth bag, put a knot in it and drop it into the pocket of his coat.

I walked up to the table and stood silently. The two cubs looked up at me and glanced nervously at Fanshawe but said nothing.

Fanshawe narrowed his eyes at me. "Yes?" he said.

"Jem Fanshawe?" I asked. He said nothing. "My name is Arnold – Sam Arnold," I continued. "I'm coachman for a house in Duke Street. A footman I know mentioned that you run a burial club, and I'd like to subscribe."

"What footman?" asked Fanshawe.

"Daniel Finch," I said. "Villiers Street."

One of the youngsters took a notebook from his pocket, examined a couple of pages and then nodded to Fanshawe, whose face brightened.

"Sit down, Mr Arnold," he said, gesturing at the empty chair.

I put my tankard on the table and sat. The lad with the notebook took out a pencil and licked its point.

"Sam Arnold," said Fanshawe and the lad wrote it down. "Duke Street. Number?"

"Twelve," I said.

"Married?" he asked.

"No," I said.

"Widowed? Kiddies?"

"No," I said.

"No family at all?" he asked.

"A sister in Norfolk – married to a farmer up there," I said. "I don't want her to have to pay when, you know, when I'm gone," I said.

Fanshawe cocked his head to one side and smiled at me. "The burial club's one option, Mr Arnold. But are you a gambling man, sir?" he asked.

I shrugged; if a man is minded to make you an offer, it's always best to hear what he has to say.

"If your sister has a farmer for a husband, she'll not be short of money," he said. "It occurs to me that if you've money for a burial club, I might be able to suggest something more interesting to do with it. Something with a good rate of return."

"You mean I'd get something back?" I asked.

Fanshawe leaned forward. "A burial club, now, that's all well and good. You pay into it and – when you've passed on – someone else gets the benefit. Very generous of you, of course," again he smiled, "but someone else gets the benefit. A tontine, now: that's an investment. And you'd get the benefit yourself."

"A tontine?" I repeated. "Foreign, is it?"

"Originally, yes," replied Fanshawe. "They've had them on the continent for a century or more – perfectly respectable. You pay into the scheme when you're young and fit, and the money is invested for you so that it grows. You receive interest every six months on the money you've paid in. And when you're old, the scheme pays out to you. The government ran them here in London, to raise money for buildings and the like, until they realised they were paying out more than they were taking in."

"I can imagine they didn't like that," I said.

"Indeed. But there are those of us," and here Fanshawe leaned in closer and dropped his voice, "there are those of us who can see the potential of such schemes. Now you, Mr Arnold. You're a coachman, you said. Aged, what, forty-five?"

"Forty-nine," I said, and the youngster scribbled that in his notebook.

"A fine profession: not too dangerous, out in the fresh air, with good, regular meals from the cook at Duke Street, I'll hazard," said Fanshawe. I nodded. "Why then, Mr Arnold," he continued, "I should say you're the ideal investor for a tontine: you'll live a long and healthy life, able to pay in for many years, and then the money will be waiting for you when you stop work and need it. You'll have no worries about being able to pay for your own funeral, I can assure you."

"Well, that certainly makes sense, Mr Fanshawe," I said. I looked around the table. "And are you all investors? In a tontine?"

The three smiled at me. "Of course, Mr Arnold," said Fanshawe. "Tell me: does your master in Duke Street tell you how much to feed his horses? Or how often to change their shoes?" I shook my head. "He does not, no, and that is because he recognises that when it comes to the care and feeding of those beasts, you know more than he does. We all of us have our areas of expertise, Mr Arnold, and mine is showing people how they can make their money work harder for them. By all means, if you wish to subscribe to a burial club, I will be more than happy to do that for you. We have the papers here." He pointed to the satchel leaning against the leg of his chair. "But if you would prefer to see your money grow so that you have a comfortable, no, a prosperous old age, well then, a tontine is the thing for a sensible, healthy fellow like you."

I stayed quiet for a few moments, to suggest deep thought, and then nodded. "A tontine it is, sir. How much am I to invest?"

♦

"Ten pounds!" gasped Martha. "Dear heavens, that is quite an investment."

"An imaginary investment, my dear," I said, "made by an imaginary coachman." I ducked as my wife threw a slipper at me.

"I know that, Sam," she said, burrowing back down under the bedclothes. "I meant simply that this is a serious scheme you have uncovered. Would a coachman have such savings, do you think?"

I pulled my nightshirt on and climbed into bed. "A bachelor coachman might," I said, stretching out my arm so that Martha could lay her head on my chest. "A bachelor without the vast expense of a wife, with her endless demands for hairpins and petticoats and slippers – which she then tosses across the room at the very fellow who works himself to the bone to provide them."

"Are you saying, Samuel Plank, that I am a bad investment?" she asked with mock indignation.

I put my finger under her chin and looked down at her. "You, Martha Plank, are the best investment I have ever made. Worth every penny." I think she liked that answer, judging by her response.

CHAPTER FIFTEEN

The worst coffee in London

MONDAY 6TH APRIL 1829

I looked up as the lightning flashed. A couple of seconds later the thunder clapped as though it were in the street with me, and I pressed myself against the wall to avoid the flailing hooves of a rearing horse. The poor beast was squealing with terror, its big eyes rolling, and the coachman leapt from his box to take the animal by the bridle and calm it.

"Come, Sam, we shall have to canter ourselves if we're to avoid a soaking," said Edward Freame, taking hold of my arm and all but pulling me along Cornhill. "Here: just on the left." We ducked into the arcaded shelter of Castle Alley just in time: fat raindrops were falling, stirring up the dust as they landed, and it was obvious that we were in for a proper April storm. Freame grinned at me. "Perfect timing, constable, I think you will agree. And who can blame either of us if we choose to wait out this deluge." He had to raise his voice as thunder rolled again and the rain now beat down on the ground with ferocity. He pushed open the door of the Bank Coffee House and I followed him inside.

We were engulfed in a cloud of smoke and steam and my eyes took a moment to adjust to the dim interior. It was apparent why my friend Freame favoured this coffeehouse, as almost every patron was dressed as he was, identifying them as clerks or bankers from nearby houses, and doubtless some from the Old Lady herself. Freame spied two seats at the end of one of the long wooden tables and made his way over to them, sitting on one and guarding the other for me. A bluff old fellow next to us nodded once in greeting and wordlessly pushed a pile of newspapers towards us. Freame raised his hand and a lad appeared at my side, putting two dishes on the table in front of us and taking a penny for each from my friend. Moments later a second lad appeared and filled the dishes, pouring coffee from a steaming pot held theatrically high. Freame lifted his dish and sniffed it.

"The peculiar thing about coffee, I find," he said, "is that it smells so much better than it tastes."

The old fellow next to me snorted in agreement and leaned towards us. "That's why they say you can have as much as you want for your penny," he said. "No-one ever wants more than one dish." He stood and retrieved his hat from the floor under his seat. "I wish you good day, gentlemen."

I took a sip of my coffee, which was both scalding and bitter. I put the dish back on the table.

Freame laughed. "It is as well that no-one comes to a coffeehouse for the coffee," he said. "Mr Grubb would soon be out of business if all he offered was this." He gestured at his own dish, which he had likewise discarded. "Luckily for Mr Grubb, he can also offer conviviality: high-minded debate and discussion, and low-minded rumour and gossip. That's worth a penny of anyone's money – even a banker's. I try to come here once a week, to keep up with the news."

"And here I am, distracting you from it all," I said.

Freame grinned at me mischievously. "Far from it, Sam," he said. "You cannot imagine how my stock is rising as I sit here with a constable – I shall be the talk of the town. Now, what shall we discuss, with all ears straining to hear us?"

"Tontines," I suggested.

The banker raised his eyebrows. "Tontines, indeed. They are hardly news, Sam."

"But still hawked," I said. "I was offered one myself earlier this week."

"And I hope you had the good sense to turn it down," said Freame primly.

I took out my notebook. "I feigned great interest," I said, "but it would be useful to know why you would counsel against such an investment."

"For the usual reason, Sam," he said. "All the odds are stacked in favour of those running the scheme." I waited. Freame leaned forward, his elbows on the table. "The very design of the scheme is open to abuse," he continued. "The subscribers to a tontine each pay in a certain sum on the launch of the scheme, receiving annual interest on their investment, and the pot of money is then invested to increase its value. When only an agreed proportion of the subscribers are left alive – perhaps a tenth of them – the pot of money is divided between them. Some schemes do not pay out until there is only one single investor left. It was perhaps worth investing in the old days, when the government ran such schemes. Indeed, we have a tontine to thank for raising the funds to build Richmond Bridge. But nowadays, you would be mad to invest. Unscrupulous organisers can claim that the invested money has lost its value, so there is nothing left to pay out, no matter how long you live. And people are often caught out by the terms of the scheme: you can choose to invest six-monthly rather than all at once, and if you do that and then miss even a single payment, your whole investment is forfeit."

"And then there's murder," I said, and two fellows further along our table stopped talking and looked at me in alarm. "If you know that your return depends on you being the last man left alive, might you not help some of the other investors on their way?"

Freame nodded. "And even worse, Sam, I have heard tell of some schemes that permit you to subscribe in the name of your child, as your child is likely to have a better chance than you of outliving all other investors. So you can imagine how the other investors might react if they find that they now have to outlive a baby to have any chance of a return." He shook his head sadly. "If I were the Lord Chancellor, I would outlaw tontines tomorrow."

"If you were the Lord Chancellor," I said, "we would see a deal more reform than we have of late."

"My goodness, Sam," said the banker, laughing. "One sip of coffee and you're spouting political opinions with the best of them."

CHAPTER SIXTEEN

An old adversary

WEDNESDAY 8TH APRIL 1829

As Wilson would learn soon enough, much of a married man's happiness depends on knowing when to stay silent. I am proud to say that I do not lie to my wife, but I have also learned when not to tell her the whole truth. When I was a young man, this was usually to spare my own feelings; nowadays, it is more often to spare hers. And so it was that I set off that morning in my uniform, divesting myself of it in the back office of Great Marlborough Street before heading on to Wych Street once again. Martha would only worry if she knew that I was returning to the Fountain.

As arranged, Tom Neale had for me a purse specially made to my direction: in the body of the bag was a weight of metal scraps, which jingled enticingly, and near the closure was a smaller internal pocket containing a few coins, for show.

"You take care, Sam," he said as he handed it over.

"The Fountain tavern at noon, Tom," I said, slipping the purse into my pocket. "You know where I shall be."

"And you do not want Constable Wilson to go with you?" he asked.

"Good heavens, Tom – you sound like my wife," I said. "Can none of you remember that I was a perfectly good constable when I worked alone? Besides, Fanshawe is expecting a footman and a purse of money, not a footman, a hulking great constable and a purse of money."

"All I meant, Sam, was that Fanshawe will not be in that tavern alone, and having another constable with you would even things up a little," said the office keeper in conciliatory tones.

"My apologies, Tom," I said. "But it's not worth taking another fellow off his duties here. However many there are of them with Fanshawe, I cannot imagine them starting a brawl in the Fountain at that time of day."

Just then the door of the police office burst open and a pair of young constables struggled in, hauling a screeching woman between them. "Aaargh," yelped one of them. "She's bit me, the cat!" And I took advantage of the diversion to slip out of the office and set off for Soho.

♦

On still days the stench of London can be considerable, particularly on those streets away from the river – which, although adding its own distinctive aromas to the mix, does serve to funnel cleansing breezes through the city. And when I turned into Drury Lane, with its overhanging buildings and narrow, close courts, the pungent stink made me stop dead to catch my breath – and I grew up in the fetid alleyways of Wapping so am not much given to delicacy. Women sat by trestle tables lining the road, selling all manner of food to the passing crowds, and swatting away flies and birds in almost equal numbers. Beggars knelt or crawled in the gutter, hands outstretched, many of them old soldiers missing a limb or more. Usually my constable's coat protected me from interference, and without it I was assailed on all sides with pleas, entreaties and offers – the latter from filthy whores hitching up their skirts and trying to entice me with gap-toothed smiles and empty promises of cleanliness. Ignoring them all, I quickened my pace and turned into Wych Street. A lad ran up to me and I shook my head to indicate that I was not interested in whatever he was selling.

"Are you Mr Arnold?" he said urgently. "Going to the Fountain?" I stopped and looked at him. He was about ten years old, thin as a weasel, and dancing from foot to foot as he looked over his shoulder towards the tavern. "Are you him, sir?" he asked again.

"Who has told you to look out for me?" I asked.

"Mr Scott, sir," he said with another glance behind him. "He says you're not to come in. You're to leave straight away." He paused and looked up at me, pleadingly. "He says I'll not be paid if you come in, sir."

"In that case, my lad, I'll do as I'm told," I said. I felt in my pocket and extracted a coin. "And now you can tell Mr Scott something from me." The boy nodded, his eyes moving from the coin to my face and back again. "Tell him that a Mr Wilson will be by tomorrow and that he can speak to him. You have that?"

Another nod. "Mr Wilson will be by tomorrow to speak to Mr Scott," he repeated.

"That's it," I said, handing over the coin. The lad took it, examined it quickly and then shoved it into the waistband of his grubby trousers before scarpering off to the Fountain to collect the rest of his wages from Scott.

I retraced my steps into Drury Lane as instructed but then stopped and peered around the corner. I saw the lad disappear into the tavern and come out again a minute later, turning away from me to loiter outside Lyon's Inn, no doubt hoping for some errands from the clerks scratching away at their books within. I waited a moment longer and the door of the Fountain crashed open. A knot of men tumbled out into the street; at the centre of the group was Fanshawe, no longer ruling the roost but now pleading with a tall man who had his back to me.

The tall man listened for a minute or two and then shook his head. He said something to the other men and two of them – I could not be sure, but they looked like Fanshawe's young cronies from our meeting in the tavern – scurried away as fast as they could. He said something else, and the two remaining men took hold of Fanshawe and dragged him into the alleyway alongside the Fountain. The tall man then turned and walked purposefully in my direction. I pressed myself into a doorway, hunching my shoulders and turning my back to the street – but not before I had spotted what he was wearing. Beneath his well-cut blue coat I caught the flash of a canary-yellow waistcoat.

♦

"And you are certain he did not see you?" asked Wilson again.

"Quite certain," I said. "The doorway was deep, and there was not the slightest alteration in his step as he passed me."

"I should have gone with you," said Wilson, shaking his head.

"And hidden in the doorway with me?" I said. "That might well have caught his attention, don't you think – the two of us cuddled up together?" Wilson shrugged. "Anyway, I was in no danger: Mr Scott saw to that. When you see him tomorrow you can tell him that I will remember what he has done."

"And what about Fanshawe?" asked Wilson.

"I waited a good five minutes to be sure that the man in the canary waistcoat had gone and then went to check the alleyway. The two bullies were nowhere to be seen and Fanshawe was getting to his feet by himself so I left him to it; I think my business with him is done."

CHAPTER SEVENTEEN

The coachman's boots

THURSDAY 9TH APRIL 1829

"I can't be whiling away the evening in a tavern," said Wilson. "Alice will have a meal on the table and plenty to say about it if I'm late."

"Thank goodness I have you to keep me on the straight and narrow," I said, putting on my coat. "With your extensive experience of, what is it now, a whole week as a married man."

"I simply mean that my time is not my own anymore," he replied, holding open the door of the office for me.

"And I simply mean one drink – I said nothing about a whole evening."

And so it was that we found ourselves a corner table in the George and Dragon, a tankard in front of each of us. Wilson took a long drink from his, wiped his mouth with the back of his hand as he always did and nodded in appreciation.

"I thought you might have had a jar or two at the Fountain," I said.

"And find myself too tipsy to defend myself?" he replied. "Anyway, Scott took me through into his quarters as soon as I arrived."

"I daresay he didn't want anyone overhearing your business," I suggested.

Wilson took another drink and then retrieved the notebook from his pocket. "Talking of business..." he said, turning the pages until he reached the right one. "It seems that whatever you said to Scott last time reminded him of his duties as a law-abiding citizen."

"Or made him recall that a victualler's licence can be revoked if he knowingly permits crime on his premises," I said.

"Either way," continued Wilson, "he now knows which side his bread is buttered. Just before you arrived at the Fountain, the man in the canary waistcoat turned up and he and Fanshawe had a disagreement. Scott said that Fanshawe told this fellow that there was a new investor on the way – that's you – and told him what he knew: your name, and how you heard about the scheme, and where you work. And then he joked that he had never seen a coachman with such polished boots, and that it must mean that you had scrubbed up special to make a good impression."

We both looked down at my boots; even at the end of the day they still retained some of the shine rubbed into them every Saturday morning by me and buffed every weekday evening by Martha.

I smiled ruefully. "Of course: a coachman's boots would be covered in horse muck. I should have thought."

"Whether they guessed you were a constable, Scott wasn't sure, but they certainly knew you weren't a coachman," said Wilson.

"And if I lied about that, what else was a lie?" I added.

"That seemed to be it," said Wilson. "The canary waistcoat said he would wait to talk to you and Scott thought it prudent to warn you."

I drained my tankard. "And you thanked him for me?" I asked. "'Twas a brave thing to do, given the man involved."

"I did," said Wilson, mirroring me in lifting his own tankard. "And now I must go; Alice will be waiting, and I like to see George before she puts him to bed."

Hippocrates

TUESDAY 14TH APRIL 1829

I walked up the three scrubbed stone steps of the doctor's premises on Savile Street and knocked on the door. It swung open, and the relief showed on Wilson's face when he saw that it was me. I left my hat on the hall table alongside Wilson's, and glanced to my left into the parlour that served – that had served – as the doctor's waiting room. Perched on the edge of one of the seats in there was the maid. She held a cup in two shaking hands.

"She found him," said Wilson quietly, "when she came back from the market. It was her screaming that sent the message lad to us. I was in early this morning and Mr Neale sent me on ahead. The message lad said she," he indicated the maid with a nod of his head, "was in a state, but he didn't know why – she couldn't tell him."

"Has anyone else been in there?" I asked.

Wilson shook his head. "The cook from next door came in to tend to the maid, and she's in the kitchen now, but neither of them will go back into the consulting room. Can't say that I blame them." He stood aside as we reached the closed door of the doctor's consulting room. "It's rather bloody." I looked at him and he swallowed hard; Wilson was a big lad, and brave when needed, but his stomach was easily turned. "Very bloody," he amended.

I opened the door and walked in. Lying slumped across his desk was Doctor Branscombe, his arms flung out as though reaching for something. His skull was comprehensively smashed, with blood and matter staining his shirt and coat, as well as the surface on which he lay and the floor around his chair.

"A frenzied attack," I observed.

Wilson nodded. I saw with approval that he had his notebook out and was jotting in it. "Anger. Temper. Passion," he suggested.

"A woman?" I asked.

Wilson's eyes widened, but he wrote it down anyway. I walked around the desk so that I was standing at the doctor's shoulder. The toe of my boot touched something and I crouched down. It was an ornament of some kind. I picked it up, and it was slippery in my hand – slippery with blood – and heavy. Marble. A marble bust, about eight inches high, with a square base. I reached into my coat pocket and pulled out my handkerchief, then wiped the bust and held it to the window. It was a man, balding, with a fine curling beard. I weighed it in my hand and looked across at Wilson.

"Solid," I said. "Heavy."

Wilson nodded. "Not something a woman might use, then?" he asked.

"I think not," I said. "You'd need a big hand to hold it, and then some strength, to wield it with force and accuracy." I lifted it to shoulder height and mimicked striking someone with it. I heard a gasp; the cook was standing in the doorway, her hand to her mouth. I put the bust down on the desk.

"Yes?" Wilson asked the woman.

She bobbed a minimal curtsey. "I've to return to my kitchen, sir," she said. "Shall I take Sarah with me? Doctor Branscombe's maid?"

Wilson looked at me and I shook my head.

"Thank you, no," I said. "I shall need to speak to Sarah, but you may go." I wrapped the bust in my handkerchief – Martha would have something to say about the blood stains, I had no doubt – and sent Wilson to the kitchen in search of a larger cloth to add to the bundle. I paused in the doorway of the doctor's room and looked around one last time before pulling the door closed behind me and placing the partially-wrapped bust on the table in the hall.

The maid was sitting where we had left her, the cup now discarded on a side table. She was turning her hands over and over in her lap. She looked up as I walked in, her eyes shadowed with shock, and I could see now that she was really no more than a girl, perhaps fifteen. I picked up a chair and placed it alongside her and sat down. I heard Wilson return from the kitchen and pause in the hall before taking up a position at the door to the waiting room. I knew without looking around that he would have his notebook at the ready.

"My name is Constable Plank," I said, "and that tall fellow standing by the door is Constable Wilson." The maid looked at me and then at Wilson but said nothing. "And you are Sarah, I understand."

"Yes," she said haltingly. "Sarah Lewis." She looked across at Wilson again.

"Constable Wilson is writing things down because otherwise I might forget them," I explained. "And we need to remember everything so that we can find out who attacked Doctor Branscombe."

"Is he... is he..." the maid asked, putting her hand to her mouth as though unable to say the word.

I nodded. "Yes," I said.

Sarah leaned closer to me. "What will happen to him?" she whispered. "Will I have to clean it up?"

"Oh no, Miss Lewis," I said. "When Constable Wilson and I return to our police office, we will arrange for the undertaker to come and collect the body, and he and his men will, well, clear up. There is no need for you to go into that room again – indeed, it is better that you do not."

The maid exhaled. "Thank you, sir. I can't get it out of my head," she tapped her temple with a shaking hand, "what I saw. I don't want to look on it again."

"You shall not, Miss Lewis. Once we have finished talking to you, you are to go straight home – you live with your parents?"

She nodded. "With my mother, yes."

"And how long have you worked for the doctor?"

Sarah thought for a moment. "Nearly two years, sir – it will be two years next month."

"And do you know of anything that might have led to this – did you overhear the doctor arguing with anyone, or anyone threatening the doctor?"

She shook her head emphatically. "Oh no, sir – the doctor was a real gentleman to work for. Quiet. Polite. I never heard nothing out of the ordinary."

"And is – was – Doctor Branscombe a single gentleman, Miss Lewis?"

"Not single, sir – a widower. Her next door – the cook – told me that he lost his wife and their baby, oh, twenty or more years ago now. Said he kept locks of their hair in his watch case, but I never saw that."

I glanced up at Wilson and he nodded.

"Now this morning, Miss Lewis. You went to the market. At what time?"

"The church had just struck nine," she replied. "The doctor said he had a hankering for mackerel, and the fish man sells out early. So as soon as I had cleared his breakfast pots, I went."

"And how long were you gone?" I asked.

"No more than an hour."

"And when you came back, you used the front door?" I asked.

The maid drew herself up a little in her chair. "Of course. I am not a scullery maid."

"Indeed," I said. "And was everything as it should be – the door had not been forced open?"

She shook her head.

"And there was no sign of disturbance in the kitchen or the back of the house? No broken windows or doors?"

She shook her head again.

"And what did you do then, Miss Lewis?" I asked.

She swallowed and closed her eyes for a moment. "I laid out the tea tray – the doctor always has tea at half-past ten. There was no-one waiting in here, and the doctor's door was slightly ajar so I knew that he was not with a patient – he always shuts the door when he is with someone. I knocked on the door to say that I was back and to ask if he wanted his tea a bit early, and when there was no reply I went in and," another swallow, "and I saw him. At first I thought he had fainted onto his desk, so I went a bit closer, and that's when I saw... everything."

I reached across and put my hand gently on her clasped ones. "I know that this is horrifying, Miss Lewis, but we are relying on you, Constable Wilson and I. You are what we call a witness – it is a very important thing. Please, if you can, continue."

She nodded and blinked. "I ran out of the house and went next door to fetch the cook – I thought she might know what to do. I don't remember this, but they say I was screaming." She looked embarrassed. "Screaming in the street, sir."

"Miss Lewis, if I had come home to what you saw, I am sure I would have screamed in the street too," I said.

♦

"Hippocrates, I should imagine," said John Conant, peering at the bust I had placed on his table, taking care to spread out a napkin first. "And is that blood?"

I nodded grimly. "And worse," I replied. "It was used to beat a man to death. About the head." I pointed at my own skull.

The magistrate looked up at me over his spectacles. "Ah yes, Thin Billy mentioned something about it when he cleared my breakfast. A doctor, I think he said."

"Doctor Branscombe, yes," I confirmed. "Savile Street."

The magistrate walked over to his window and gazed down into the street. I used to think that he was looking out for someone, or keeping an eye on the business of the court, but I now knew that he was all but unseeing at these times: if John Conant was looking out of his window, he was thinking. After a couple of minutes, he turned back to me.

"Do you think that one of his patients might have done it? Perhaps the doctor gave some unwelcome news or advice?" he asked.

"Possibly," I said. "I looked at the doctor's diary and he was not expecting anyone this morning, but the maid – she came home from the market and found the body – the maid said that there was no sign of anyone breaking into the house."

Conant nodded. "So the doctor knew his caller and let him in." He put his head to one side. "Or her?" He walked over to the table and picked up the bloodied bust, using the napkin to shield his hand. "Unlikely. It would take some strength to clout a man with that." He replaced the bust carefully. "Were there other ornaments he could have used, or did he select Hippocrates deliberately?"

I took out my notebook; Wilson and I had gone over his notes when we had returned to Great Marlborough Street and I had written a few reminders and annotations in my own book. "There were two busts on the mantel-piece – well, one still in place and a square in the dust where Hippocrates had lived. The other was John Donne."

"The poet?" asked Conant. I nodded. "Perhaps Hippocrates was simply the nearest to hand. A robbery, do you think?"

"That was our first thought," I agreed, "but the maid mentioned a watch-case of which Doctor Branscombe was very fond, and Wilson checked the body and found it in place – and quite obvious to any robber. We did not ask the maid to check the room, to confirm if anything was missing, but there was a handsome silver letter knife on the desk and some banknotes in the pocket of the doctor's coat, so I think not." I paused. "One more thing, sir. Doctor Branscombe was the family physician for the Fosters, in Villiers Street. It may be a coincidence, of course."

The magistrate stood quietly for a few moments. "Or it may not," he said eventually.

♦

Martha shivered. "Clubbed over the head with a bust?" she said. "There must have been a deal of anger behind that. A bust of who, did you say?"

Wilson swallowed his mouthful quickly so that he could answer. "Hippocrates. The Greek physician," he explained. "The father of modern medicine, they call him. Which is why all doctors take the Hippocratic oath."

"Indeed," said Martha, catching my eye and looking away quickly. "I had no idea." She had no doubt guessed that Wilson was simply repeating what I had told him, but then how is a fellow to learn, if not by listening and remembering what he is told? She gestured at the pot on the stove, and Wilson held out his plate. I kept reminding Martha that Wilson now had his own wife and kitchen, but she took such pleasure in feeding him. And every meal he ate with us was one fewer meal that had to be provided by Alice on the junior constable's wages that Wilson brought home, and on which relied not only Alice and George but also Wilson's widowed mother and her two daughters.

"I thought I knew him," I said, leaning back in my chair.

"Hippocrates?" asked Wilson, pausing with his spoon partway to his mouth.

Martha hooted with laughter, finally reduced to dabbing tears from her eyes with the corner of her apron. I gave her a stern look, but in truth seeing her merriment was always one of the delights of my life.

"Sam's not that old, William," she said when she had eventually stopped laughing. "I think he meant the doctor."

"The doctor, yes," I said. "You remember a couple of years ago, Martha, when Wilson and I were trying to find out who was providing medical services to the girls in Harrison Street? And I went to visit a doctor in Savile Street."

Martha nodded. "More like three years ago now, Sam, but yes, I remember. And this was the same man?"

I shook my head. "No: the same premises, but a different doctor. The fellow we knew must have scarpered."

"Although that might be relevant," suggested Wilson, reaching into his coat pocket for his notebook. "If this Doctor Branscombe was in the same line of business, perhaps he gave a patient some bad advice, or talked about their – their condition to someone else."

Martha nodded as she cleared the table. "Doctors must hear all sorts of things. But I'm sure they are not supposed to tell anyone – like priests in the Catholic church, they say."

"The seal of the confessional," I said. "That's what they call it. Whatever the priest hears, he cannot tell anyone."

Wilson looked at me. "But what if someone confesses to a crime? To a murder? Surely then the priest must go to the magistrate."

I shook my head. "Not even then."

"Well." Wilson blinked a few times. "And are doctors the same?"

"The next time I see my old pal Hippocrates," I said, winking at Martha, "I shall ask him."

CHAPTER NINETEEN

Scars and wagers

WEDNESDAY 15TH APRIL 1829

The next day I returned alone to Savile Street. As instructed, the undertaker's men had removed the body and then delivered the key to Great Marlborough Street; the note with it confirmed that Sarah Lewis had returned home as soon as she had let them in and that they had "removed the unpleasantness". And indeed the doctor's office had been put to rights, with only the asymmetry of the single bust on the mantelpiece suggesting that anything was out of the ordinary. I looked at the rug beneath the desk and a few dark spots remained, all but hidden in the pattern. Bloodstains were more obvious on a few letters on the desk, which had been straightened neatly. I sifted through them, making a note in my book of the patient names mentioned; as the doctor had willingly let his murderer into the house, it was possible that a patient was responsible. The doctor's diary was in the drawer of the desk and I took it out and turned to the page for the previous day. The space for morning appointments was blank, so the caller had been unexpected.

Remembering what Mrs Godwin had said on the day of Hugh Foster's funeral, I looked around for any notes the doctor might have made about his patients and their ailments. And in a cabinet next to the bookcase I found an ingenious system, revealing the late doctor to have been meticulous man. Perhaps to the doctor's design, a carpenter had divided the space inside the cabinet into twenty-five cubby-holes, a letter of the alphabet painted on each – X being the missing letter – and in each cubby-hole were papers relating to the patients whose surname began with that letter. Cleverly, the dividers could be moved along grooves in the wood, allowing each cubby-hole to be expanded or reduced as required: the Z one, for instance, was narrow and empty while the S one contained the most papers.

I extracted all the papers from the cubby-hole labelled with an F and took them over to the desk. I leafed through them until I found those relating to Hugh Foster and James Foster. Hugh Foster, I read, had suffered from failing eyesight and "general decline", and had complained of a loss of interest in food after the death of his wife. He had died from angina pectoris – a heart condition. I turned to the notes the doctor had written about James Foster, whom he had known since birth. There were the usual childhood ailments, including a broken arm when the boy had fallen from a tree at the age of seven. I smiled; there is not a boy in the land who has not fallen from a tree. The notes were silent for several years, coinciding with the years that James Foster had been in the Cayman Islands, and then, as Mrs Godwin had said, there was a record of the doctor's visit to Villiers Street on the morning of Saturday 7th March. "Patient has been brawling," the doctor had written. "Bruises to chest, tenderness to ribs – possible fracture. Cuts on knuckles – no fractures. Black eye – no damage to socket or eyeball." And then alongside this dry record of the doctor's examination was this, underlined twice: "No scar from broken arm".

♦

As I was leaving the doctor's premises I saw a young man standing on the other side of the street, looking up at the building I had just left. I waited for a coach to pass and went to cross over to him, but he caught sight of me and set off in the direction of Piccadilly.

"Excuse me, sir," I called, but he simply quickened his pace. He had looked familiar, although I could not quite place him, and nothing catches the attention of a constable like running away from him. I kept my distance, and after glancing behind him a couple of times he obviously decided that he had given me the slip and slowed down again. He carried on into Albany Row and then turned right into Piccadilly, dashed across the street, causing a hackney to swerve and its jarvey to swear, and turned left into St James's Street. I stuck my nose round the corner just in time to see the man striding up the steps of an elegant building on the right of the road. I crossed to look more closely at the building and at the top of the steps, set into the wall, was a discreet nameplate: Crockford's.

The heavy glazed door swung open. The doorman who appeared had certainly been hired for his imposing appearance, as he towered over me and was easily as broad as Wilson.

"Can I help you, sir?" he asked, managing to make it sound threatening.

"Perhaps," I said mildly. "I am Constable Samuel Plank, acting on the instructions of John Conant Esquire, magistrate. Can you tell me the name of the gentleman who entered these premises just before I arrived?"

"As a gentlemen's club, Crockford's offers its members privacy and discretion," he replied – it was obviously a phrase he repeated often.

"And as a magistrate, Mr Conant is able to issue warrants to have all such premises – and their members – searched," I responded. "On the other hand, if Mr Conant were to come by the information he requests without obstruction..."

The doorman looked over his shoulder and then leaned down towards me. "James Foster," he said. "A recent member, but very, very welcome, if you get my meaning."

♦

"And what was his meaning?" asked Martha, standing to clear the table.

"Well, I took it to suggest that Mr Foster is gambling heavily," I said. "He's come into this money from his father, and no doubt Crockford has sniffed him out."

"Sniffed him out?" repeated Martha, lifting the cloth that had been protecting the rhubarb pie and reaching for a knife to cut it.

"William Crockford is a canny man," I explained. "From what I hear, he makes it his business to know all the wealthiest men in London – who has inherited what, who owes what to whom – and then he targets them. He sends out private invitations, offers them a free wager or two to get them started – and he has hired the best French chef to fill their stomachs while they fill his coffers. Word of James Foster's inheritance will have reached his ears. Don't forget that young Foster has been living in the Caribbean for some years; he won't be wise to our cut-throat

London ways. And Miss Lily said that he was boasting about his prospects at that rout back in the spring."

Martha sat down again and pushed the jug of cream towards me. "It's terrible what it does to young men, this gambling," she said. "Too much money and too much time on their hands, and not enough sense in their heads."

We both fell silent as we ate our pie.

CHAPTER TWENTY

Hazard

TUESDAY 21ST APRIL 1829

J ust as I turned the corner into Great Marlborough Street, Mr Conant's coach was drawing to a halt outside the police office. Fred Dawson jumped down from the box and opened the door for Miss Lily, who stepped out into the street and caught sight of me.

"Constable Plank," she said. "Just the man I wanted to see."

I offered her my arm and we walked up the steps leading to the staircase to her father's room, but when I bowed in farewell, she looked surprised.

"That was not a polite turn of phrase, constable," she said. "You really are the person I need to see. Come, let us find my father."

The magistrate was in his dining room, seated at the table and flanked by piles of paper. His spectacles were perched on his nose and he looked over them at us as the door opened, smiling broadly when he saw his daughter.

"Lily, my dear," he said, walking over to us and taking both her hands before kissing her on the cheek.

"Papa," she said warmly, unpinning her hat and putting it on the sideboard. "I have collected Constable Plank and need to speak to you both."

Conant looked enquiringly at me and I shook my head.

"Coffee, my dear?" the magistrate asked his daughter, indicating the pot.

Miss Lily settled herself into one of the armchairs. "No thank you, papa – this is not a social call. Come, gentlemen." And she waved at the other chairs. Her father and I did as we were told.

"Constable Plank," she began, "some time ago we spoke about James Foster. Recently returned from his family's plantation in the Caribbean."

"I recall, miss," I said.

"This morning I called on his sister, Mrs Moncrieff." Miss Lily stopped and looked at me. "You will need your notebook, constable," she said.

"My apologies, Miss Lily," I said, standing so that I could retrieve the book from my pocket. I sat down again, opened the book on my knee, licked the end of my pencil, and waited.

Miss Lily nodded approvingly and continued. "I barely remember her from when I was a child, but Catherine – Mrs Moncrieff – and I have become friends since she invited me to her rout, for St Valentine's Day." She flashed me a warning look; plainly she had said nothing to her father of the unpleasant end to that evening. "She spent several years in the country – in Suffolk – and has limited social connections here in town. And with no mother or sister to confide in, well, she has formed an attachment to me."

"And she has told you something that concerns her, Miss Lily?" I asked. "About her brother?"

"She has, Constable Plank," replied Miss Lily, "and I know that you and Papa have some doubts of your own about him – about whether he really is James Foster."

"A sister would surely know," said Conant.

"But after six years apart, and..." I replied.

Miss Lily held up her hand. "You can put your minds at rest on that score," she said. "I explored the possibility with Catherine – with great discretion and cunning, so you needn't look so worried, both of you – and she has no doubts at all: the man who has returned is indeed her brother James Foster."

"But the dog," I said. "The dog who had been so loyal to the son before he went away."

"Six years is a long time," said Miss Lily. "And during those years Orthez transferred his affection to Catherine's father, who came to depend on him – dogs can sense when they are needed, I believe."

"That's true," said Conant, nodding. "You remember your grandmother's little dog?"

His daughter nodded. "Darling, she was called, Constable Plank, which was funny as she was a foul-tempered little thing and not at all darling. But near the end she would not leave Grandmama's side, sleeping on her bed and always within reach; I think she knew that Grandmama was frightened of dying alone. And when she did die, the howling from Darling was just awful – we wondered how a tiny dog could make such a sound. It was as though her heart had broken too."

We all paused for a moment until Conant spoke. "If the sister is not worried about her brother's identity," he asked, "what is she worried about?"

Miss Lily smoothed her skirt and sat a little more upright. "His behaviour," she said. "His moods and his temper."

The magistrate looked alarmed. "Is he violent?" he asked. "If he is, Lily, you must not return to that house."

His daughter reached across and patted her father's knee reassuringly. "Not violent, no, papa," she said, "but ill-tempered – quick to anger. But Catherine thinks she knows the reason. She asked one of the footmen to follow her brother, to find out where he was going. She suspected an unhappy attachment and wanted to know the name of the lady involved – she thought she might be able to help."

The magistrate and I glanced at each other, both wondering what type of woman might have ensnared a young man who had recently inherited a fortune and where the footman might have been led.

Miss Lily continued. "But it was not an affair of the heart. The footman said that for three days in a row Mr James went to the same place: a gentlemen's club on St James's Street."

"Crockford's," I said.

Miss Lily looked surprised. "That's right," she said.

"So it's gambling," said her father, shaking his head. "Foolish fellow: his money won't last long in that place. He's a sharp one, Crockford."

"What do you mean, papa?" asked Miss Lily.

"I've heard a few complaints about Mr Crockford," he explained. "Son of a fishmonger, if you can believe that, and uneducated, but a genius at calculating the odds – knowing a good wager from a bad one, my dear. He started out taking bets at boxing matches and horse races, and then he had the good fortune to meet a butcher who thought he was good at cribbage. Crockford took the man for all he had – which was plenty – and used his winnings to buy the place in St James. An honest gambling den is bad enough, but Crockford likes to be sure of the outcome. I'm told that he pays fellows to pretend to win, and to spread rumours that the club is in trouble because it is losing money to its members. Hazard is the game of choice in Crockford's – with loaded dice, of course – and he employs only the sharpest dealers for his card games."

Miss Lily looked indignant. "But if he is cheating, papa, why do his members not sue him?"

"It is hard to prove his actions, my dear," said Conant, "and those who lose money at his club may not want the world to know their business. The few matters that have been taken to court have failed, because Mr Crockford takes care to engage the finest legal minds in London."

"Poor Catherine, then," said his daughter. "If her brother is in the clutches of this Crockford man, their money will soon be spent."

"Surely she has her own money," I asked. "Her father will have left her provided for – and the little lad." I paged back through my notebook.

"Arthur," said Miss Lily, smiling. "He's a shy little boy, although perhaps it's not surprising: London must seem huge after Bury St Edmunds, particularly to a fellow only just turned seven. Catherine has a small legacy from her mother," she confirmed, "and a little from her father. Mr Foster's intention was to leave the majority of his fortune to the Quakers, to support the campaign to outlaw slavery and to be used for other good works. But when James returned, Mr Foster changed his will; he said James would need the money to set up his own household once the plantation had been sold. He made James promise to support Catherine and Arthur for as long as they needed it – I think he imagined that Catherine would remarry one day. But if James is gambling it all away, what will happen to Catherine – a widow with a child and very little money of her own?"

♦

Conant returned to the dining room after he had seen his daughter safely into his coach, having asked me to wait for him.

"Well, Sam," he said, taking the seat next to me as I looked back through the notes I had made. "A familiar story, I am afraid."

"It is indeed," I agreed. "Mrs Plank described it well the other evening: young men with too much money and time on their hands, and not enough sense in their heads."

"Ha – that is it exactly," the magistrate said.

"But there is something that troubles me," I said. Conant looked at me and waited. I chose my words carefully, not wanting to betray any confidences. "After Miss Lily went to the rout in Villiers Street, she mentioned to me that James Foster was telling everyone that he was soon to come into a fortune. She dismissed it as the drunken blustering of a fool – and I encouraged her to think that."

"But you do not think that?" asked Conant.

"It is the timing of the thing," I said. "When I visited Mr Foster in February he was on good form: elderly, yes, and with the frailties of age, but in excellent spirits after the return of his son. And only a month later – barely a fortnight after that rout – he is dead."

"You think the son may have been impatient to inherit?" asked the magistrate.

"If he had debts at Crockford's, perhaps he had them elsewhere too," I said. "And after an absence of six years – an absence forced on him by his parents – perhaps he was not as fond of his father as his father was of him."

"If Hugh Foster really was his father…" mused Conant.

"Indeed," I agreed.

CHAPTER TWENTY-ONE

Yellow wheels and a red body

THURSDAY 30TH APRIL 1829

I was just getting ready to go home when the door to the back office was thrown open and Wilson appeared.

"I'm glad I've caught you," he said. "There's a report come in and you'll want to hear it."

He vanished again and I shrugged on my coat, following him to the front desk. Standing there was a lad of about fourteen.

"That's Constable Plank, there," said Thomas Neale to the lad, pointing at me. "Now you tell him what you've just told me."

The boy was wearing thick trousers, muddied at the knee, and a workman's coat that was slightly too large for him, with boots in good if grubby condition, and a cap twisted in his hands. He looked back at Tom, who nodded encouragingly, and then at me.

"Out with it, lad," I said. "Name?"

"George Smith, sir," he said. "I work in Hyde Park, with the keepers – apprentice gardener."

"And what are you doing all the way over here?" I asked.

"There's been an accident in the park," he said, twisting that poor cap all the more. "There's a gentleman dead – thrown out of his carriage."

I looked at Tom. "Another young fop driving too fast with horses he can't control," I said. "I'm sorry for his mother, but it's nothing to do with the constables, surely."

Tom held up his hand. "Tell Constable Plank what you saw before the accident, Mr Smith," he said.

"I saw the carriage go past me. I was having a break, sitting under a tree and eating an apple, and I saw it." Young George looked at Tom, who nodded. "It was a curricle, with a pair of bay horses. And two people in it. And the woman was driving."

I frowned. "A man and a woman in the carriage, and the woman was driving?" I asked. The boy nodded. "You're certain?" He nodded again.

"And when I heard later about the accident," he continued, "there was no mention of the woman. I asked one of the keepers – he'd just come back from where it happened. There was the carriage on its side, he said, with the horses still in harness, and the man on the ground nearby, dead."

"It might have been a different carriage that you saw," I suggested.

The lad shook his head emphatically. "No, sir – it was the same one. Very fancy: yellow wheels and a red body."

I looked at Tom. "Sounds like the same one to me, Sam," he said. "That's not a livery you see on many carriages."

"All right, lad," I said. "I'll make some enquiries – ask some questions." I put on my hat. "But tell me: why did you come here? Why not leave it to the keepers?"

"My gran, she runs a stall in Oxford Market," he said. "Fruit. And she always tells me, if there's any trouble, to go straight to the constables in Great Marlborough Street. She says you're honest here."

"Hah!" I said. "She's a wise woman, your gran."

◆

I have often thought that there is something about a fellow sitting down to a well-deserved hot dinner that angers the gods. No sooner had I lifted the first spoonful of stew to my mouth than there was a knock at the back door.

Martha put her hand on my arm. "You carry on, Sam," she said. "I'll go." She went to the door, spoke to whoever was there and then called back to me over her shoulder. "It's a message," she said, "from Mr Conant, the lad says. No reply needed." She passed the note to me before taking an apple from the bowl and a coin from my coat pocket and handing them both to the lad. I knew that the message runners tussled over who would deliver our messages, with Martha always handing out food, but it gave her pleasure and it was a small enough thing.

Martha returned to the table. "Well?" she said, picking up her fork.

"You're not going to believe this, Mar," I said. "There was a carriage accident in Hyde Park today; a young fellow overturned his curricle and broke his neck."

"I certainly can believe it," she said smartly. "I've seen the way they drive – no concern or consideration for anyone."

"Not the accident," I said. "The young man. It was James Foster."

CHAPTER TWENTY-TWO

Hands in supplication

SATURDAY 2ND MAY 1829

I was sitting in the yard in my shirt, my boots and Martha's on the ground in front of me and a brush in my hand, when I heard the front door knocker. Martha had not mentioned anyone coming to call, and my visitors generally came to the back door; no-one wants to advertise their business with a constable by banging on his front door. I heard voices in the kitchen: Martha and another woman. My wife's head appeared round the door.

"You'd better come in, Sam," she said seriously.

I sighed and rinsed my hands in the bucket before rolling down my sleeves and going indoors. Sitting at the kitchen table, as pale as a ghost, was Mrs Godwin, the housekeeper from Villiers Street.

"I was just telling Mrs Godwin how sorry we were to hear about Mr James," said Martha, putting the kettle on the stove. "What a terrible shock, and coming so soon after his poor father."

The housekeeper looked from me to my wife and back again. "And Mr Harding," she said in a hoarse whisper, almost as if she thought we might be overheard. "That's three sudden deaths since the turn of the year, constable, and I don't mind telling you I'm scared."

I pulled out a chair and sat down opposite the woman, deliberately keeping my manner and tone as calm as possible and taking out my notebook. "Scared, Mrs Godwin?" I asked. "Scared of what?"

"When Mrs Moncrieff heard the news last night," said the housekeeper, "she fainted. Right there in the hallway, at my feet."

"The poor woman," said Martha, measuring tea into the pot – it was an extravagance but she could see that Mrs Godwin needed something reviving. "It must have been a terrible shock for her."

"Terrible," echoed the housekeeper. "We carried her into the parlour and laid her on the sofa and I administered the smelling salts. As soon as she came round, she started talking about the household being cursed."

It was my turn to be the echo. "Cursed!" I said. "Surely you do not believe that, Mrs Godwin." Martha shot me a warning look.

The housekeeper drew herself up in her chair. "I most certainly do not, Constable Plank. I am a sensible woman, not a silly chit given to superstition. And as a sensible woman, I notice things." She took a sip from the cup that Martha had put in front of her. "Hands, for instance." She put down the cup and turned her own hands over, showing us the palms and then the backs. "I am a housekeeper – no longer a maid of all work, but still, I do not have the hands of a lady. Mrs Moncrieff has beautiful hands – soft and pale. But when I was tending to her yesterday I noticed that they were marked – here." With one hand she made a slashing motion across the palm of the other. "The skin was not broken but there were angry red marks, as though a rope had been pulled through her grasp."

Martha inspected her own hands as she listened. "But that is not what has frightened you, Mrs Godwin," she said.

The housekeeper shook her head. "Mrs Moncrieff may talk of curses but the wickedness in this world is done by men and women, not by," she waved her hand in the air, "spirits and demons. As you know only too well, I am sure, constable," she said.

"Do you suspect that the carriage accident was not an accident?" I asked. "That it was deliberate?"

"That Mr James killed himself?" added Martha.

Mrs Godwin bit her lip. "I do not know – I simply do not know. But he was not happy, not recently." She leaned forward and spoke urgently. "Daniel – the young footman you met, constable – told me a few days ago that he had been woken in the night by a man calling out. Daniel's room is above Mr James and he was sure it was coming from there. I told him to fetch me the next time it happened, and that was the night before last. I thought a maternal voice might calm Mr James and so Daniel and I went to his room. We could hear him shouting from outside. It was mostly just nonsense – you know how it is with nightmares – but more than once he said, clear as anything, 'No, I will not'."

I glanced up from my notebook. "Those were his exact words – you are sure?" I asked.

The housekeeper nodded. "'No, I will not.' I knocked on the door but he did not wake and so we went in. The bedclothes were thrown off and Mr James was thrashing about, as though he was struggling with something, or someone. I touched him on the shoulder and then shook him, and his eyes opened suddenly. He looked… haunted. That's the only word for it, Mrs Plank. And then he said something that has preyed on my mind. He said, 'We should not have done it'."

"And did you ask him what he meant by that?" I asked.

Mrs Godwin shook her head. "I don't think he was fully awake when he said it – I think it was part of his nightmare. When I spoke to him – something soothing, I can't remember what – he looked at me as though he had only just seen me, and asked what I was doing in his room. I explained and offered to make him a warm milk to help him sleep more peacefully, but he refused. And the next morning Daniel said that Mr James acted as though nothing had happened. But if he was disturbed in his mind or guilty about something, and then the opportunity presented itself when he was out in the curricle..." Her voice tailed off.

"Did Mr James often have nightmares?" I asked.

"I had known him only a few months, of course, but no," said the housekeeper. "You could ask Doctor Branscombe about his medical history..." She clapped a hand over her mouth. "I clean forgot: that's four deaths, not three." She looked at me imploringly. "Now that surely cannot be a coincidence, constable. Or a curse."

"It seems unlikely," I agreed.

"And then there is this," the housekeeper said, reaching into her bag and handing me a book. "I was checking the linen in Mrs Moncrieff's room and I found this slipped into the drawer with her nightgowns. I checked, and it's from a set in Mr Foster's study – it's the third volume of five. Now if Mrs Moncrieff is interested in plants, why would she feel the need to hide the book?"

It was a small, sturdy book, obviously well-thumbed, and there was a scrap of paper tucked into it, marking a page. I took the book to the window and examined it. "Hortus Kewensis" was written on the title page, followed by the explanation that it was a catalogue of the plants cultivated in the Royal Botanic Garden at Kew. I turned to the page in the book that had been marked. Two plants were described there: *Abrus* and *Pterocarpus.* I looked again at the scrap of paper that had served as a bookmark and on it was scribbled the single word *Abrus.*

"May I borrow this, Mrs Godwin?" I asked. "I can guess at some of it, but need time to work it out. It may well be nothing, and I will make sure that the book is returned to you quickly, in case Mrs Moncrieff looks for it."

"Don't worry about that, constable," said the housekeeper, standing to leave. "If she does, I shall blame Mary; I shall say that she found it in the drawer and returned it to the study."

♦

I was keen to decipher the information and so I called on Mr Conant at Portland Place that afternoon, to see if he could spare me half an hour.

"My own Latin is not what it was," he said when I explained my request, "but between us I daresay we can stumble through. And it's probably far more interesting than these papers I am supposed to be reading. Here: show me."

I handed the book to Conant. He went to his bookcase and pulled out his Latin dictionary, taking both books to his desk and reaching for his spectacles as he sat down. He beckoned me; I picked up another chair and set it down next to him so that we could work on the translation together. He slid a blank piece of paper over to me and I took out my pencil.

"*Quadrilobus* – four lobes, I should imagine," he said. "Then nine filaments and," he reached for the dictionary and checked something, "they are attached to the base of the flower, with petals opening at the back. This first part is a description of the look of the plant." He paused as I wrote down his translation. "And next we have the full name of the plant: *Abrus precatorius*. Now that sounds familiar – yes, here it is in the dictionary: *precator* means a prayer or petition. I suppose the petals are shaped like hands in supplication. And its common name is Jamaica wild liquorice, which tells us that it is native to that part of the world – as the catalogue said, native of both Indies. And this reference to Bishop Compton – I think there was a bishop of London who was a renowned botanist, so I

202 | SUSAN GROSSEY

assume he had a specimen of this plant in his collection."
He sat back in his chair. "And that's it."

I read again what I had written on the sheet of paper
before folding it and tucking it into my notebook. "Jamaica wild liquorice," I said. "It may be nothing. But why
is this particular plant of interest to Mrs Moncrieff? It
was the only volume of the catalogue that she had taken,
and the only page that she had marked."

"The catalogue has only the skeleton of the story,
Sam," said the magistrate, taking off his spectacles and
polishing them on his handkerchief. "You need to flesh it
out. A botanist, perhaps, or a keen gardener might be
able to tell you more. Perhaps Mrs Plank would enjoy a
visit to the physic garden in Chelsea."

"I'm sure she would," I replied. "There was one other
thing." I opened my notebook to make sure I made no
mistake in what I told Conant. "I checked Doctor Branscombe's notes about his recent treatment of James Foster
– he had been involved in a fist-fight and came home the
worse for wear. But the doctor had also written this: 'No
scar from broken arm'. When James Foster was a lad of
seven, he broke his arm falling out of a tree."

"So did I, at much the same age," said the magistrate,
smiling.

"In the case of James Foster," I continued, "the break
was a serious one, and the bone pierced the skin. There
should have been a scar, about four inches long. Longer,

even: James Foster's arm is considerably larger now than when he was seven years old."

"So Doctor Branscombe had his own suspicions about James Foster – or the man claiming to be James Foster," said the magistrate.

"And now he is dead," I said. "Just as the butler had his suspicions, and he is dead."

CHAPTER TWENTY-THREE

Sam in the suds

MONDAY 4TH MAY 1829

"It is simply that as we are making enquiries on behalf of Mr Conant we are permitted to take a coach, and he thought you might enjoy the outing," I said as Martha pinned on her hat. I was puzzled at her mood; when I had arrived home the previous evening she had initially been excited at the thought of a jaunt to Chelsea but the more I explained, the quieter she became until she said barely anything at all. She was silent as we walked to Oxford Street, where I knew we stood the best chance of spying a coach for hire, although she was pleasant enough to the jarvey who pulled up in answer to my wave. Her argument, then, was with me, and I was determined to find out what it was.

I waited until the jarvey had negotiated the turning into Regent Street and then took Martha's hand. She did

206 | SUSAN GROSSEY

not squeeze mine in return but did not snatch it away either.

"Come on, Mar," I said gently. "I know I'm in the suds with you; what I don't know is why."

"That's a vulgar term, Sam," she said primly – and I know of old that when Martha turns prim it's because she thinks she's in the right.

"It is, my love, and I apologise," I said. "But I'm just a buffle-headed fellow who knows no better."

I glanced at her and she turned away quickly, but not before I saw her trying to keep a straight face. I squeezed her hand. "Tell me, Mar: what have I done?"

She looked at me for a long moment. As chance would have it, just then the coach jolted into a pothole and my wife was thrown against me, giving me the opportunity to take hold of her other hand and kiss it.

"It's nothing, Sam," she said. "I'm being silly." She retrieved her hands and smoothed down her skirt. I stayed quiet; there was no point denying it or agreeing, until I knew what she meant. "It's just seeing William and Alice. He's so attentive. He rushes home to be with her and George. The other day he bought her a hatpin he thought she would like – not for her birthday, but because he saw it and thought of her. And I know they're new-married and we've been married for nearly three decades…" Her voice trailed off and she looked out of the window. "And then yesterday you came home and proposed this outing, and I thought," she turned to look at me and took a deep breath, "well, I thought that you wanted to do something nice for me, a treat. And it turns out that it's just work. Not for me at all. Not even your own idea – a suggestion from Mr Conant." And a tear spilled from her eye and moved slowly down her cheek. I reached up and dried it with my thumb.

Martha smiled wanly at me. "Silly, you see," she said.

"Not silly at all," I said. "Foolish, perhaps." Her eyes flashed and I continued quickly. "Foolish of me, I mean, to take you so for granted. It may be a while ago now but I remember that I made three promises on our wedding day. The first I made to your father, standing outside the church: I promised him I would take care of you. The second I made at the altar: I promised to love and honour you all the days of our lives. And the third I made to you that night, when we were alone at last. Can you remember the promise I made?"

Martha shook her head.

"I promised you that I would do everything in my power to make you happy," I said. "And I have forgotten that promise too often. Taking care of you and loving you and honouring you is easy, because you are the best wife in the world. But because you are such a good wife and because you put up with me, I assume too often that you are happy. It makes me lazy, and you are right to ask more of me. After all, you make me happy every single day – with your smile and your warmth, and with your excellent pies."

Martha pouted and bumped me with her shoulder. "I thought food might come into it somewhere," she said.

"We're simple creatures, we men," I said. "A pie for dinner and a cuddle afterwards that's all we ask." I winked at her and she laughed.

♦

The rest of the journey passed happily enough, with me pointing out places of interest that we passed, until the coach drew to a halt at the entrance to the physic garden in Swan Walk. I helped Martha down and told the jarvey to have a drink at the Old Swan and return to collect us in an hour. As he turned his horses around, I lifted the knocker on the wooden gate in the wall and rapped loudly.

After a few moments the gate opened and a man looked out at us. He was quite short but sturdy, with the ruddy complexion of those who work outdoors, and dressed in a coat and breeches of pale yellowish brown; a roll of paper was in one coat pocket and the handle of a gardening implement poked out of the other. Beneath his coat was a dark brown waistcoat and beneath that a once-white shirt, with a reddish kerchief knotted at his throat. Thick grey stockings, muddy shoes and a rather battered black hat with a damaged brim completed his outfit. "May I help you?" he asked in a thick country accent.

"I am Constable Samuel Plank," I said, "and this is my wife."

The fellow looked at Martha, took off his hat and bowed. "Madam," he said.

"I have a letter from John Conant Esquire," I explained, handing over the letter, "magistrate at Great Marlborough Street, requesting assistance with a botanical matter."

He read the letter, which I knew said no more than I had already told him, and stood aside to beckon us into the garden.

"My name is Burling," he said. "Thomas Burling. I am one of the gardeners here. You have caught me on a good day; often I have to spend my time accompanying medical men around the place as they look at our specimens – botanising, as they like to call it – but today I have been left to my own devices." He led us into the garden. "It is not what it was," he said sadly. "London has caught up with us – you saw the new brewery next door, and Coal Wharf on the other side – and with the soot and the smoke and the constant building work..." He shook his head. "But we battle on. We have the river to cool us in summer and warm us in winter, and the soil here is excellent – it used to be a market garden, Mrs Plank."

"You are not from London yourself, Mr Burling," said Martha.

"I am not, no," said the gardener, "although I have lived here for twenty years or more. I'm from Kent. I worked in the gardens of a grand house there and my master had an interest in physic gardens. He sent me here for a year, to learn how to create a garden for him."

"And you met a London girl and married her," said Martha.

"You have it exactly, Mrs Plank," said Burling with a smile. "My poor mother: all those lovely lasses in Kent, she said, and I had to choose a city girl. But my Marjory – I would have moved to Alaska for her, let alone London. She was a prize, my Marjory."

Burling paused as he led us through the garden and Martha touched him lightly on the arm. "When did you lose her, Mr Burling?" she asked quietly.

"A year ago next month," he replied. "One day she was fine, then the coughing started and she was gone within the week. I have my girls, of course: Mary's nearly eighteen and Grace, she's fifteen and the image of her mother. And I have the garden. There's nothing like a garden to remind you that life goes on." He smiled at Martha and she hooked her arm into his.

"Come, Mr Burling: tell me more about your garden," she said. "And then Sam can ask his questions."

♦

Once we had seen the various beds dedicated to different types of plant and toured the glass house – "one of the first in Europe to be heated, with pipes under the floor delivering heat all winter long from the stove", explained the proud gardener – Mr Burling led us to the small stone building that served as his office and sitting room. A kettle stood on the tiny range in the corner and a sagging armchair was drawn close to the fireplace, its back to us. Papers covered a desk under the window, spilling onto the chair and the floor. Against the wall, within reach of anyone sitting at the desk, was a lopsided bookcase stuffed with books and more papers.

"You will excuse me, Mrs Plank," said the gardener as we looked around the room. "I am not a tidy housekeeper and my girls rarely venture here to the gardens. This is a male domain, with just me and Sloane." He walked across to the armchair and bent over it. "This is Sloane – named after Sir Hans, who did so much to create this garden, back in the last century. He's old now, and not very steady on his legs, and completely deaf, but excellent company for all that." And as we watched, a scruffy little brown terrier jumped down from the armchair and turned his nose towards us. He yawned widely and then tottered over on stiff legs to sniff our shoes. Martha bent to stroke his head and he snuffled her hand in contentment.

"Sloane and I will make some tea and then sit by the fire while you two discuss Mr Conant's questions," Martha said.

"You see, constable," said Burling. "There's been a woman in the place for less than a minute and already it's feeling more homely."

♦

Once Martha had brought us tea in a couple of chipped and mismatched cups, she went over to the armchair. The little dog – already smitten – followed her and, with great concentration and determination, jumped into her lap. Burling retrieved a crate from outside the door and put it down next to the desk, sitting on it while waving me into the chair from which he had removed all the papers, simply adding them to the piles on the floor. I took out my notebook and showed him what we had learned from the entry in the catalogue.

"*Abrus precatorius*," he read. "I can see why a constable might be interested in this particular plant."

"It is dangerous?" I asked.

"Poisonous, yes," said Burling, reaching across to his bookshelf and pulling out a large journal. As he leafed through it I could see that it was full of handwritten notes, in a variety of hands. "Our own record of what we know," he explained. "Whenever the gardeners learn something new about a plant – from our own collection or by visiting others – we write it down here. Once we are sure of the details we add them to our *Index Seminum*, which is used to exchange plants and seeds between all physic and botanic gardens, so that we can all increase our collections and our knowledge."

"What a clever idea," said Martha from her fireside seat.

"Yes, madam," agreed the gardener. "The index was dreamt up here in Chelsea and now links gardens all around the world. Ah, here we are: *Abrus precatorius*. A tropical native. Also known as false liquorice and rosary bead. The roots are sometimes used as a substitute for liquorice – boiled up and taken to ease stomach conditions."

I looked up from my notebook. "But you said it was poisonous."

Burling nodded. "Aye, it is, but there are many plants that heal if taken in one quantity or form and harm if taken otherwise. Digitalis, for instance – foxglove. An excellent treatment for dropsy if taken very diluted, but fatal in stronger doses." He returned to his ledger. "And the leaves of *Abrus precatorius* can be mixed with other plants to make a syrup to treat chest colds, sore throats and other internal inflammations. But then there is this warning – see, here, the skull and crossbones." He turned the ledger towards me and indeed someone had inked the familiar symbol for poison against the entry. "It seems that the poison is in the seeds: ingestion of even a single seed can be fatal." He looked at me. "Is that what has happened? Someone has been poisoned by this plant?"

"Not exactly," I said. "There have been four deaths in one family and hidden in the house I found a copy of the Kew catalogue with the page marked for this plant. Mr Conant and I thought it might be relevant."

Burling closed his ledger. "I hope so," he said. "Sensational poisonings are good business for us, as it reminds everyone – particularly those with money to donate – why a physic garden is so essential."

♦

"I liked Mr Burling," said Martha as we rattled home. "It is hard for a man to be left with two daughters – well, young women now. He needs a wife."

I smiled at her. "You think all men need a wife."

"All good, decent men need a wife," she corrected me. "The others do not deserve one."

We drove on for a few minutes in companionable silence, relishing the luxury of being carried through the crowded streets in our own coach.

"Does William seem worried about anything?" asked Martha after a while.

"Worried?" I asked. "In what way?"

"I don't exactly know," she replied. "Alice is concerned. She said he seems… uneasy. As though he has something on his mind."

"He has probably just realised what it means to be married," I said jovially.

Martha turned to look at me. "And what does it mean, Sam?" she asked.

I put my hand over hers on the seat, but she pulled it away and turned again to look out of the window.

CHAPTER TWENTY-FOUR

A metaphorical hatpin

TUESDAY 5TH MAY 1829

The young turnkey looked me up and down and held out his hand again.

"Warrant, constable," he said.

"As I explained," I replied, "I have no warrant. I am neither delivering nor collecting a prisoner, and I am not visiting a prisoner prior to a trial. I am here simply to have a word with Mr Wontner."

"And as I explained," he said, "we cannot let you in without a warrant. This is a prison, not an assembly rooms."

I heard another voice from within the prison and the turnkey disappeared, pushing the gate closed in my face.

After a few moments it opened again and there was the prison keeper himself. He rolled his eyes at me.

"A new recruit," he said, beckoning me in, "keen to show that he knows the rules. I don't like to discourage him; it's best they start out keen and then the years take less of a toll on their enthusiasm."

I followed John Wontner past the gatehouse where the turnkeys gathered and I nodded at the young fellow to show that there were no hard feelings.

"I remember knowing the rules," I said as Wontner and I walked to his office.

"Aye," said the keeper, unlocking his door and then standing aside to let me go in. "Back when we both had more hair and less gut." He patted his own stomach and sighed. He sat at his desk, which was, as ever, covered with papers arranged in an order discernible only to its owner. The usual jug of barley water was at his elbow and he poured out two tumblers, passing one to me and then raising the other in a silent toast before drinking deeply from it.

"Talking of earlier times," I said, "do you recall that investment fraud some years back? A man killed himself, leaving a widow and young son, and there was a schoolteacher involved." Wontner frowned in concentration but said nothing. "And a man in a canary waistcoat," I added.

The keeper's face cleared. "Ah yes, that I remember – he was one of the magpies for the scheme, as I recall."

"That's the fellow," I said. "He never answered for his part in that matter, and I think he's risen up the ranks."

"You've seen him again?" asked Wontner, standing to lean over the desk and refill my tumbler.

I told him about the burial club and the tontine, and about my near miss in Drury Lane with the man in the canary waistcoat. "And I was wondering whether any of your noses had mentioned someone like that. He's obviously confident of his place; no-one scared of being arrested would go around in that signature finery."

"But you're thinking that no-one reaches the upper ranks in the rookeries without making a few enemies along the way," said the keeper. "I'll drop the question in the right ears and let you know."

"Thank you, John," I said, raising my own tumbler in salute. "That's a fine example of knowing when to ignore the rules."

"I'll have a word with young Richards on the gate," said the keeper with a smile. "He's a smart one – he'll soon learn to pick his battles." We sat for a moment or two, Wontner looking at me expectantly, until he said, "Is there something else troubling you, Sam?"

"You and Mrs Wontner," I started. "You've been married a long time."

"Fifteen, no, sixteen years," said Wontner.

"And does she still baffle you?" I asked.

Wontner's concerned face broke into a broad grin. "Of course she does!" he said. "Not every day, but on occasion. And I daresay I confound her too, on occasion. How dull life would be if we knew everything about our wives, Sam." He grew serious again. "But this is troubling you, my friend. I do not mean to make light of it. Tell me what has happened and let's see if we can puzzle it out between us."

I took a deep breath and told him what Martha had said to me in the coach on the way to Chelsea. Wontner listened carefully. When I had finished, he shrugged.

"I cannot see what is confusing you, Sam," he said.

"My wife thinks that I am not attentive enough. Why does she think that?" I asked.

"Ah, and here we have the problem," said the keeper, sitting back in his chair and steepling his hands in imitation of a learned man about to deliver a lecture. "You are trying to understand why your wife thinks a certain way, no?" I nodded. "That is not possible: not even the most intelligent man in London will understand why his wife thinks something, let alone a lowly constable," he indicated me, "or humble prison keeper," he indicated himself. "You must abandon this attempt as a lost cause. But," and here he held up one finger, "you are a very lucky fellow. It does not matter why she thinks you are inattentive; all that matters is that she has told you how she feels, and – even more wonderful – she has told you herself how to remedy the situation. For the modest price of a hatpin, you can restore happiness to your wife and harmony to your household."

"But Martha is not bothered about hatpins," I started.

"The hatpin is metaphorical, Sam," said Wonter with a degree of exasperation. "Your wife needs evidence – there, you know all about evidence – she needs evidence that you are thinking about her as you go about your daily duties, that you do not forget her when she is not in front of you, remembering her only when she dishes up your pie for dinner."

"But that's nonsense," I said hotly. "I think of Martha often – sometimes she is the only soft and kind and generous part of my day. She must know that."

"And yet she tells you that she does not," said the keeper. "Telling her that she is wrong will not solve the problem. A hatpin – a metaphorical hatpin – will."

◆

And so it was that, later the same day, I found myself in Burlington Arcade. A few weeks earlier Martha and I, out for a walk on a Sunday afternoon, had taken a stroll past its gorgeous windows. As always, my wife had gasped at the splendours on offer, shaking her head at the extravagance of those who spend so much on such un-necessary objects. But she had gazed rather longingly at a display of gloves. As it happens, I knew the shop that had caught her eye: Wilson and I had once rescued a starving and terrified pickpocket from the outraged grasp of its proprietress. The lad was now earning an honest living in a coach yard, and as I had refrained from hauling the woman before the magistrate for allowing her upstairs room to be used by ladybirds and their gentlemen, I thought she might give me a good price.

The display in the window of Madame Fontaine's shop was certainly striking; although Madame Fontaine herself was no more French than I was, she had an artistic eye. And the engraving on the fanlight promised that Parisian touch: "Purveyor of fine Continental ladies' gloves and hosiery". The gloves in the window were arranged as though a lady of taste – or more realistically, her maid – were packing for a journey: a dressing table stood with its drawers open, gloves spilling out of them, while a trunk on the floor was half-filled with more gloves, each pair draped to show it to best advantage. There were day gloves and evening gloves, winter ones and summer-weight ones, short gloves and long ones. I sighed.

Madame Fontaine had seen me at the window and bustled out from behind her counter to poke her head out of the door.

"May I 'elp you, sir?" she said in what she obviously thought was a convincing French accent. She spotted my coat, took a closer look at me and dropped all pretence. "Oh, it's you, is it. Where's your tall pal?"

"Mrs Fontaine," I said. "This is not an official visit. I wish to look at some gloves, for my wife."

She raised an eyebrow – or the line painted to resemble one – and stood aside to let me enter the shop. She then brushed past me to take up her station again behind the counter. "Evening gloves or day gloves?" she asked.

"Day gloves," I said.

"Leather or fabric?" I paused, realising that I had not paid that much attention to the specific gloves that had caught Martha's eye. Madame Fontaine tilted her head to one side. "Constable, you may not care for me, but I am good at what I do, if you will let me. Now, these gloves. Where will your wife be wearing them?"

"On visits to friends," I said, thinking of Martha's calls on Mr Freame at the bank and on Mrs Wontner. "And sometimes to church. Outings – with me."

"A more practical glove, then – nothing too delicate or lacy. A glove to serve a purpose, not just for show," suggested Madame Fontaine.

"But not too practical," I added. "Something that she would not buy for herself. To show her that – that I have thought of her and chosen carefully."

She nodded once, business-like. "And your wife's colouring?" I must have looked perplexed. "Is she fair-haired? Dark? Her skin and eyes?"

"Ah," I said. "Mrs Plank is dark-haired, with curls. Her eyes are brown – a soft, deep brown. And her skin is like buttermilk. Neither pale nor dark, but smooth."

Madame Fontaine smiled. "Why, constable, you have made a study of her. Many men cannot tell me the colour of their wives' eyes."

"Constables are trained to notice details," I said.

"If you say so," replied the shopkeeper, smiling again. "With that colouring, and for a pair of gloves that is practical but special, I think dark cream leather would do well." She turned her back and bent down to take out a drawer from the cabinet behind her that filled the back wall of the shop. She put it on the counter and then retrieved a piece of black cloth from under the counter. From the drawer she took out a pair of gloves and placed them on the black cloth. "There," she said. "Finest kid leather, made in France."

The gloves were made of pale yellow leather, with a cross-hatching design painted on them. In each diamond created by the cross-hatching was a tiny picture – a bird or a flower or a dancing child. I picked up one of the gloves; it was soft and light, and draped over my hand like silk. I hesitated.

"Not quite right, then," said Madame Fontaine. She was right: she was good at this. I did not think I had given away my thoughts in my face, but she had read them nonetheless.

"Too... showy," I said, putting down the glove. "Mrs Plank prefers hidden quality."

"Hmmm," said the shopkeeper, looking at me appraisingly – perhaps to assess my hidden quality. She returned the gloves to the drawer and then turned to select another one from the cabinet. She peeped into it, put it back and pulled out a third. "Ah, yes," she said, almost to herself.

The gloves she offered this time were a similar colour, perhaps a little paler. The fingers and hands were plain, although as I lifted a glove to examine it I could see the tiny stitches that held it together. Around the wrist of the glove was painted a most delicate design: a yellow garland with pink roses at intervals and a green vine twisting around it. Next to that – further up the arm, as it were – a series of small slashes had been made in the leather and a narrow pink ribbon was threaded through them, tied in a bow at the inner seam. And each glove was finished at the wrist with a delicately snipped scalloped edging.

Madame Fontaine pointed at the glove I had left on the cloth. "To the outside world," she said, "this is a plain leather glove. All of the interest – all of the quality – is known only to its wearer, hidden under her sleeve."

They were perfect.

♦

Once we had finished dinner that evening I went into the sitting room while Martha tidied the kitchen. I retrieved the gloves from where I had hidden them behind a cushion and put them on Martha's armchair before settling down and opening the newspaper. Martha came in and bent over her mending box, selecting a nightshirt of mine, a needle and the white thread. When she reached her chair she glanced down and saw the small package.

"What's this, Sam?" she asked.

"Just a little something I saw today," I said casually, peeking around the side of my newspaper. "For you."

Martha laid down the nightshirt on the arm of the chair, then picked up the package and turned it over in her hands. Mrs Fontaine had created a dainty parcel, with the gloves protected by a length of white gauzy fabric and then tucked into an envelope of brown paper and secured with a striped ribbon.

"Shall I open it?" she asked.

I put down my newspaper; I wanted to enjoy her surprise. "Of course – it won't open itself, will it?"

Martha sat down and put the package on her lap, carefully undoing the ribbon, winding it around her hand and then slipping it into her pocket. She unfolded the brown paper and then the gauze – and stopped. She said nothing.

I leaned forward, the newspaper discarded. "What is it, Mar? Did I make a mistake? There was another pair if you want to…"

Martha looked up at me and I could see the tears standing in her eyes. "You could show me every pair of gloves in England, Sam, and I would choose this pair."

I knelt in front of her chair and took her hands in mine. "And you could show me every woman in England, Martha, and I would choose you. I'm sorry I gave you cause to doubt that."

CHAPTER TWENTY-FIVE

A quiet Sunday

SUNDAY 10TH MAY 1829

"Wave goodbye to papa and Sampa," said Alice, taking hold of George's chubby arm and waving it for him. The little one gurgled and looked up at her, and Alice beamed down at him. Wilson and I both waved like fools and then caught each other's eyes and stopped.

"Off with you, gentlemen," said Martha, shooing us with her apron. "The sooner you go, the sooner you'll be home, and there'll be a nice bit of roast meat waiting for you."

Wilson put on his hat and held the door open for me, and we set off into the quiet of a Sunday morning. London is such a bustling, relentless place that it is a pleasure to see it on its day of rest.

"I'm sorry about the Sampa business," said Wilson after a minute or two. "Alice says it will be easier for him than 'Uncle Sam'. Perhaps when he's a bit older and can say his letters more clearly we can try again."

"Don't you change it," I replied. "Anyone can be an Uncle Sam, but I'll wager I'm the only Sampa in London." We crossed Oxford Street, mercifully free of carts and with only the occasional coach taking the faithful to church. "Was Alice vexed that we have to go out this morning?" I asked.

Wilson shook his head. "She's spent enough time with Mrs Plank to know what life is like when you're married to a constable. She's quiet, Alice, but she listens and learns."

"A quiet wife who listens," I said. "You'd be the envy of many husbands. Although you may like to bear in mind that Mrs Plank was a quiet little thing when I married her." I laughed at the look on his face.

A few minutes later I spoke again. "When Mrs Plank and I were at Chelsea," I said, "she mentioned that Alice is worried about you. That she thinks you have something on your mind." I deliberately did not look at him and kept my tone light. "Is there something?" He said nothing. "Something at the office?" I asked. Again, he said nothing. "Or just the responsibilities of a new husband?"

"That's it," he said. "Responsibilities."

I was not convinced but, unlike women, men can rarely be persuaded to talk of things they wish to keep to themselves.

◆

As requested, we went straight to the tradesman's entrance at 14 Villiers Street and knocked quietly. Mrs Godwin appeared and quickly beckoned us inside.

"Alone as hoped, Mrs Godwin?" I asked.

She nodded. "Mrs Moncrieff and Master Arthur have gone to church in the carriage with Jeffreys and Daniel, Miss Napier and cook have the day off, and I've sent Mary to visit her mother. We are a much-reduced household these days, constable," she said sadly.

I put a comforting hand on her arm as she shook her head. "Indeed, Mrs Godwin. But come, we have work to do, and sermons – although usually a sight too long, in my opinion – do not last all morning. Constable Wilson will go to Mr James's room and you and I will go to Mrs Moncrieff's."

The housekeeper looked uneasy. "It feels disloyal," she said. "I know I asked you to come, but now..."

"Mrs Godwin," I said soothingly, "Constable Wilson and I will be very respectful. We will not poke or pry into irrelevant matters. We hope only to find something to explain the terrible misfortunes that have blighted this family in recent weeks – as you yourself said to me, it cannot be a coincidence." I dropped my voice. "If we do not find out what is going on, misfortune may strike again – and we have to think of Mrs Moncrieff, and the boy."

The housekeeper wrung her hands but nodded, and led us upstairs. Mrs Moncrieff's room was at the front of the house, with two tall windows overlooking the street, and another door that the housekeeper explained led through to Arthur's bedroom. The bed was made and the curtains tied back neatly, but the room was not particularly tidy; the dressing table was strewn with things, as though the occupant had been disturbed in mid-toilette, and a pair of gloves was lying across the stool.

"Where is Mrs Moncrieff's maid?" I asked.

Mrs Godwin huffed. "She brought one with her from Suffolk but the silly girl didn't like London – too busy, she said, too dirty and not enough fields. Fields! Well, we sent her back to her fields last month and since then Mary and I have managed between us – you cannot imagine how hard it is to find a good lady's maid these days, constable, with so many girls preferring to work in shops and the like."

I smiled. "I cannot, no," I said. "Does Mrs Moncrieff keep a diary? I know that some young ladies like to write down their thoughts and concerns."

Mrs Godwin raised an eyebrow. "Something of an in-
dulgence, to my mind, but no, she does not. She has an
appointment book, of course, but she takes that with her."

I walked over to the wardrobe and opened the door.
"Can you see anything out of the ordinary? Is anything
missing?" I asked the housekeeper, who came across and
looked through the items hanging there and shook her
head.

I crossed to the dressing table. There were various
items for beautification – an open pot of powder, a trio of
perfume bottles, a brush and comb set with enamel deco-
ration. A jewellery box stood with its lid open, and again
I asked Mrs Godwin to examine the contents.

"She is wearing the earrings that her husband gave her
on their wedding day," said the housekeeper, leaning past
me and pointing, "and this is the pair that she inherited
from her mother, along with these pearls. This bracelet
was a gift on her twenty-first birthday from her parents."
She reached into the jewellery box. "But the necklace her
brother brought back for her from the Caribbean – where
is that?"

"Perhaps she is wearing it," I suggested.

Mrs Godwin shook her head. "Goodness me, no – it's
a rough little thing, made by one of the... workers on the
plantation. But she is fond of it, particularly now."

I opened the drawer in the dressing table and carefully
looked through the delicate items stored there. Under a

pile of handkerchiefs, wrapped in a cloth, was the missing necklace. I lifted it and coiled it into my hand. As the housekeeper had said, it was a rather crude effort, with shiny red beads about the size of peas threaded onto a thin brown cord. The cord had snapped and a couple of the beads had been cracked, spilling some powder onto my palm. I sniffed it and touched it with my tongue; it was bitter.

"They're beans, Mr James said," explained the house-keeper, "from some local plant. It's a shame it's broken; I wonder whether she will want it re-threaded."

There was a cough and I turned to see Wilson stand-ing at the door. He shook his head.

"Well, I think we've finished here, Mrs Godwin," I said. "I am sorry that we cannot give you any answers today, but we will send word if there is news."

♦

"Slow down, lad," I said as Wilson marched up the Strand. "I know you're keen to fill your belly, but it's im-portant to go over what we have learned before we forget anything."

Wilson opened his mouth to object but thought better of it and did temper his pace a little.

"Nothing at all in James Foster's room, then?" I asked. "You looked for everything we discussed?"

"I did," said Wilson, ticking things off on his fingers as he spoke. "No weapons. No threatening letters – to or from James Foster. No IOUs from other gamblers. No laudanum."

"And yet we're meant to think that he was so disturbed – so alarmed – that he would drive recklessly enough to kill himself, either by accident or by design," I mused.

"Meant to think?" repeated Wilson. "But you don't?"

"Do you?" I asked in turn. Wilson shrugged. "You've told me what you didn't find in his room," I said, checking both ways before we stepped out into Charing Cross. "Now tell me what you did find."

Wilson retrieved his notebook and started reading from it. "The bed was made and the chamber pot had been emptied. There was one pair of cufflinks and a collar stud in a little dish next to the basin and ewer. There was a clean shirt and cravat hanging on the valet stand, with evening shoes next to it. There was a book... What?"

He stopped reading because I had held up my hand. "A clean shirt, cravat and evening shoes," I said. "What does that tell you?"

"That he was going out for the evening," replied Wilson. He nodded slowly. "And no man who plans to kill himself in the afternoon asks for a clean outfit to be prepared for that evening."

♦

Wilson leaned back in his chair and patted his stomach with satisfaction. George, sitting on Martha's lap, held out the soggy remains of the biscuit on which he had been gummy gnawing.

"Very kind of you, lad," said Wilson, smiling, "but I couldn't manage another bite." He reached over and pinched the lad's cheek. "You have it, my boy."

"Ouf," said Martha, shifting in her seat. "I'm not sure you need the rest of that biscuit, Georgie-boy – you're quite a weight these days. Are you going to grow up into a big strong constable, like your papa?"

Wilson beamed, and I remembered the conversation he and I had had about the true nature of fatherhood. Martha looked across at me with a smile and then her face changed.

"Sam?" she said. "Are you feeling ill? You look grey, and you're sweating." She passed George to Alice and came to my side, putting her hand to my forehead where it felt wonderfully cool.

A griping pain spread across my middle and I clutched my stomach. "Excuse me," I gasped, and staggered to my feet, gripping the edge of the table. "The privy," I said between clenched teeth, and pushed my way past Martha into the yard. I was only just in time.

A few minutes later I heard a soft tapping on the privy door. "Sam," said Martha gently, "can you come out yet?"

I considered my answer. The urgency seemed to have passed. "I need a cloth, Mar," I said. I heard her walk away and then return a moment later and her hand appeared under the door with two cloths: one damp and one dry. I tidied myself as best I could and threw the cloths down into the privy. I stood up gingerly and opened the door. Martha was sitting on the chair by the back door and came over to take me by the elbow. The kitchen was empty.

"Alice thought you might be embarrassed, or might need to come back in in your underclothes," Martha explained. "She's a thoughtful girl, that one. And now you, Samuel, are going up to bed to sleep it off. William said he will come by in the morning as usual."

CHAPTER TWENTY-SIX

Gingerbread

MONDAY 11TH MAY 1829

It was not a comfortable night for either of us; I endured another two hurried visits to the privy and also cast up my accounts into the chamber pot. As dawn broke, I felt as weak as a kitten and turned my head slowly to look at Martha. She was barely asleep, alert to any movement, and she put out her hand to stroke my face.

"My poor Sam," she said softly. "How do you feel?"

"Empty," I said, and my lips stuck to my teeth as I spoke. I grimaced.

Martha sat up and reached for the shawl that she had thrown over the end of the bed. "I'll go down and fetch you something to drink," she said. "Barley water, or would you prefer some milk?"

"Barley water," I croaked. "And perhaps something dry to eat – a plain biscuit."

"I can do better than that," she said, standing up and looking around for her slippers. "I made some gingerbread on Saturday, as William is so fond of it. Ginger is just what you need for a sore belly."

♦

As usual, my wife was right: after two tumblers of barley water and a fair-sized piece of gingerbread, I felt much improved. I tottered downstairs and went into the kitchen where Martha had put a bowl of hot water on the table for me to have a thorough wash. While I did that she went upstairs to strip the bed and by the time she came downstairs with her arms full of linen I had cleaned myself. Dangling from the fingers of one hand Martha had a fresh shirt for me and I put it on.

"I couldn't manage your trousers as well," she said, dumping the bedlinen in a pile by the back door. "But you'll need to dress soon; William is on his way, I should imagine."

♦

I had just gone back upstairs to finish dressing when I heard a knock at the back door, followed by voices. Then Martha called up the stairs for me to hurry.

"I'll be down in a minute, Mar – tell Wilson to hold his horses," I replied.

I heard footsteps on the stairs and then Martha's head appeared round the bedroom door. "It's not only William," she whispered. "Mr Conant is with him. And that big pile of soiled linens sitting there in plain sight. Do hurry, Sam." And she trotted off downstairs again.

By the time I returned to the kitchen, the magistrate was sitting at the table with a cup of tea in front of him. Wilson was standing by the back door – his usual position on official visits – and the pile of bedlinen had disappeared.

"Delighted to see you up and about, Sam," said Conant, reaching up to shake my hand. "Wilson's note yesterday evening alarmed me and I decided to come and see you – and ran into him on the way here."

"There was no need to send word to Mr Conant," I said to Wilson, taking my own seat at the table. Martha gestured to the tea but I shook my head; instead, she poured me another tumbler of barley water and then put the plate of gingerbread on the table. Wilson glanced at it but stayed where he was – a restraint which I knew was costing him.

The magistrate took a piece of gingerbread, broke off a morsel and popped it into his mouth. "Delicious, Mrs Plank – quite delicious." Martha smiled and smoothed down her apron. "And I disagree, Sam: young Wilson was quite right to let me know. Too many coincidences, to my mind. You go to a house connected with three recent deaths…"

"Four deaths," said Martha and then put her hand to her mouth.

"Four deaths?" asked Conant.

"The doctor," I replied, raising my eyebrows at Martha.

"Ah yes, Mrs Plank – quite right," said the magistrate. "So you go to a house connected with four recent deaths, and within hours you are taken violently ill." He took another piece of gingerbread and the look on Wilson's face was so pitiful that I held out the plate to him and nodded. He took some and ate it quickly. "Of course your quick recovery suggests that you simply ate some contaminated food that has now, well, passed."

I glanced at Martha. She was nodding. "Yes, Mr Conant," she said, "that was my thought too. But everything that Sam ate yesterday, we ate with him." She pointed at herself and at Wilson. "And we're not ill."

"Did you eat anything at Villiers Street?" the magistrate asked. I shook my head. "Nothing to drink? On the way home from Villiers Street?"

Again I shook my head. "It was Sunday morning," I said. "There was nothing about. And we knew that Martha would have a meal waiting for us. Anyway, I was already feeling a bit... peculiar by the time we sat down to eat, before I had even a mouthful."

"There was one thing," said Wilson suddenly, and we all looked at him. "In Mrs Moncrieff's room," he continued. "The broken necklace. You tasted the powder on your hand."

"Only a tiny bit," I said. "Less than a pinch."

"Nonetheless," said Conant, "there are some substances that can be deadly in even the smallest quantity. From a necklace, you said?"

I described the necklace to him and as I did so, Martha gasped. We all looked at her. "Your notebook, Sam, from when we went to Chelsea." I gestured to my coat hanging near the door and Wilson checked the pockets, found the notebook and handed it to me. "What did Mr Burling say about that plant again?" asked Martha

I turned to the relevant page, read it quickly and looked up at her. "Poison in the seeds. Ingestion from even one can be fatal." I looked at Conant. "*Abrus precatorius*. The Kew catalogue called it Jamaica wild liquorice, but the gardener at Chelsea said it is also known as the rosary bead plant because the seeds look like rosary beads."

"Just like the beads on that necklace," said Wilson.

"Goodness, Sam – you must warn Mrs Moncrieff," said Martha. "If she touches that powder, or the young boy…"

"She may know already," I said.

Conant frowned. "But Hugh Foster and his butler both died of heart failure," he said, "while James Foster died in a carriage smash and Doctor Branscombe was bludgeoned to death – excuse me, Mrs Plank."

Although over the years both my wife and his daughter had heard more disturbing details than most men, the magistrate still thought of them as delicate creatures to be protected from the nastier side of life. Martha nodded slightly to show that she accepted his apology.

"It is puzzling, I know," I replied, "but where else are we to go? Who else can be involved?"

"We know that the doctor was murdered," said Wilson, "but we also know that it could not have been a woman – Hippocrates was too big and heavy for a woman to lift."

"That's true," I said, sitting back in my chair.

"But it wouldn't hurt to know a little more about Mrs Moncrieff," said Conant. "When you are feeling more robust, Sam, perhaps you and Wilson could go to wherever it was in the country that she lived for those years."

"Suffolk," I said. "I will ask Mrs Godwin – the housekeeper – for the address."

◆

That night in bed, I held out my arm as usual for Martha to curl into me and rest her head on my chest. The poison had had no lasting effect and in fact I had eaten like a horse all day, with Martha watching every mouthful. I was just drifting off to sleep when I felt Martha shivering against me.

"Are you cold, my love?" I asked, pulling the blanket tighter around her shoulders.

She did not answer, simply burrowing against me, and I realised that she was not shivering, but crying.

"Martha," I said coaxingly, "what's all this? There's nothing to be upset about – I'm perfectly well now."

"I know," she said without lifting her head, her voice muffled. "But it might have been different."

"Here now, that's no way to think, is it," I said, putting a finger under her chin to force her to look up at me. "It might be different every day – I might be run down by a coach or knifed in the gut by a rogue."

"If you're trying to comfort me, Sam Plank," she said, "you're going about it the wrong way." But there was the slightest beginning of a smile. She put her arm across me and squeezed hard. "I couldn't manage without you, and I don't think you take enough account of that when you go around the place like you do, walking in front of coaches and tasting strange powders. And it's not just me anymore, is it: there's Alice and George to think of. And if I'm reading the signs right, there's soon be another little one calling you Sampa – Alice looked as sick as a horse yesterday, even before you started. So you and William need to be more careful, especially on this jaunt to Suffolk."

CHAPTER TWENTY-SEVEN

A jaunt to Suffolk

THURSDAY 14TH MAY 1829

"Good heavens, lad, what's in that bag?" I asked as Wilson loomed out of the gloom with a bulging duffel bag on his shoulder.

He came up to me and put the bag onto the ground. "Alice insisted," he said. "Clean clothes in case of bad weather, warm clothes in case of cold, light clothes in case of heat. And enough food to feed the whole coach." He smiled sheepishly. "You'd think we were off to Australia, not Bury St Edmunds."

For all his talk I knew that Wilson was nervous about our excursion; London born and bred, he had never been outside the city, and Suffolk was a foreign land to him. We stood aside to let a coach manoeuvre its way into the spacious yard of the Swan with Two Necks which, despite the early hour, was teeming with people and horses, as befitted one of the busiest and most important coaching inns in London. We followed the coach into the yard and walked across to the office, which had a board outside advertising the numerous routes offered by the enterprising Mr William Chaplin – I had heard tell that his company owned upwards of four hundred horses. Here at the Swan, with tight city streets pressing in on all sides and no room for building more stables, Chaplin had solved the problem by housing his horses in chambers underground. I collected our tickets from the clerk and he pointed at our coach, the "Times", with its distinctive two-necked swan painted on the back panel and its name emblazoned on the doors. With only twenty minutes to go until we set off, preparations were well underway, with passengers already sitting on top, and one fellow in the prime outside position next to the coachman.

"We are fortunate that Mr Conant has approved inside tickets for the journey," I said. "My days of sitting up top and being soaked to the skin or picking flies and dust from my teeth are over. We could have taken the speedier mail coach, of course, but I thought you would like to enjoy the scenery rather than travel through the night."

"Alice says that I am to remember everything and describe it to her and to George," said Wilson, grinning like a schoolboy.

"The first rule of coach travel," I said, indicating the way, "is to use the privy before setting off."

♦

Right on time, just as a church struck five, our Norwich-bound coach rumbled out of the yard and onto Lad Lane, the horses straining to pull their load while the coachman flicked his whip high above them and called out encouragement. A late passenger ran alongside, beseeching the coachman to allow him to board, but the timetable is sacrosanct and the coach moved on as the sky started to lighten ahead of us. The first hour of our journey was familiar enough, as we made stops at the Blue Boar in Aldgate and then the Bull Inn in Bishopsgate to pick up more passengers, but then we headed out of London into the country and Wilson fell silent as he gazed out of the window at the expanse of fields and trees. He even forgot to fidget, although he did sigh from time to time as he tried to rearrange his duffel bag into a more comfortable position at his feet, and I was grateful for my own much more modest luggage. Martha is wise to the ways of a travelling constable; she knows that there will be little call for fresh clothes if I am simply to sit in a dusty coach.

Onwards we rolled, covering the miles, until we stopped for an early midday meal at the White Hart in Braintree. Wilson leapt from the coach and ran for the privy, and I was not far behind him. The coachman said we would be stopping for three-quarters of an hour only and we made our way quickly to the parlour, ordering a serviceable meal comprising a roast meat roll, a tankard of ale and a slice of fruit pie. We were just wiping the pastry crumbs from our lips when a porter stuck his head into the parlour and yelled, "Times for Norwich – leaving in five minutes!".

Wilson stood and stretched his arms above his head. "My backside's sore," he said to me in a low tone.

"Then you might want to sit on some of those spare clothes of yours," I replied. "The road so far has been in good condition but from now on it might be a different story, depending on how well each parish is maintaining its section of the route. Just be thankful it's not raining. And talking of water…"

"I know," he said. "The privy."

♦

Suffolk is certainly a pretty county. The gently rolling fields, with their low hedgerows, were dotted with the sheep that had once brought so much wealth to this part of England. The villages we passed seemed frozen in time: since the decline of the wool trade, no-one had had the money to rebuild or renovate, and the buildings – from the grand merchants' houses to the humble weavers' cottages – stood as a picturesque reminder of former prosperity. On we travelled, making shorter stops at Halstead and Sudbury and Long Melford, before rumbling into Bury St Edmunds. By this time, the early morning and the jolting of the coach had caught up with both of us and Wilson and I had to be shaken awake by the coachman.

"Bury St Edmunds, gentlemen," he said. "Get yourselves down, or you'll be coming with us to Norwich."

"What time is it?" I asked thickly.

The fellow pulled a watch from his pocket and opened it. "Just gone three," he said proudly. "Right on time."

◆

"It's much grander than I had expected for the country," said Wilson as we stood in front of the Angel, gazing up at its three elegant storeys, generous sash windows and the large but surprisingly delicate fanlight over the doorway.

"London may be our capital," I said, rolling my head to relieve the knots in my neck, "but there is plenty of life outside it. Look behind you."

Wilson turned around and I indicated the cathedral and the abbey. "Bury St Edmunds has been an important ecclesiastical town for centuries," I explained. "The abbey was sacked in the sixteenth century, and there are only ruins left, but St James's Church – there – and St Mary's Church survived. I read about it in Mr Conant's encyclopaedia."

Wilson nodded. "I shall try to find a print to take home for Alice – it is a pretty scene."

"It is indeed," I said. "But this town is good for the body as well as the soul. Take a deep breath and tell me what you smell."

Wilson sniffed and frowned, then sniffed again and smiled. "That's hops," he said.

"Aye," I said, picking up my bag. "There's a brewery just around the corner and I hear good reports of its beer. Shall we find our beds and then explore the lie of the land?"

CHAPTER TWENTY-EIGHT

The house on Guildhall Street

FRIDAY 15TH MAY 1829

The next morning Wilson looked a bit the worse for wear when I nudged him awake; knowing when to say no to another tankard was a skill he had yet to learn. There was a knock at the door and a sturdy maid came in with a bowl of hot water and two towels over her arm; she put them on the dresser and then glanced over at Wilson, who was groaning as he hauled himself upright.

"The bacon and eggs at breakfast will soon soak up the beer," she said in her soft, broad accent. "Cook prides herself on being able to revive anyone." She looked at me and winked. "Even him." She curtseyed and left.

"You hear that?" I said loudly, watching Wilson wince. "Bacon and eggs downstairs."

♦

An hour later, the bacon, eggs, toast and several cups of tea had done their work and Wilson was ready to start his day. We walked out onto Angel Hill, following the directions offered by the porter with whom we had left our bags at the inn. We passed a beggar on the corner, one empty leg of his trousers pinned up, and I remembered reading how the end of the wars had been particularly harsh for soldiers sent home to agricultural parts of the country; now that food could once more be imported from the Continent, local prices slumped and farming work disappeared. I handed the fellow a coin and he touched his cap in thanks.

Wilson and I turned into Abbeygate Street, the abbey now directly behind us, and walked up the gentle slope. We passed a few little streets of half-timbered houses before turning left into Guildhall Street. We spent a few moments gaping at the ornate entrance to the guildhall itself, which Wilson declared was like a castle in miniature, before continuing to the address that Mrs Godwin had given us. The house was a solid, grand affair entirely suited to a banker, which was the profession of the man we had come to see.

I knocked on the door and a footman answered. I stated our business and he showed us into a pretty parlour, where I occupied myself by looking at the sketches on the wall while Wilson stood by the window. After about ten minutes the door opened and in came a woman with not an ounce of softness to her; her thinness made her look taller than she was, an effect she exaggerated by tilting her head back slightly and looking down her long nose at me.

"Mason tells me that you are constables from London," she said with distaste.

"Yes, madam," I said. "I am Constable Samuel Plank and this is Constable William Wilson, and we are conducting enquiries on behalf of John Conant Esquire, magistrate at Great Marlborough Street in Piccadilly."

She glanced over at Wilson, turned her gaze to me, sniffed and then indicated that I should sit.

"We were hoping," I said formally, "to speak to Mr Knight."

"My husband is at his banking house," she said. "If it is a matter of finance, you should call on him there, and not at his home."

I felt my hackles rising but kept my tone cordial. "It is a personal matter, madam, to do with your niece, Mrs Moncrieff."

Mrs Knight closed her eyes for a moment. "My niece by marriage, constable – we share no blood." She caught sight of Wilson writing in his notebook. "What are you doing there?" she barked, and he stopped and looked at me.

"As constables we are required to report our findings to the magistrates," I explained, "and it is part of Constable Wilson's duty to make sure that we report everything accurately. If you wish to inspect his notebook before we leave, you are welcome to do so."

"Hmph," she said, turning down her mouth. "I may well do that. But you may continue," and she waved her hand at Wilson. He raised his eyebrows at me but said nothing. "Why do you need to know about Catherine?" she asked. "She left here months ago, and good riddance."

"Why do you say that, Mrs Knight?" I asked. "Are you not fond of your – of Mrs Moncrieff?"

"Constable Plank," she said, "my husband is a banker. An important man in Bury. And as his wife I have worked long and hard to give him a home and family that befit his station, with never a breath of scandal. Others do not have the same concern for his standing. Others who live far away and do not appreciate the way in which idle gossip spreads in a small town."

"You refer to Mr Knight's family in London?" I asked.

She drew herself, if it were possible, even more upright in her seat. "Mr Knight was inordinately fond of his older sister, the late Mrs Foster. And when she said that her foolish daughter had… fallen, Richard – Mr Knight –

immediately suggested that the girl come here, where no-one knew her and live as a young widow."

"So there was never a Mr Moncrieff?" I asked.

"Good heavens, no," said Mrs Knight. "What self-respecting man would marry a girl in that condition? Of course, my main concern was the protection of my own darling Emily. She was only fifteen when her cousin came to live with us, and despite my concerns the two of them became as thick as thieves. When the child was born, Emily doted on him."

"Just to be clear, Mrs Knight," I said, speaking carefully, "as this differs from what we have been told elsewhere. When Mrs Moncrieff came to live with you, she was expecting a baby, and had a son. It is not your daughter – Emily – who had the child."

Mrs Knight looked horrified. "Constable Plank! Emily was brought up by her father and me as a young lady of perfect morals. When she married she was untouched. Who on earth would suggest otherwise and blacken the name and reputation of a dear woman who is no longer here to defend herself?" Tears sprang to her eyes and she retrieved a handkerchief from her pocket and wiped them away almost angrily.

"I am sorry to distress you by reminding you of your daughter," I said.

Mrs Knight shook her head tightly. She took a deep breath and looked at me, and for the first time I saw a softening of her features. "When you have lost a child, constable, you do not need reminding of her. She is in my thoughts every day."

"Nevertheless, I am sorry," I said, and I meant it. "What we had been told is that Mrs Moncrieff – Miss Foster as she was then – came to live with you. While she was in your home her cousin – your daughter – had a child who was subsequently orphaned, and when Mrs Moncrieff returned to London she took the boy with her, to bring him up as her own. But you now tell us that the child's mother is Mrs Moncrieff herself."

"If our darling Emily had been his mother, constable," said Mrs Knight, "why would we give up our grandchild? Why would we not just bring him up ourselves? No, we were glad to see the back of her when she decided to stay in London after my husband's sister's funeral. Mr Foster begged his daughter to stay, apparently, and agreed to take the boy into his home. I will admit that we miss Arthur – he was a bright little thing."

"So Mr Foster did not know that Arthur was actually his grandson?" I asked. I looked over at Wilson who was scribbling as fast as he could to keep up.

"Well, we didn't tell him, if that's what you're asking," said Mrs Knight, prickling at the idea. "As far as I know, Catherine and her mother agreed to keep the whole business from her father; he doted on her and it would have broken his heart. He was a kind man – at least in later life, after he came back from the plantation. It's a shame the place didn't have the same effect on that shiftless son of his."

♦

"Well," said Wilson, after taking a long drink from his tankard.

"Well indeed," I echoed.

"And I thought our family was complicated," he added, "with George and all." He drained his tankard and then used his finger to dab the last pie crumbs from his plate. "I'd like to take a little present back for him," he said. "And a picture for Alice – she's never been out of London and it would be nice to show her a bit of the country."

I managed not to smile at his worldly tone. "I asked the porter," I said, "and he said that there are several booksellers in Abbeygate Street selling prints."

Wilson stood. "What time does the mail coach leave?" he asked.

"Seven o'clock," I said. "Shall we meet here at five for a bite to eat?"

♦

From our vantage point in the dining room of the Angel we saw the smart mail coach, painted in the black and maroon livery of the Royal Mail, draw up outside at half-past six. A fellow wrapped in a greatcoat clambered up as soon as it halted to reserve his spot next to the coachman; I did not envy him his exposed position and once again was grateful for our inside tickets. The coach was immediately surrounded by porters who set about hauling boxes, trunks, packages, bags, baskets and more into every spare space that had been left by the porters at earlier stops and securing them with rope.

"Did you find a suitable print for Alice?" I asked.

"I did," said Wilson, reaching down into his bag and carefully taking out a slim package. He untied the string and opened the envelope that the bookseller had fashioned out of old newspaper, extracting a small but very fine print of the abbey ruins. I laughed. "What?" asked Wilson indignantly. "Is there something wrong with it?"

I shook my head and reached into my own bag for a similar package, which I undid to show an identical print that I had bought for Martha. Wilson looked put out for a moment and then roared with laughter. "Alice will be delighted," he said. "She's always telling me that Mrs Plank has such good taste, so to have the same print as her, well, she'll be pleased."

"And George?" I asked, carefully wrapping up Martha's present.

Wilson delved into his bag again and brought out another little package and handed it to me. I unwrapped it and in my hand was a small sheep, about the size of an egg.

"There was an old girl in the market," he explained. "She said that her husband made the body," he pointed at the wooden frame of the animal, carved and stained black, "and then she made its little coat from wool. At least I think that's what she said – she was a real countrywoman, and not a tooth in her head."

"It's just right," I said, giving the little creature a stroke on the muzzle and then wrapping it up and handing it back to Wilson. "Now drink up, and remember…"

Wilson lifted his tankard. "I know, I know: the privy."

♦

Our two fellow inside passengers were already in place when Wilson and I boarded the coach – an elderly couple from Norwich, he as thin and silent as she was fat and talkative, who were going down to London to meet their first grandchild. Before we had even left Angel Hill we knew that their daughter was married to a lawyer – "An important lawyer, constables, of whom I am sure you will hear more in the future, given your line of work" – and that the new grandson was sure to follow in his father's profession. I caught the husband's eye and he gave me a slow wink before turning to gaze out of the coach window. He evidently knew his wife well; by the time the coach had left the town and picked up speed on the road to Newmarket, her head had fallen forward onto her generous bosom and she was snoring softly.

Our route back to London was different to that of the stage coach but there was little time to take notice of the towns where we stopped very briefly to collect mail. Both Wilson and I slept in snatches, jolting awake as the coach sped on its way and then dropping once more into a fitful doze. All seven passengers – the four of us inside and the three on top with the coachman – were travelling all the way to London, and we had to get out only once to spare the horses, while they negotiated a steep little hill outside Harlow. As Wilson and I walked alongside the coach in the moonlight, the Post Office guard spotted us from his perch at the rear of the coach, next to the mail box.

"Excuse me, gentlemen," he called down. "Are you constables?"

"Aye," I replied. "Constable Plank and Constable Wilson, from Great Marlborough Street."

"Might I ask a favour, constables?" he said. "For the final part of the journey, could you exchange seats with the two gentlemen sitting on the bench behind the driver? We're heading into Epping Forest, and having two constables visible on the coach…"

Attacks on coaches – particularly mail coaches – in Epping Forest were common enough for this proposal to make sense, and when the coachman pulled the horses to a halt at the top of the rise we made the switch. The two outside passengers were only too pleased to be able to spend the final hours of their journey in relative comfort, and Wilson was young enough to be excited at the prospect of seeing off a highwayman. For my own part, I sincerely hoped it would not come to that and instead concentrated on enjoying watching the sun rise as we galloped towards London.

A question of inheritance

MONDAY 18TH MAY 1829

It was almost noon when I knocked on the door of 87 Hatton Garden. A young clerk let me in, indicated a seat and went to tell his master that I was waiting to see him. A few moments later I heard boots thundering down the stairs and James Harmer appeared. His fondness for food and wine showed in his generous girth and in his jowls, but his delight in life spread far beyond the table. By dint of hard work and an exceptional brain he had hauled himself up from humble beginnings – his father had been a weaver in Spitalfields – and now was one of the most respected (or feared, depending on your situation) lawyers in England. Unlike many of that breed, however, he had retained his compassion for his fellow man, and often took on cases for no fee when he felt that the cause was just. He also enjoyed discussing and debating the law, always looking for ways to make it fairer and more effective, and it was his legal curiosity that had brought me to him today.

"Constable Plank," he said with genuine pleasure, holding out his hand. He pulled his watch out of his pocket and consulted it. "Now you're a clever fellow, coming to see me at this hour."

"I thought you might be appearing at the Old Bailey at two," I said, "and wondered whether you might like some company on the walk, and perhaps a little refreshment at the Saracen's Head."

Harmer held out his hand and his clerk passed him his hat, which he clapped onto his head, and his satchel, which he tucked under his arm. "I promised Henrietta – my wife – that I would eat nothing at noon," he patted his belly, "but if it is a matter of urgent court business, well, what's a fellow to do?"

♦

A quarter of an hour later we were sitting at a table in the tavern, a tankard and a roast meat roll in front of each of us.

"What d'you think of this new police force, then, constable?" asked Harmer, taking a large bite of his roll. He chewed for a moment and then continued. "It seems likely that Peel's police bill will pass, and not before time, in my opinion."

"I think it rather depends on who will be in charge," I said, taking a drink from my tankard. "I can't deny that something more organised would be welcome – Great Marlborough Street has excellent men, but some of the other police offices, well, I don't need to tell you. But the man in charge, he will have to know what he's about."

Harmer wiped the back of his hand across his mouth. "From what I hear," he said, "they are thinking of two men. Joint command. One fellow a soldier, for discipline and organisation, and the other a lawyer, for legal exper-tise."

"That's a sound idea," I said, "as long as the two are the right men."

The lawyer lifted his tankard. "I'll drink to that," he said, draining it and then waving it at the pot boy. The lad brought over another tankard and pointed at mine; I shook my head. "Will you sign up?" asked Harmer. "The new force?"

"You're not the first to ask," I replied. "Wilson – you remember Constable Wilson?"

Harmer held his hand up in the air to indicate great height. "That tall young fellow of yours?" he asked.

"That's the one," I said. "He and I were discussing it, and I told him that I'm too long in the tooth to get used to a new way of doing things. But I am encouraging him to do it; he's a good constable – although I take care not to tell him that, in case he sits on his laurels. He's a married man now, with one child and another on the way, so he'll need steady work."

The lawyer shook his head, smiling. "There's nothing like a nest full of gaping beaks to make a fellow work hard," he said. He swallowed his last mouthful of meat roll and sat back in his chair. "But you didn't drag me in here and force food on me to talk about the new police force, so what's on your mind, sir?"

"Inheritance law," I said promptly. Harmer picked at a back tooth and said nothing. "There has been a series of deaths, all connected with one family, and I have my concerns," I continued. "I have been wondering whether money is at the heart of it. And I have recently found out some facts about the family that paint a rather different picture to the one I was originally given." Without mentioning any names, I told the lawyer what I now knew of the structure of the Foster family. He listened without interrupting.

When I had finished, he said, "Well, they are not the first family to spin a yarn to protect the reputation of a daughter, and they certainly won't be the last. Although," he continued as he saw me about to object, "it is slightly unusual that the father was kept in the dark – not unheard of, but usually the parents act in tandem. Now, you said your concerns were about inheritance law – not strictly my area, but I have a working knowledge. Ah, out comes the notebook: this is serious."

"Another symptom of age, I fear," I said, opening my notebook on the table. "I find I need to write things down otherwise they vanish from my head. Now, the father of the family – the old man who has recently died – became a Quaker in his later years, and made out his will in favour of the Society, leaving only small bequests for his daughter and the boy he thought she had adopted."

I stopped as Harmer held up his hand. "There is no entail on the family's property? No title?" he asked. I shook my head. "Then primogeniture is not a concern and the father could do as he saw fit with his will."

"And he intended to," I said. "He was a great supporter of the abolitionists and wanted them to use the money to further their cause." Harmer nodded approvingly. "But when his son returned from the Caribbean, the father changed his will and named the son as his heir, which is understandable. And soon after that, the father died."

"And the son inherited the lot," said Harmer.

"And then the son died," I continued.

"Intestate?" asked the lawyer.

"I suspect so," I said. "He was a young man, unmarried, and would not have had much thought to his own mortality. No doubt the family lawyer would have advised him to draw up a will when he came into his inheritance, but I doubt he had time to do so."

"Then your first task is to find out whether the son had a will or not," said Harmer. "If he did, the situation is clear. With no children of his own – no legitimate children of which we are aware, I should perhaps say – then it was entirely up to him how he distributed his fortune. But if he did not, well, then, that is more interesting."

"Who would stand to benefit in that situation?" I asked.

"His parents and older brother are all deceased," said Harmer, "and he has no children. His next of kin, therefore, is his sister. The Prerogative Court at Canterbury would grant her a letter of administration, authorising her to dispose of the estate as she wishes – almost certainly to herself, I would imagine, unless she is of the same charitable nature as her father. She is a widow, you say? No, unmarried – that's right. Either way, she is of age and has no father, no brother and no husband, and so will be the mistress of her own assets – a comfortable position for her."

"But she does have a son," I said. "A child."

"Did her brother know that he had a nephew, rather than an adopted…" he frowned as he worked it out, "cousin once removed?"

"I don't know," I admitted. "They were close, the brother and sister, but I do not know whether she confided in him about her child. And there is another complication."

"Another one?" asked Harmer. "Thank heavens I asked for this second tankard." He lifted it and drank.

"It is possible that the son is not the son at all," I said. Harmer's eyes widened. I explained what I had read in the doctor's notes, and what the butler had told the housekeeper, and I even mentioned the dog.

"It sounds like the plot of a theatrical melodrama," observed the lawyer.

"Aye," I laughed. "It does, but there it is. And if it were proved that the man who returned was not the son at all, and that the son did indeed die in the Caribbean, what then would happen to the inheritance?"

Harmer leaned back and stroked his chin. "An interesting dilemma, constable – very interesting. I daresay there would be arguments on both sides but, working from first principles, I would say that the Quakers would be in luck. After all, if the father had wanted his daughter to inherit everything, he would have written that in his original will, but he did not. He changed it only when his son was restored to him. If that son is once again removed, then we must revert to the original wishes of the father, as though the son had died before the father made his will. Which, you think, he had."

I shrugged. "That is still to be shown," I said.

The lawyer took out his watch and leapt to his feet. "Good heavens, constable, I shall be late." He stuffed his hat onto his head, reached down for his satchel and then shook my hand vigorously. "Thank you for entertaining me – a fascinating story, and a knotty legal problem thrown in for good measure. Now I must be off." He reached into his pocket for some money but I shook my head.

"I will not hear of it, sir," I said.

Harmer tipped his hat in thanks. "Then I am in your debt, constable, and shall look forward to our next meeting – and our next dilemma." He paused for a moment. "That sister; she must be hoping it really was her brother who showed up, otherwise she can bid farewell to her fortune." He bowed and was gone.

CHAPTER THIRTY

Such a nasty thing

TUESDAY 19TH MAY 1829

After my discussion with Mr Harmer I had read through my notes several times, to make sure that I understood what he had told me about probate and inheritance, and by the next morning I knew that I had to call on Mrs Moncrieff. Wilson did not come for me, as his first duty of the day was to collect a prisoner from Coldbath Fields to attend a hearing at Great Marlborough Street, and I used the walk to rehearse the careful questions I would need to ask her.

My opportunity came sooner than I had expected. I was sitting in the back office, waiting for any warrants from the morning's business in court, when Tom Neale appeared at the door.

"You're wanted, Sam," he said. I stood and reached for my hat but he shook his head. "Upstairs. I'm not sure what's going on, but Mr Conant has adjourned his hearings and sent for Miss Lily, and he wants you upstairs straight away."

"I hope he's not unwell," I said.

"He made no mention of calling the doctor," said Tom, following me down the corridor to the front office.

I passed Thin Billy on the stairs as I went up to the magistrate's rooms.

"What's going on, Billy?" I asked quietly. "I can't remember the last time he adjourned a court."

The footman glanced up the stairs and whispered, "There's a lady up there with him – very distressed. I've been sent for chocolate." He lifted the empty pot he was carrying and edged past me.

I knocked on the door and could hear the relief in Conant's voice as he called out, "Come in, constable".

I entered the dining room, closing the door behind me, and saw the magistrate standing by the fireplace. In one of the armchairs, her back to me, was a woman.

Conant spoke to her. "This is Constable Samuel Plank, one of our most experienced officers." I walked over to the woman and as she looked up at me, I recognised her from the funeral at Bunhill Fields. "And this is Mrs Moncrieff, Sam – her father was Mr Hugh Foster, and her brother James Foster."

I bowed to her. "Please accept my condolences, Mrs Moncrieff," I said. "The past few months have not been kind to you."

She was a beauty, to be sure, but it was a hard kind of beauty. It was too contrived for my taste: the skin was a shade too pale, the lips slightly too red, the lashes too sooty. She shook her head sadly, and her hair did not move, anchored as it was with pins and pomade.

"Thank you, constable," she said. "My father was advanced in years and had been frail but my brother..." she dabbed at her eye with a handkerchief, "I did not expect to be mourning my brother for many years yet. But now that he has gone, I feel I must tell the truth about him."

Of course that caught my attention but I mastered my reaction and kept my expression as one of sympathetic concern.

"Do not distress yourself, madam," said Conant gently. "My daughter will be here soon."

Mrs Moncrieff sighed. "Miss Conant has been a good friend to me," she said. "And I know that James was fond of her. I did wonder whether he might propose, and she and I would be sisters – but that is of no consequence now."

From the way the magistrate simply nodded I knew that his daughter had not told him of the events of the evening of St Valentine's Day, though perhaps – to echo Mrs Moncrieff – that was of no consequence now.

The door opened and in came Lily with a pot in her hand.

"I met Thin Billy coming from the kitchen and I said I would bring this up, to save him the journey," she said, going across to the sideboard and setting down the pot. "It's not like you to drink chocolate, papa," she said, walking over to embrace him but stopping when she caught sight of Mrs Moncrieff.

"Catherine," she said, bending down to kiss her friend. "I am sorry that I have not visited you since... since the accident. I hope my note reached you?"

"It did, Lily, thank you," said Mrs Moncrieff. "And I cannot tell you what a comfort it was to me to be reminded that I have such a dear friend, and one with a distinguished magistrate for a father. Otherwise I would not know where to turn with this."

She reached into her reticule and took out a folded piece of paper. She opened it and read it before handing it to Conant with the very tips of her fingers, as though it were soiled.

"*All is known,*" read the magistrate aloud. "*Pay now.*"

Miss Lily looked shocked. "Goodness, Catherine," she said, "who on earth sent you such a nasty thing?"

Miss Moncrieff shook her head. "It was not sent to me," she said. "It was sent to James – by Doctor Branscombe."

"Doctor Branscombe?" I repeated. "How can you be sure?" Conant passed me the note and I looked at it. "It is not signed."

"James recognised the hand," said Mrs Moncrieff.

"When did the doctor send it?" I asked, copying the words into my notebook.

"I cannot remember the exact date," she said. "It was before Easter – perhaps the week before. James was very angry when he received it, I do remember that."

"Do you know what the doctor meant when he wrote 'All is known', Mrs Moncrieff?" I asked. "What is known?"

Mrs Moncrieff took a ragged breath and closed her eyes for a moment. Miss Lily leaned forward and touched her knee. "James is gone, Catherine," she said, "and so is Doctor Branscombe. It cannot hurt either of them, but it is distressing you – otherwise you would not have come here today. If you know what the note means, you should tell papa and Constable Plank – it may be important. But first, perhaps a cup of chocolate – you look pale."

Conant went over to the sideboard and poured out two cups of chocolate for the ladies while I brought over two dining chairs so that he and I could sit down. Once we were all settled and Mrs Moncrieff had had a reviving sip of her drink, she began.

"Doctor Branscombe was our family physician for as long as I can remember," she said. "But when James came back from the Caribbean, he and the doctor had a falling out." She shook her head. "It sounds foolish even to my own ears, but Doctor Branscombe claimed that James was not who he said he was. That he was not James at all, but another man claiming to be James."

"Did he tell your father of his suspicions?" asked Conant.

She shook her head. "No: only James. James refused to entertain his ridiculous accusations, and then he received that note."

"But why would the doctor need money?" I asked.

"I wondered that too, constable," said Mrs Moncrieff, "but then it came to me." She leaned forward and gazed intently at me, as though willing me to understand. "I am certain that my father would have left a bequest to Doctor Branscombe in his will – the will that he wrote when we thought James had perished at the plantation. When James was so mercifully restored to us, my father wrote a new will, leaving everything to James, and the doctor's bequest vanished. I believe he was counting on that bequest, constable, perhaps even had borrowed against it, and saw this as a way to extort money from James."

The magistrate and I glanced at each other. "That could make sense, Mrs Moncrieff," he said.

"You will forgive me asking," I said. "Constables always ask too many questions. Are you certain that the doctor's allegation was ridiculous? Are you sure that the man who returned from the Cayman Islands was your brother James Foster? I think it only fair to tell you that a good friend of your father's, Edward Freame, has expressed the same doubts."

"Mr Freame the banker?" asked Mrs Moncrieff. I nodded. "But surely Mr Freame was in the same position as Doctor Branscombe," she continued. "Before my brother returned, my father's will left the majority of his fortune to the Quakers. Mr Freame and his Quaker friends would have been glad to see James declared an impostor. But he was not: he was my brother. Although I wish to God he had not been!" And she burst into tears. The magistrate produced a clean handkerchief from his pocket and handed it to her; she nodded in thanks and pressed it to her face.

"What an odd thing to say, Catherine," said Miss Lily, whom I knew had little patience with histrionics. "What on earth can you mean?"

Mrs Moncrieff sniffed and took a deep breath. "James was always hot-tempered, even as a boy. I think papa hoped that sending him to the plantation – putting him to work – would calm him down. But I fear it did not. When he received that note from Doctor Branscombe, he was furious – more angry than I have ever seen him. I told him to ignore it, that the doctor would never follow through with his threat, but he wouldn't listen. He said he would go to see the doctor and make him promise not to spread his vile lies." She slumped in her seat. "And you know the rest."

Miss Lily put her hand over her mouth. I knew she was thinking of that February evening when James Foster had pressed her up against a wall, because it was in my mind too.

"Mrs Moncrieff," I said. "I need to be sure about what you mean. Are you saying that your late brother, James Foster, killed Doctor Branscombe?"

She nodded. "Yes. He went to see the doctor that morning and came home wearing a greatcoat that was not his own and refused to let Finch take it from him. I followed him to his room; at first he would not let me in but I said I would scream if he did not. And his clothes – there was blood on them. He had taken the doctor's coat to cover them. He said he and the doctor argued, that the doctor threatened to go to the newspapers with his allegation – and James lost his temper."

I looked up from my notebook. "What did you do with the soiled clothes, Mrs Moncrieff?" I asked.

"His shirt and coat," she said. "We cut them into small pieces and put some on the fire and discarded the rest when we went out."

"And why did you not report the matter, Mrs Moncrieff?" asked Conant. "You could have come to me, as you have today."

"Were you scared of him, Catherine?" asked Miss Lily.

Her friend nodded. "I had to think of Arthur as well as myself," she said. "If he could do that to Doctor Branscombe for threatening to tell the newspapers, what would he do to me for reporting him to the magistrate?"

"Indeed, Mrs Moncrieff," said Conant. "I am only thankful that your father did not live to see this – from what I hear, he was so proud of James, and so pleased to have him home again. I'm sure it would have broken his heart to see what his son had become."

A look of anguish crossed Mrs Moncrieff's face and she put out her hand. "Oh please, Mr Conant, you must not think too harshly of James. It was a wicked, wicked thing that he did, but he regretted it so bitterly. He wept like a child in my arms for days afterwards. He said he would confess were it not for the shame it would bring on the family. He had hopes that I would marry again one day, but what man of quality would take me, knowing my brother to be a… murderer." She shut her eyes at the word. "In the end, he could not stand the guilt. He was drinking more and more, and that afternoon he took the curricle – I begged him not to, but he was beyond my reach. The moment the message arrived that evening, I knew what had happened. It was an accident, they said, and perhaps it was."

Miss Lily leaned across and squeezed her friend's hand. "It is best to believe that it was, my dear," she said.

Mrs Moncrieff paused a moment and then nodded. "Thank you, Lily," she said. "And thank you, Mr Conant. I feel much lighter in spirit, now that you know the truth." She picked up her reticule and stood up. "But I have taken up enough of your time. And there is so much that I have to attend to; there is the plantation to be sold, and the house here in London."

"You are leaving London?" asked Miss Lily, getting to her feet.

"I think it best," said her friend. "There has been too much sadness here for me. Once everything is settled I have a mind to move to the coast – Ramsgate, perhaps, or Brighton. Arthur's health is not robust and I am told that sea-bathing is the very thing." She glanced into her reticule and then looked at me. "Please may I have the note, constable? I should like to destroy it myself, so that I know it cannot fall into the wrong hands."

"If I may, madam," I said, "I would like to keep hold of it for a day or two, but I will return it."

Mrs Moncrieff considered for a moment and then nodded. "Of course, constable. I am grateful to you for taking the matter so seriously. And I know I can count on your discretion."

I looked at Conant. "Mrs Moncrieff," he said, "we will do all that we can to minimise the distress for you, but there has been a murder. There cannot be a trial, of course, and your brother's confession was not witnessed by a third party, and we cannot know that he was in his right mind when he made it. But the matter will have to be recorded officially, and Doctor Branscombe's family notified."

"I quite understand, sir," said Mrs Moncrieff smoothly. "I know that you will do all you can for me. May I ask one more small favour? Would you permit your daughter to stay as my guest for a night or two? I confess that I find Villiers Street rather a melancholy place, and the presence of a dear friend," she held out her hand and Miss Lily took it, "a dear friend who now knows all the secrets of my heart, will be the greatest comfort to me."

◆

It is not often that Martha is struck dumb, but when I had finished recounting to her the events of the afternoon she simply gaped at me.

"Dear heavens, Sam," she said eventually. "What a family. It is a blessing that the poor father did not live to see it. What do you think: was it really James Foster who came back? Mrs Moncrieff certainly thinks so."

"Or says she does," I said. "You know, Mar, watching her going on like that, with Miss Lily sitting so quiet and calm next to her – I kept thinking that it was a performance worthy of Mrs Siddons in her prime."

My wife's eyes widened. "You mean she was play-acting?" she asked.

I shrugged. "Perhaps exaggerating, and certainly trying to gain our sympathy. There's one thing that does trouble me." I reached over to my coat and retrieved my notebook from the pocket. I opened it and took out the note that Mrs Moncrieff had let me keep, unfolding it and handing it to Martha.

She read it and shuddered. "Nasty, and to the point," she observed.

"But not," I said, "in the hand of Doctor Branscombe. I have seen his diary and the notes he made about James Foster, and his hand is plainer, more upright."

"But if he did not write it, then who did?" asked Martha.

CHAPTER THIRTY-ONE

Wilson pays

WEDNESDAY 20TH MAY 1829

Wilson and I were engaged in separate business all day but as I was walking home along Great Titchfield Street, my mind on my dinner, I heard someone calling my name. I turned to see Wilson walking as fast as he could to catch up with me; when he was a younger constable I had had to remind him on several occasions that a running constable lacks dignity and causes panic, and these days he nearly always remembered my advice.

"Constable Plank," he said, panting slightly as he reached me. "You are on your way home."

"Plainly," I said. I waited.

"It is a fine evening," he observed.

"Constable Wilson," I said, "you and I are not in the habit of discussing the weather, and particularly not

286 | SUSAN GROSSEY

when Mrs Plank has promised me a nice piece of fish for my dinner. Now is there something else?"

He nodded. "There is, sir. Could we stop at the George and Dragon – I would prefer not to talk in front of Mrs Plank." He smiled wanly. "I'll pay."

We said nothing until we were sitting with a tankard each. I had no doubt Martha would say something about the stench of the tavern when I reached home, but an ale at the end of a day of work is always welcome.

"Well, then," I said, once we had each taken a long draught.

"George Fanshawe," said Wilson.

"The runner involved with the burial club, and the tontine?" I asked.

Wilson nodded. "That's him. He's been threatening me. Well, not me exactly – but Alice and George."

I put my tankard down and leaned forward. "What do you mean, threatening Alice? Has he spoken to her?" I asked.

"If he had I wouldn't be sitting here talking about it," said Wilson grimly. "No: he has sent me three messages – nothing written down, of course – three messages saying that I am to leave well alone or they will pay the price. Alice and George."

"Mr Vickery's daughter said he was a nasty piece of work," I said, recalling our visit to Coldbath Fields and its keeper.

"I suppose one of his lackeys reported back to him when I went to see Scott at the Fountain," continued Wilson. "I thought we'd been careful, but perhaps someone recognised me, or had me followed. Either way, he knows I'm a constable and that I can make trouble for him."

"Aye," I said, draining my tankard. "And you certainly will. I've dealt with bigger and nastier bullies than George Fanshawe before now, and I'll show you how it's done – but it can wait until tomorrow. Now you go home to that lovely wife and son of yours and give them a kiss from me."

CHAPTER THIRTY-TWO

An elegant little piece

THURSDAY 21ST MAY 1829

"Just a small bowl, thank you, Mrs Plank," said Wilson as he took off his hat and pulled out a chair at the table.

"Does Alice not feed you in the mornings?" I asked, as Martha ladled porridge into a large bowl and put it in front of him.

"Of course she does," he said, "but it's a fair step from Brill Row to here."

"Don't you listen to him, William," said my wife, putting a hand on Wilson's shoulder. "And who's that now?" She went to the back door and opened it. A message lad stood there and she took the note from him and handed it to me before paying him with a coin and a heel of bread.

"It's from Mrs Godwin, at Villiers Street," I said. I read the note again. "Finish up, Wilson – quickly, now."

Martha looked at me with concern. "What is it, Sam?" she asked.

"I'm not sure," I said, putting on my coat. "'Constable Plank,'" I read aloud, "'please come immediately – it concerns Mrs Moncrieff and Miss Conant. Yours, Elizabeth Godwin'."

♦

I flagged down the first hackney we saw and the jarvey turned his horses to head south. It took us a few minutes to cross the flow of traffic on Oxford Street but soon we were trotting as fast as we could along Regent Street.

"I am sorry that we cannot deal with Fanshawe this morning," I said to Wilson. "This afternoon – it's next on my list."

"Of course," said Wilson. "He's going nowhere, the more's the pity."

As the jarvey turned into Villiers Street, I spotted Mrs Godwin standing on the corner. She waved to indicate that we should stop and the jarvey pulled his horses to a halt alongside her.

"Constable Plank," she said, "oh, and Constable Wilson. Perhaps it is as well. Please, leave the coach here. We don't want her to see or hear you arriving."

Wilson looked at me and I raised an eyebrow, but we did as we were asked. I paid the jarvey and we followed the housekeeper quickly along the street and then down the steps at number fourteen to her room. A pot of tea was waiting, with two cups, and Mrs Godwin returned to the kitchen for a third. As she poured, I could see a slight tremor in her hand.

"Mrs Godwin," I said, nodding my thanks as she handed me a cup and indicated the armchair. "Perhaps you should sit down as well, and tell us what is wrong." She passed a cup to Wilson, who put it on the table so that he could take up his usual position at the door, notebook in hand, and then she sat in the chair next to her bureau.

"Perhaps it was wrong to summon you, constable," she began, "but I do not know what else to do." She took out a handkerchief and twisted it in her hands. "It is at times like this that I most miss Mr Harding; he always knew what to do in a crisis."

"You knew well enough to call us, Mrs Godwin," I said.

She nodded and straightened her back. "I did, constable, yes. The day before yesterday, Mrs Moncrieff came home with Miss Conant, who was to stay for the night. I was glad to see her, I will admit: Mrs Moncrieff has been very upset – understandably – since her brother's death, and I thought Miss Conant might be a comfort to her.

Mary made up the room next to Mrs Moncrieff's – Arthur's room – and cook prepared a supper tray for them."

"And the lad?" I asked.

"Well, that's one blessing in all this mess," said Mrs Godwin. "With Mrs Moncrieff so distressed, Miss Napier – the governess – suggested that she could take Arthur home with her, to stay for a while with her mother in Clapham. It's a perfectly respectable household, constable; Mrs Napier is an old friend of mine, the widow of a clergyman. In fact I was the one who suggested her daughter for the post here. Miss Napier's married sister lives with their mother, with a couple of kiddies of her own – I thought it would be company for Arthur, and a sight more cheerful than us at the moment." She smiled sadly. "He's to stay there until tomorrow."

"And it was Tuesday evening, when Miss Conant arrived," I said.

"That's right," said the housekeeper. "Mary went up last thing on Tuesday to collect the supper things, and the tray was outside the door of Mrs Moncrieff's room. She knocked, she said, to see if the ladies wanted anything but there was no reply. She went up again the next morning – yesterday morning – and knocked, but Mrs Moncrieff called out that they were not to be disturbed and just to leave a breakfast tray outside the door. And it's been the same at every meal since: yesterday luncheon and supper, and breakfast today. I went up myself, of course, and the doors of both rooms are locked."

"The meals – are they being eaten?" I asked.

"Yes," said Mrs Godwin, "and the dirty plates left outside the door. Now I know grief can take people in different ways, and Mrs Moncrieff can be quite… excitable. I thought a day or two of weeping, with Miss Conant for sensible company, would be no bad thing. But this morning, cook found this hidden under a plate on the tray when Mary brought it down." She reached into one of the cubbyholes in her bureau and took out a slip of paper which she handed to me. "I think it must be Miss Conant's hand – it is not Mrs Moncrieff's."

I looked at the paper; it was a page torn from a small notebook. On it were only three words: *Call Constable Plank.* I passed it to Wilson, who read it and handed it back to the housekeeper.

♦

Mrs Godwin led us up the stairs and along the corridor to Mrs Moncrieff's room. We stopped outside and she pointed to another door next to it and mouthed "Miss Conant". I nodded. As we had agreed, Wilson moved slowly and quietly to the second door while the housekeeper knocked on the first. There was no reply.

"Mrs Moncrieff," she said, "it's Mrs Godwin. I'm here with Constable Plank; he has a message for Miss Conant, from her father."

There was silence for a long minute and then, "Tell him to slip it under the door," called Mrs Moncrieff.

"I cannot do that, madam," I said. "I am instructed to give Miss Lily the message in person."

I heard scuffling in the room and put my ear to the door. The two women were whispering, but angrily, perhaps desperately. After what seemed an eternity the door of Mrs Moncrieff's room opened, but only wide enough for Miss Lily's face to appear. She looked dishevelled and tired – and frightened.

"Hello, constable," she said, and I could hear the effort to sound calm.

"Miss Lily," I said. "Your father wonders when you will be coming home – he misses you."

"And I miss him," she said, tears coming to her eyes. I moved towards her and her eyes widened in panic, so I stepped back again.

"Can you not give me any indication, Miss Lily?" I asked again. "He will worry if I cannot give him a reply."

From inside the room, Mrs Moncrieff spoke. Her voice sounded determined but shrill. "It is entirely up to Miss Conant when she leaves – she knows what she has to do."

I looked at the housekeeper; she had her hand to her mouth and looked as concerned as I felt. I glanced over at Wilson who was on his knees in front of the other door, carefully jiggling a pick in the lock.

I spoke loudly to cover any sound he might make. "What do you mean, Mrs Moncrieff? What does Miss Lily have to do?"

Miss Lily looked intently at me. "I am to tell papa that he cannot make the doctor's murder a matter of record. That it must not be put down anywhere for anyone to know that it was a murder. But I have told Catherine that it is not for me to tell a magistrate what he can and cannot do – it is a matter of law."

"That is indeed the case, Mrs Moncrieff," I said, again keeping my voice up. "Mr Conant cannot change the judicial system simply to please his daughter."

"Then you must tell him that it is not to please her, but to save her," came the reply.

Miss Lily's hand came out towards me and then there was the sound of a crash behind her and she leapt back. I looked along the corridor and Wilson had disappeared into the room. I pushed open the door and grabbed for Miss Lily, pulling her towards me and all but throwing her out into the corridor. Wilson had come through the connecting door into the room and now had hold of Mrs Moncrieff, his arms wrapped around her from the back, pinning her own arms to her sides. He had lifted her off the ground and she was kicking and struggling to get free but he was taller, broader and much stronger. He glanced down at the floor and I saw a pistol. I bent down and picked it up carefully; it was an elegant little piece, about five inches long, with a dark wooden handle and a finely engraved silver muzzle. I checked the safety slide; it was in place. Mrs Godwin came across to me and looked down at the pistol.

"That's one of Mr James's," she said. "He won it at his club one night – he was showing it off to everyone the next day, how the mechanism worked. It frightened the life out of poor Mary."

"It frightened the life out of me," said Miss Lily, who had come into the room behind the housekeeper. "Could you take me home now, do you think, constable?" And I stepped forward to catch her as she fainted.

♦

Martha looked from me to Wilson and back again as we recounted the events of the morning. After we had taken Miss Lily to Portland Place and sent word to Mr Conant to come home, and then given him a very abbreviated version of what had happened, he had insisted that we both go home early. Once we were there, Martha had taken one look at us and refused to listen to anything we had to say until we had each eaten a bowl of thick pea soup – "I was intending this for dinner but we'll worry about that later" – and a hunk of bread. Only once our bowls were wiped clean would she allow us to speak.

"Poor Miss Lily," she said at the end. "She must have been terrified."

"She was very brave," I said. "Her father's daughter through and through."

"And so were you, William," said Martha, reaching over and patting Wilson's hand. He flushed but looked pleased. "Although I am very cross with you for taking such a chance. You're not a bachelor any longer, William – how would Alice and little George manage without you?" She stood and cleared the bowls. "A slice of cherry tart to follow?"

Wilson smiled broadly. "Cherries are my very favourite, Mrs Plank – I just wish they grew all year round."

Martha served us each a slice of tart and then sat down again. "I have heard of grief sending people mad," she said. "And Mrs Moncrieff has had a great deal of it in the last twelve months, losing both her parents and her brother – and grieving for that brother for a second time. Perhaps it's no surprise that the balance of her mind has been affected. That said, it was a wicked thing she did to poor Miss Lily. Just think: she could have killed her."

I shook my head. "She certainly intended to frighten Miss Lily, to force her to do her bidding. But I don't think she ever intended to hurt her. The safety slide was in place when I picked the pistol up – unless you engaged it, Wilson?" His mouth full, he shook his head. "And the housekeeper said that James Foster showed the pistol to everyone, demonstrating how it worked, so Mrs Moncrieff would have known how to use – and disengage – the safety slide."

"The poor woman," said Martha, shaking her head.

I smiled at her. "You have the most compassionate heart in the world, Mrs Plank."

"And why shouldn't I?" she asked. "Compassion costs nothing to give, and may mean the world to someone."

She glanced over at Wilson, who was busy using his finger to wipe the last drops of cherry juice from his plate, and I knew that she was thinking about that night three years ago when I had brought home a desperate young girl I had found in the alleyway, a young girl who was now lucky enough to call herself Mrs Wilson.

Sensing himself the centre of attention, Wilson looked up. "What?" he asked.

"I wanted to ask you one thing," I said as Martha stood again to clear the table. "Where did you learn to pick locks?"

"A cracksman showed me," he said. "I caught him by the legs as he was breaking into a house and pulled him out. He was only a nipper and I knew what would happen if he went before the judge. I put the fear of God into him and then we made a deal: he would show me how to pick a lock and give me his picks, and I'd give him a chance to go straight. It was your idea, sir," he nodded at me. "You're always telling me to take every opportunity to learn from experts."

I am sure my chin all but hit the table. "That wasn't the sort of expert I meant," I said. "I meant lawyers and the like. Ten pounds to a crown he went round the corner and jumped through another window."

"Then you're ten pounds out of pocket," said Wilson. "He's kept to his side of the bargain. He's one of our regular message lads – and no, I won't tell you which one."

Martha stood there, her hands on her hips, and laughed until tears streamed down her face.

CHAPTER THIRTY-THREE

Catherine's baby

SATURDAY 23RD MAY 1829

Miss Lily was sitting in an armchair by the fireplace in her father's dining room.

"Come over and say hello, Constable Plank," she called out. "I dare not move from here, under strict orders from papa. Luncheon has been set out and we will eat when he arrives."

I walked over to the fireplace and smiled at her. For all her brave words, she looked drawn and pale, and her smile was not quite as easy as usual. She had a blanket tucked around her and her feet propped up on a low stool. "You see," she said, indicating it all, "I am considered an invalid today. And you will have to amuse me until papa arrives." The clock on the mantelpiece struck the hour. "Which should be any minute now," she added.

I sat in the other armchair. "You are not an invalid, Miss Lily," I said, "but you have had a frightening encounter."

She nodded and bit her lip. She leaned towards me and held out her hand; I took it. "It was frightening, constable, and I wanted to thank you for coming. You and Constable Wilson. I was so happy to see your face at the door." She squeezed my hand. "Thank you." I nodded; as Martha will tell anyone, I have a soft spot for Miss Lily and it angered me to see her brought low. "But let us not alarm papa," she added. "He is not as robust as we are, I think."

The door opened and in came Mr Conant. He looked questioningly at me, the worry clear on his face, and when I nodded encouragingly he walked over to his daughter and made himself smile at her. He kissed her cheek and then held out his hand to escort her to the table.

"I am not ill, papa," she said, but she did not really mind his concern.

♦

After a meal during which the magistrate and his daughter both loaded morsels onto each other's plates while neither ate very much, Conant settled Miss Lily back into her armchair.

"Are you sure you feel strong enough to do this, my dear?" he asked her, pulling the blanket around her.

"Papa," she said, "how much strength do I need to talk? You and Constable Plank need to know what Catherine told me, and until I can tell you it will go round and round in my head." She smiled at him. "Now sit, both of you."

Conant took the other armchair and I brought over my chair from the dining table.

"Do you have your notebook, constable?" she asked. I nodded and held it up for her to see. "The first important thing to tell you is that you were right, Constable Plank: the man who returned from the Caribbean was not James Foster."

"We should recruit that dog," said the magistrate. "He knew all along."

"Papa!" said Miss Lily reprovingly, but she smiled. "The man who claimed to be James Foster was actually Matthew Dunn. He and James Foster became friends in Grand Cayman; Mr Dunn was working for a shipping company. They had plenty in common: they were both pale-skinned and red-haired, they were both disgraced younger sons, and they were both dependent on their fathers for money. Begrudgingly dependent. James Foster did die in July last year, as his parents were told, of a fever. And towards the end, when he was in the grip of the illness, he spoke to Mr Dunn of what had happened before he left England."

"The falling out with his father?" I asked.

"In a way, but more specifically what led to the falling out," she said. She shifted in her seat and looked down at her hands. "You know that before James Foster was sent out to the Caribbean, Catherine went to stay with her uncle and aunt in Suffolk. Catherine's mother told her husband – the late Mr Foster – that this was to protect Catherine from her brother's bad influence." She looked up at her father and he nodded.

"A sensible decision, I always thought," he said.

"But not the whole story, papa," said Miss Lily quietly. "Catherine told me that when she was sent to Suffolk, she was expecting a baby. James Foster's baby."

Her father stumbled to his feet and looked at me, horror on his face.

"And did you believe her, Miss Lily?" I asked.

She thought for a moment. "At first, no," she admitted. "But then I worked out the dates and it all fits: when James went to the plantation, when Catherine went to Suffolk, Arthur's age." Her voice broke a little on the boy's name. "Catherine's mother knew: that's why she was so keen for James to go. She feared that if she told her husband, he would blame her for not bringing up James properly – and she feared what he would do to his son. She forgave James eventually, I suppose, otherwise she would not have mourned so when he died. Catherine never forgave her mother, though, for not protecting her: that's why she stayed in Suffolk until Mrs Foster died."

"Did the uncle and aunt know?" I asked, thinking of the prim woman we had met in Bury St Edmunds.

"Good heavens, no," said Miss Lily, shaking her head. "They knew she was going to have a baby, of course, and that she was unmarried, but Mrs Foster told them there had been an unwise and unhappy liaison with a married man and therefore no hope of a wedding. She sent an allowance to the aunt for the care of Catherine and Arthur, and they agreed that all anyone in Suffolk need know was that poor Mrs Moncrieff's husband had been carried off by consumption." She gave a hollow sort of laugh. "Catherine said the name Moncrieff was in a newspaper that her uncle had been reading when she arrived, and he checked the local trade directory and there were no Moncrieffs in Bury St Edmunds who might ask awkward questions." She held out her hand. "Sit down, papa – please."

The magistrate reluctantly took his seat again.

"And then Matthew Dunn returned to London," I prompted her.

She nodded. "And then Matthew Dunn returned to London," she continued. "Knowing everything about James and Catherine and Arthur. And he had a plan. As I said, he bore a resemblance to James Foster – same age,

306 | SUSAN GROSSEY

similar colouring – and had spent enough time with him to be able to mimic him well enough."

"And of course James Foster had been away for six years," I said, counting up in my head. "A young man can change a great deal in that time, in a harsh climate, with illness and hard work to shape him."

"At least enough to convince Mr Foster, with his failing eyesight," said Miss Lily. "But Catherine knew straight away. And that's when Mr Dunn proposed his plan. He knew from James Foster that his father planned to leave his fortune to the Quakers and the abolitionist cause. But he calculated – correctly – that if a beloved son were to return from the dead, a reformed character, then his father would want to change his will to pass everything to that son. And he also guessed – again, correctly – that the father would accept him as James Foster, while the daughter might not, and could expose him as an impostor."

"Are you following this, Sam?" asked the magistrate, holding up a hand to make his daughter pause.

I nodded distractedly, writing as fast as I could in my notebook. "Carry on, please, Miss Lily," I said once I had caught up.

"And so Mr Dunn suggested to Catherine that they cooperate," she said. "He proposed that if she went along with his pretence – if she recognised him as her brother – he would keep the secret of Arthur's paternity, and when Mr Foster died and he came into the inheritance, he would share it with her, so that Arthur would be provided for."

I held up my own hand this time. "Did Catherine not think that her father would provide for her himself, in his will – I understand that he was pleased to have her home, and very fond of Arthur."

"I can explain that," said Conant. "I discussed it once with Captain Henderson, when we were talking of Hugh Foster – we are all fathers of beloved daughters. And Henderson told me that Foster was concerned about fortune-hunters. He believed that if he left too much to his daughter, she would attract the attention of unscrupulous fellows with an eye to her money, and so he preferred to leave her a regular, sufficient allowance. I do not think he trusted his daughter to have the sense to see off the rogues, whereas I have no such misgivings." He smiled at Miss Lily.

"I see," I said. "Mrs Moncrieff saw this as a way to secure a greater portion of her father's estate, for herself and for her son."

"Yes," said Miss Lily. "And as a way to safeguard her secret. And so they struck their agreement. Catherine also insisted that Mr Dunn – in the guise of James Foster – make his own will naming her as his heir, should he die before marrying. What could be more natural than a loving brother wanting to secure the future of his widowed sister and her child?" She sighed. "But after years in the Caribbean, Mr Dunn found the temptations of London irresistible. He gambled, he drank to excess – Catherine begged him to calm down, fearing he would give them away. And then he received that note from Doctor Branscombe."

I turned back through my notebook. "'All is known – pay now'."

Miss Lily nodded. "After that, Catherine was frightened of him. He seemed to lose all control. She says she thought about confessing everything and taking the consequences, and then there was the accident in Hyde Park." She gazed into the distance for a moment. "Poor Catherine. I think it was too much for her to take. I think it broke her… her mind, her spirit."

Her father leaned forward and patted her knee comfortingly. "One shock after another can have that effect," he said.

"She was like a cornered animal, papa," said Miss Lily quietly. "I could see it in her eyes: she did not know which way to turn."

"Do not distress yourself, my dear," said Conant, kneeling in front of his daughter and taking her hands in his. "Mrs Moncrieff is being cared for by people who understand her condition and will do all they can to help her recover."

♦

Once he had seen his daughter into his carriage and given Dawson the coachman strict instructions to take her straight home to Portland Place, Conant returned to his dining room.

"What do you think, Sam?" he asked.

"I think Mrs Moncrieff told your daughter only half the story," I said bluntly.

"And so do I," the magistrate agreed. "I certainly didn't want to add to Lily's anxiety about her friend by asking any more questions, but it seems to me that anyone who stood between Mrs Moncrieff and her fortune – her father, Doctor Branscombe and Matthew Dunn – did not last long."

"And the butler," I added. "He told the housekeeper that he thought Dunn was an impostor. And she said it was all too much to be a coincidence."

"Ah, the wisdom of mature ladies," said the magistrate. "We ignore it at our peril." He went to his desk and picked up a sheet of paper. "Mrs Moncrieff has been admitted to an asylum in Sussex – Ticehurst House Hospital. You and I shall go and visit her on Monday. Come to the house... no: I do not want Lily to know. Wait on the corner of New Cavendish Street and I shall pick you up in the chaise. It's a journey of fifty miles or more – we shall be away overnight."

CHAPTER THIRTY-FOUR

Ticehurst House

MONDAY 25TH MAY 1829

Martha had been rather tight-lipped when I told her that I was going away again, but she was pleased to hear that it would be a more comfortable journey for me. I had packed my bag the night before, and as I picked it up she handed me a parcel of food that weighed nearly as much.

"Bread, sliced cold meat, boiled eggs, apples, walnut loaf and four bottles of ale – not all for you," she said, looking me over and brushing imaginary dirt from my shoulder. "You're to share with Mr Conant."

"It's not a school outing, Mar," I said in protest. "And I'm sure Mr Conant will prefer to stop at an inn for his midday meal."

"Then more fool him," she said, "but I am not having you risk your stomach again". She reached up and gave me a fierce kiss before pushing me towards the door. "You take care, Sam, and I'll see you tomorrow evening."

♦

By ten minutes to eight I was standing on the corner of New Cavendish Street, looking northwards along Portland Place. And at eight o'clock exactly, just as the three bells of All Soul's in nearby Langham Place started to ring the hour, Mr Conant's chaise appeared. The postillion pulled it to a halt alongside me; the magistrate leaned over to open the door and I climbed into the seat next to him, pulling the door closed and putting my two bags on the floor at my feet. Conant knocked on the roof and we set off.

"Good morning, Sam," he said. "That bag," he nudged it with his boot, "made an interesting clanking sound as you set it down. Is it one of Mrs Plank's famous packed luncheons? With bottles of ale? I'll give you a crown for it, if it means I don't have to eat a lukewarm bowl of fatty stew at a dreadful inn."

"Your money is safe, sir," I said. "Mrs Plank packed enough for two – four, probably. And maybe even the horse."

We fell silent as the postillion did his best to steer us through the busy streets; the lightness and speed of our carriage would not come into its own until we had a clear road in front of us.

♦

In the event, we turned into the driveway of Ticehurst House at nearly four o'clock.

"It's a far remove from Bethlem," I commented as I looked out at the grand building and the extensive grounds in which it sat.

"Ah well, Ticehurst House has private patients as well, and their families will pay handsomely for their care," said Conant. "I sent word that we would be calling to see Mrs Moncrieff – I hope my message arrived."

We stopped at the entrance to the hospital, which had the appearance of a well-kept country home of three storeys, with elegant proportions, a castellated parapet and plenty of windows. A footman of sorts – a guard, I supposed – opened the chaise door and escorted us into the hallway, off which closed doors led in every direction, and asked us to wait. There was a sweeping staircase ahead of us, but we were separated from it by half-glazed doors, which again were closed.

After a few minutes the footman returned with a woman who had the air of a housekeeper. She held out her hand first to Mr Conant and then to me, introducing herself as Mrs Thurley, matron in charge of the female patients.

"Mr Newington received your letter on Saturday, Mr Conant," she said, "and passed it to me. Ordinarily, of course, our patients can be visited only by their doctor and certain close family members, but I can see that this is a special case."

As she spoke, she led us to one of the doors and lifted the large ring of keys which was hanging at her waist, unlocking the door and ushering us through it before locking it again behind us. We were in a small vestibule; Mrs Thurley walked to the door on the other side of it and again unlocked it, took us through and locked it again.

"Do many of your patients try to escape, Mrs Thurley?" I asked.

"Not many," she said, "but it is as well to be prepared. You will see that we have an enlightened approach to our patients, gentlemen. We do not use any restraints unless absolutely necessary." We were now walking through a long drawing room, furnished in good taste and with light pouring into it through the large windows. "We try to make them feel that they are at home, or at least in a congenial temporary lodging. We provide good food and encourage all sorts of pastimes; many of our ladies do excellent needlework." The matron nodded to an elegant woman who was sitting in an armchair leafing through a magazine, with a small dog curled at her feet. "We have theatrical and musical entertainments, and in the winter months we host weekly dances. All of this calms the mind and tames any wildness. But you must not think that we do not take the medical side of our treatment seriously." We reached the end of the drawing room and Conant held open the door; Mrs Thurley inclined her head in thanks and stopped outside another door, unlocking it and standing aside to let us go in. It was her office, and she sat in the chair behind the desk and indicated that we should take the two seats ranged in front of it. The matron opened the ledger that was on the desk, to a page marked by a ribbon.

"Mrs Moncrieff was brought here on Friday last – the 22nd of May – in a state of confusion, after threatening a woman with violence," she read.

"My daughter," said the magistrate. "Her friend."

"It is often those closest to the patient who suffer the most in such situations," said Mrs Thurley pragmatically, but not unkindly. "As is usual, Mrs Moncrieff will be confined to her room for the first few days, while we observe her condition and decide whether she presents a risk to herself or to others. After that, she will join the other ladies and, as her state of mind improves, she will be given more liberty, to join in our activities and to move about the grounds."

"The grounds are lovely," I said.

"They are the brainchild of Mr Newington," said Mrs Thurley, turning in her chair to look out of the window. "The landscaping was done, oh, more than ten years ago now, by veterans of Waterloo. No matter his injuries, a man can always do something in a garden to heal his body and his mind. You might like to have a walk later, gentlemen: we can offer you a pagoda, various summer-houses, a bowling green and three aviaries. Watching birds is very restful." She turned back to us and smiled. "Several of our patients today choose to spend their time working in the grounds." She glanced down at the ledger again. "And for now, that is all that we at Ticehurst know of Mrs Moncrieff. The supervising physician will visit her regularly, assessing her condition and talking to her – if she wishes to talk." She stood. "Shall we go to see her, gentlemen? It is time for afternoon tea and Mrs Moncrieff may be glad of your company."

We followed the matron through another pair of locked doors into a corridor running along the side wing of the house. Some of the doors on this corridor were ajar, and I glanced into what looked like ladies' bedrooms, each with two windows looking out into the grounds. Mrs Thurley stopped at one point to have a quiet word with a young woman who was dressed in a plain dark dress, with her own ring of keys at her waist. "That is Miss Johnson," she said as the young woman walked ahead of us down the corridor. "She has been trained by

Mr Newington to work with our female patients." The matron halted outside a closed door. "Here we are." She knocked on the door and I heard Mrs Moncrieff call out, "Come in". Mrs Thurley unlocked the door and entered the room; Conant and I followed her.

Mrs Moncrieff was sitting in an armchair, a pot of tea and a plate of sugared biscuits on the low table in front of her.

"You have some visitors, madam," said Mrs Thurley politely.

Mrs Moncrieff smiled in welcome. "Mr Conant," she said, rising to her feet, "and Constable Plank too. How nice to see you. Please, sit down." She indicated the other two armchairs that had been provided – Ticehurst House patients obviously received guests as a matter of course. Miss Johnson appeared with two more cups and put them on the table.

"There now," said Mrs Thurley. "I shall leave you to your conversation. I shall be locking the door, Mrs Moncrieff, but Miss Johnson will be sitting just outside the door and will come if she is called. I shall see you later, gentlemen." And the matron left us, locking the door behind her as she had promised.

Mrs Moncrieff busied herself pouring the tea, handing us our cups and then passing the biscuits. It had been a while since the last of Martha's supplies had run out and I took two.

"How is Lily, Mr Conant?" asked Mrs Moncrieff. "I am mortified to think of the distress I caused her while I was," she waved her hand in the air, "not in my right mind."

"She is recovering, thank you, Mrs Moncrieff," replied the magistrate, "and asked me to pass on her regards." He put his cup of tea onto the table. I did likewise and retrieved my notebook from my coat pocket.

"You have some questions for me," said Mrs Moncrieff.

"Yes, madam, we do," replied the magistrate. "Lily has told us what she knows of your," he paused to find the word, "situation. And we understand the difficulty and delicacy of that situation. For a young woman to go through such an ordeal – you have our sympathies, Mrs Moncrieff."

"Thank you, sir," she said softly.

"However, we do not think that you told Lily everything," he continued. Mrs Moncrieff's eyes narrowed slightly but she said nothing. "There are some parts of your situation that are still unexplained, and Constable Plank and I are of the view that you have those explanations."

"Indeed," said Mrs Moncrieff. "Explanations for what, may I ask?"

Conant glanced at me and I nodded. "Since the arrival of Mr Dunn," he said, "four people connected with your family have died: Mr Harding, your father, Doctor Branscombe and Mr Dunn himself. Constable Plank and I have worked at the police office for many years and during that time we have dealt with all manner of deaths: murders, self-murders, illnesses and accidental deaths. And we have developed an understanding of what is normal and what is not. What has happened in your family is not normal, Mrs Moncrieff."

If we had expected a show of grief or a tearful confession or even an outraged denial, we were to be disappointed. Mrs Moncrieff simply sipped at her tea and said calmly, "I am afraid you will have to elaborate, sir. I am quite at a loss to understand your concerns. My poor dear father died of heart failure, as I understand was the case with Mr Harding. They were both men of mature years – such a thing is not unexpected. The doctor was killed in a rage by Mr Dunn, just as I told you."

"You told us he was your brother," I said.

Mrs Moncrieff gave me a long stare. "That does not change the facts of Doctor Branscombe's death. He tried to blackmail Matthew, Matthew became enraged, and the doctor came off worse."

I wrote down that phrase; it seemed oddly unsympathetic.

"And the death of Mr Dunn?" asked Conant.

"Again, as I said before," answered Mrs Moncrieff, "Matthew found London's attractions too tempting. He drank too much, and after he had killed the doctor, it preyed on his mind. I tried to comfort him, but..." she shrugged.

"You did more than that," the magistrate reminded her. "You protected him. You hid the evidence – the bloody clothes."

"That was a mistake," she said. "And I am paying the price. I may not have gone as far as Matthew – taking reckless chances with my life – but then I have a son to care for. Mrs Godwin and Napier are all very well but they are no substitute for me – his mother. But my mind," again she waved her arm overhead, "my mind has been under great strain."

Conant looked at me. "Nonetheless, it would be reassuring if we could check where you were on the dates of the four deaths," I said, pencil poised above my notebook.

"Of course," she said graciously. She walked across to the small bureau by the window and picked up a small black book.

"Constable Plank will check the dates," said the magistrate smoothly, standing and holding out his hand for the book, "while you and I look out at these wonderful gardens. Is that one of the aviaries we can see?"

Mrs Moncrieff hesitated for a moment but handed the book to Conant who passed it to me before steering our hostess to the window by her elbow. I quickly found the blackmail note that Dunn had allegedly received from the doctor, tucked into the back of my notebook, and compared the hand with that in the appointment book. It was the same.

"Thank you, Mrs Moncrieff," I said, standing to return the book to her.

As he walked back to his seat, the magistrate spoke again. "I hope you won't take offence at this question, Mrs Moncrieff," he said, "but we are obliged to ask it, if we are to understand the whole... situation. Were you and Mr Dunn lovers? Was that part of the arrangement you reached with him?"

"Matthew and I?" she replied with amusement. "Good heavens, no. Matthew Dunn was a weak and foolish man, Mr Conant – as you can tell from his actions, and indeed his reactions. I was willing to go along with his plans while they suited me, but tying myself to him for life did not suit me. I allowed one man to take advantage of me – never again."

"And yet," I said, reaching into my pocket and pulling out a handkerchief, "and yet you kept this memento that your brother bought for you in the Cayman Islands, and that Mr Dunn kindly brought home for you. Mrs Godwin found it in your room and thought you might like to have it as a reminder of home." I unwrapped the broken necklace and picked it up by one end, the broken seed dangling at the bottom of the thread. Mrs Moncrieff had held out her hand to take the necklace from me, but when she spotted the cracked seed she snatched her hand back quickly, so that the necklace fell onto the floor between us.

◆

Mr Conant leaned back in his chair in the parlour of the Bell in Ticehurst. The remains of a passable meal were on the table in front of us; by unspoken agreement we had eaten and drunk our fill without discussing our visit to the asylum. The landlady Mrs May saw that we had finished and sent her daughter over to clear the dishes, leaving the decanter behind. I filled the magistrate's glass and handed it to him and then poured myself a drink.

"You know," said Conant, waving his glass at me for emphasis, "if James Foster had had half the wit and cunning of his sister, he would have made his fortune at that plantation and probably avoided catching the fever."

"She is certainly sure of herself," I said. "Do you think it was all an act, the disordered mind?" I waved my hand above my head in imitation of Mrs Moncrieff and Conant smiled.

"Possibly," he said. "Maybe even probably. But she had not reckoned on anyone taking such an interest, had she? And she had certainly not reckoned on your notebook and its ability to remember everything."

"She knew that necklace was poisonous," I said. "She looked it up in the Kew catalogue and perhaps elsewhere too. She knew enough not to touch the broken seed."

"As did you, I hope," said the magistrate. "Mrs Plank would never forgive me if we poisoned you for a second time with the same necklace."

We both sat silently for a few minutes.

"What will happen to her?" I asked eventually.

"I want to consider it overnight," he replied, "but there seems to me to be enough doubt about each of the deaths to commit her for trial. Mr Harding, a man of previously robust health, had concerns about James Foster and died suddenly. Mr Hugh Foster died while alone in the house with Matthew Dunn, who had entered into a pact with Mrs Moncrieff which meant that they both had much to gain from the old man's death. Doctor Branscombe also doubted the story about James Foster and was beaten to death. Mrs Moncrieff would have us believe that Dunn lost his temper when the doctor tried to blackmail him, but her evidence for this explanation – the note demanding money – was written by her and not by the doctor. And then Matthew Dunn is so overcome with drink and guilt that he steers his curricle into a tree – the very vehicle that only minutes before was seen being driven by a woman. Mrs Moncrieff, his grieving sister, then stands to inherit his recently-acquired fortune. Have I missed anything?"

"The poison?" I suggested.

"Ah yes, the poison, which you were good enough to test for us yourself," he said. "A few grains of that – who knows what effect it might have on an elderly man? Or on a young one already enfeebled by drink?"

"Will you recommend an insanity verdict?" I asked.

"I can mark the papers, certainly," said Conant. "When we are back at Great Marlborough Street tomorrow, we can write our report on today's visit, giving our opinion on Mrs Moncrieff's state of mind. Did you find her to be beyond reason, Sam – with no understanding of her surroundings and unable to tell the difference between right and wrong?" I shook my head. "Nor did I," he agreed. "So a *non compos mentis* verdict is out of the question. On the other hand, do you consider her actions – if it all happened as we suspect – to be those of a sane person?"

"They cannot be," I said.

"I agree," said Conant. "And that is what our report will say. If the judge thinks as we do, he will direct the jury to find a verdict of guilty but insane. And Mrs Moncrieff will be detained in an asylum."

CHAPTER THIRTY-FIVE

Off to America

THURSDAY 28TH MAY 1829

"Now you stand there," I said to Wilson, pointing to a spot at the top of the steps leading to the front office at Great Marlborough Street, "and I'll stand here."

I looked down the street and a coach turned the corner from Poland Street. The coachman raised his whip in greeting and I watched as they drew closer. A group of message lads stood by the railings as usual, ready to run errands for a coin or two.

"Here he comes, Constable Wilson," I said loudly, to catch the attention of the lads, and any passers-by. It worked: several heads looked in our direction.

"Yes, here he is," carolled Wilson in reply.

The coach drew to a halt and Wilson walked down the steps to open its door. Out came two constables – junior colleagues of ours – flanking their prisoner.

"Jem Fanshawe," I said at the top of my voice, and then repeated it for good measure. "Jem Fanshawe. It is good of you to come to speak to us – I look forward to hearing what you have to tell us."

The fellow looked terrified, as well he might. He had been dragged from his bed by two constables, held under their none-too-gentle protection for a couple of hours until his arrival in Great Marlborough Street could be witnessed by as many people as possible, and then welcomed by Wilson and me as an old friend. I glanced at the message lads; most of them were simply gaping at the spectacle, but one was already haring off down the street as fast as his scrawny legs could carry him.

Jem stumbled up the steps, Wilson's hand on his elbow, and we went into the front office.

"Jem Fanshawe," I said to Thomas Neale, dropping all pretence at friendliness. "To answer this warrant from Mr Conant." I passed over the paper that the magistrate had given me the previous evening. "Suspected of fraud and of threatening behaviour."

Jem looked at me in astonishment. "Threatening who?" he asked. And then he stopped short. "Hold on now, don't I know you?"

"That's Constable Plank," said Tom, looking up from the ledger in which he was writing the details I had given him. "And all that matters is that he knows you." He closed the ledger. "Now Constable Plank and Constable Wilson would like to have a few words with you, Mr Fanshawe," he continued. "Don't look so scared, man. This is a respectable police office, and we follow the rules here: it's not Bow Street. The constables won't lay a finger on you." Tom winked at me, and Wilson walked off down the corridor with Fanshawe while I followed them.

In the back office, Wilson pulled out a chair for Fanshawe and took the one next to him. I sat opposite them.

"Now then, Jem," I said pleasantly, "you are in a maze, aren't you."

Fanshawe looked at me sullenly, his shoulders hunched and his nose twitching like a rabbit, but said nothing.

"I imagine you're needing a drink," I said, leaning back in my seat. "Those young constables who turned you out of your bed this morning, I'll wager they didn't offer you so much as a crank to get you started."

Again he was silent, but this time he licked his lips; four hours with no grog in the morning is a trial for any toper.

"If you help us, Jem," I said slyly, "I reckon we can help you. Mr Neale always keeps a nip of brandy about the place, for medicinal purposes."

"What d'ye want to know?" he croaked at last.

"That's better," I said. "Constable Wilson and I want to talk to you about your burial club, and about tontines."

"That's it," he said, pointing a skinny finger at me. "That's who you are. From the Fountain. You're the coachman from Duke Street. Arnold."

"So now you know that it would be a waste of time to deny your involvement," I said. "I have in here," I tapped the notebook that I had put on the table at the start of our conversation, "all the evidence I need for the magistrate. Fraud is a serious business, Jem. Years, we're looking at." I shook my head. "But..." I saw the flicker of hope in his eyes. I leaned forward. "But if you help us to get to whoever is pulling your strings, well then, Constable Wilson and I might be able to put in a good word for you."

Fanshawe shook his head. "I can't," he said. "He'd kill me."

"Ah, well, that is certainly a consideration," I said. I stroked my chin as though thinking. "Constable Wilson," I said, "perhaps you could remind Mr Fanshawe of the unenviable position in which he finds himself. Tell him what we know."

"Certainly, sir," said Wilson, pulling out his own notebook and reading from it. "Jem Fanshawe runs a burial club from the Fountain Inn in Wych Lane. A gang under his command collects subscriptions from members on a fortnightly basis. The club is fraudulent and does not pay out as promised. He also offers a tontine to wealthier targets. He collects these larger investments himself, at the Fountain and elsewhere. The tontine is also suspected of being fraudulent."

"Suspected," interrupted Fanshawe. "For all you know, it might well pay out at the appointed time."

"That's a fair point, Jem," I said. "And I am sure that if you show the magistrate the money that people have paid into the tontine, safely stowed in a bank or in investments, he will take that into account."

Fanshawe sank further into his chair. Wilson continued. "We also know that Jem Fanshawe is the younger brother of George Fanshawe, a Principal Officer operating out of Bow Street." I observed Jem carefully as Wilson said his brother's name, and he flinched minutely. Wilson glanced at me and I nodded. "George Fanshawe is suspected of accepting bribes to protect others from prosecution. He is suspected of threatening behaviour towards a magistrate's constable and that constable's family. And he is suspected of assault to commit mayhem on his former cook."

"He's a vicious one, your brother," I said, shaking my head. "And now he knows you're here, helping us. That was quite a welcome this morning, I thought – I hope you appreciated the effort. And I noticed that one of George's little spies was off to tell him the glad tidings before you were even in the door."

This time Fanshawe whispered it. "He'll kill me."

"I think it's likely," I said. "Which means that we're your only hope, Mr Fanshawe. Tell us what we want to know, and we'll get you out of London this afternoon."

♦

"And where is he now?" asked Conant when I went up to his dining room to tell him what we had discovered.

"Wilson has taken him to the Gloucester Coffee House on Piccadilly," I said, "and will stay with him until the Bristol mail coach sets off at eight o'clock. Jem fancies his chances in America, it seems. Tom Neale gave him the price of an outside ticket and an old coat and hat."

The magistrate nodded. "No family?" he asked.

"I think that's part of the problem for Jem," I said. "He lost his wife and children to disease last year, and took to the grog. And his brother saw his chance."

"Poor fellow," said Conant. "Perhaps a clean start in a new country is what he needs." He walked to the sideboard and held up the decanter. I glanced at the clock and nodded. He poured two glasses and brought them over to the fireplace and we settled into the armchairs. "To a clean start for Jem," he said, lifting his glass.

"Aye," I said, lifting my own before taking a drink. "To give the fellow his due, once he realised there was no way out, he was very helpful."

"With information about his brother?" asked the magistrate. "Enough information for me to submit to the judge?"

"I think so," I replied. "I need to check a few details, but that won't take long. He did tell us something we had not anticipated." I sat forward in my seat. "Most of the subscribers to the club we were concerned with were servants in houses in the area around Villiers Street – Mrs Godwin, for instance. We suspected that there was someone local promoting the burial club, and I should have realised sooner. It was Samuel Harding."

"Harding the butler?" repeated Conant.

I nodded. "Rather than putting in his own money," I explained, "Harding persuaded others to subscribe and he took a cut of their dues. Not much from each one, but every fortnight, it added up." I took another drink. "We were puzzled, Wilson and I, to understand how the person collecting the subscriptions from the house knew not to come once Harding had died – Mrs Godwin said they just disappeared and never came back. It wasn't because they feared a claim on the club, as we thought: it was because they knew already that he had died, and they feared his participation would be uncovered. And it might have been, had we thought to look, but when Mrs Godwin said she thought Mr Harding was looking through his papers for evidence about James Foster, we thought the same.

Perhaps he was actually trying to hide evidence of his involvement with the burial club."

"Shall you tell Mrs Godwin?" asked the magistrate.

"I can't see that it will help," I replied. "She already knows that the burial club was a racket and has resigned herself to the financial loss. I think it would be kinder to let her keep the fond memories she has of Mr Harding."

"You're a soft-hearted fellow, Sam," he said, smiling.

"Aye, well," I said, draining my glass and standing up. "There's enough wickedness and unhappiness in the world without adding to it when there's no need."

CHAPTER THIRTY-SIX

Devious women

THURSDAY 11TH JUNE 1829

I had every intention of attending the trial of Mrs Moncrieff, but I was kept so busy that morning with warrants that by the time I arrived at the Old Bailey the court had been adjourned for lunch. I was looking for a clerk to ask about the verdict when I heard my name being called.

"Constable Plank, over here."

I turned around, and sitting on a bench in the corridor leading to the courtroom was the housekeeper from Villiers Street. She looked dignified and calm in the chaos of her surroundings.

"Mrs Godwin," I said, pushing my way over to her through the stream of people.

"Please," she said, moving along the bench to make room for me.

"It is a warm day," I observed, "particularly in this crush of people."

"I have never been here before," she observed. "I had no idea that so many people would attend."

"I am afraid that people have an appetite for the seamy side of life," I said apologetically. "And a trial involving a lady of Mrs Moncrieff's standing in society would certainly bring out the busybodies. Were you in the courtroom?"

"I was, yes," said Mrs Godwin. "I thought it only right that she should see someone she knew. Miss Napier said I should not come – so did Mary. But it is not Christian, is it, if we abandon people in their hour of need?"

"So I am told," I said. "Did you hear the verdicts, Mrs Godwin?"

♦

I sat quietly and waited for the storm to pass. "I know it's not what we expected, my love," I said, as Martha stood with her arms crossed.

"But not guilty for those deaths, Sam," she said. "Those murders. It makes no sense."

"The judge's job is to listen to the case made by the lawyer and then to tell the jury what he thinks of that case, and where its strengths and weaknesses lie," I said.

"And it was a strong case," she insisted.

"It provided an explanation for everything that happened," I agreed, "but there was no evidence – the judge said as much. The apothecary's opinion was that Mr Harding died of heart failure, and Doctor Branscombe had recorded the same for Mr Foster. Matthew Dunn killed the doctor, as we know, and then apparently himself – perhaps accidentally, perhaps not. And Mrs Godwin said that Mrs Moncrieff had the jury on her side. She dressed the part and wept prettily."

"Did the lawyer tell the court about the deal she made with Dunn?" asked Martha indignantly. "That she agreed to trick her own father?"

"It was all in the papers submitted by Mr Conant," I said. I held out my hand and Martha tutted. "Come here, Mar," I said coaxingly, and after a moment she put her hand in mine. I pulled her onto my lap. "The law is a slippery thing – you of all people know this, after more than twenty years listening to me complain about it."

"That's true," she said grudgingly.

"And what we must do in this case is remember that we did get the right ending, even if the way there was not what we expected. The blackmail note that she wrote proved that Mrs Moncrieff meant for Dunn to be enraged and to confront the doctor – that she encouraged him to commit a crime. Perhaps she didn't know that Dunn would kill the doctor, but she certainly knew that there would be an argument – and she knew that Dunn was, well, a troubled and volatile man. The jury found her guilty of perverting justice, for which she could be sent to prison. But, taking into account the report Mr Conant and I had written, along with the views of the presiding physician at Ticehurst House Hospital, the judge decided that she should be detained in an asylum instead."

Martha sighed. "I suppose you are right, Sam." She leaned her head against mine. "Her poor little boy – what will happen to him, I wonder?"

"I asked Mrs Godwin, and he is to return to Suffolk and live with his uncle and aunt," I replied. "They were always fond of him, she said, even if they didn't care for his mother, and Mr Knight has a mind to take him into the bank when he's older, so he will have a steady profession."

"Won't he inherit the Foster fortune, then?" she asked.

"He will not, no," I said. "Mr Conant and I discussed this very question on our way home from the asylum, and he checked with his lawyer." Martha slid off my lap and into her own chair so that she could listen more carefully. "The father's original will, which he wrote after the death of both of his sons, left the bulk of his fortune to the Quakers, for them to spend on the abolitionist cause. His wife and daughter were provided for, but he did not want to leave so much to Mrs Moncrieff that her money would attract fortune-hunters." I looked at Martha and she nodded. "When – as he thought – his son James returned from the dead, he rewrote his will, leaving his fortune to him."

"Yes," said Martha, "and that was the start of all the trouble: Mrs Moncrieff saw a way to inherit more, and to pass it on to her own son."

"But as it was only Matthew Dunn pretending to be James Foster, the new will cannot be applied – and so we go back to the old will."

Martha nodded. "The Quakers and the abolitionists."

"Exactly," I said.

"After all this nastiness, at least the money will do some good," said Martha, leaning back in her chair.

I nodded. "But four men died," I added.

Martha stood and kissed my cheek. "Take your own medicine, Sam: forget what has happened and remember that we have the right ending." She turned to the stove to check the pot that was bubbling on it; she stirred its contents and took a taste from the spoon. "Nearly done," she said. And then a thought struck her and she turned to me. "You know, Sam. Perhaps if Mrs Moncrieff had told her father that James Foster was Arthur's father, he might have changed his will again. You never know: he was so fond of James and of Arthur, he might have decided to make the best of it. Then she would have achieved what she wanted, without all this fuss."

I stared at her, thinking it through, and then roared with laughter. "Until this minute, Martha Plank, I thought that Catherine Moncrieff was the most devious woman I had ever met. It seems I was wrong. I shall have to keep a very close eye on you."

CHAPTER THIRTY-SEVEN

Rumours
and whispers

MONDAY 15TH JUNE 1829

"There's not much more I can do, Sam," said Thomas Neale, shrugging. "You've all had your turn with this warrant, every constable in the office, and you've none of you run him to ground."

I looked again at the warrant that Mr Conant had issued for the arrest of George Fanshawe on the second of June – nearly a fortnight ago. It was a bit grubby now, having been folded and unfolded many times and, as Tom said, carried in the coat pocket of every constable at Great Marlborough Street. It was hard to imagine how a Principal Officer from Bow Street could just disappear, but that is just what had happened. None of his fellow runners knew where he was, we had checked all of his usual haunts, and his landlady said she had not seen him since the end of May but assumed that he had been sent out of London for work.

As though he had read my thoughts, Tom said, "Maybe he's been hired by someone in the country. Runners don't often turn down work, if the money's right."

"It's possible," I agreed, "but surely one of his colleagues would know about it."

"Not if it's unofficial," said Tom, touching the side of his nose. "You know the Bow Street boys." Our office-keeper was justly proud of the way Great Marlborough Street was run; we kept to the right hours and did our work within the law. Honest constables like to work with honest magistrates, and John Conant attracted the best. In particular, any constable seeking to supplement his pay by taking bribes would soon be out on his ear. Other police offices, however, did not hold themselves to such high standards. "But this has just come in for you," added Tom, reaching under his counter and handing me a note.

I opened it. "Dear Constable Plank," it said. "There is a matter we should discuss, at your earliest convenience. I have instructed the turnkeys to bring you to me whenever you arrive. I remain your servant. John Vickery."

"It's from the keeper at Coldbath," I said to Tom. "He wishes to see me."

"Then we are in luck," said the office-keeper. "There's a cracksman downstairs who's on his way there; if you can accompany him I'll tell young Edwards he's free to attend to other duties, and we'll kill two birds with one stone. Save your poor old feet, too."

♦

The coach stopped outside the entrance to the prison on Dorrington Street, the horses sweating and steaming in the noonday sun. My young prisoner had been silent during the journey, staring out of the window, but his composure cracked a little as he looked up at the grey walls of Coldbath.

"My brother was in here," he said. "On the wheels."

"Then you were a fool to follow him," I said.

I rapped loudly on the door and heard the bolt being pulled back. A turnkey looked around the door. "Constable Plank," I said, "with a prisoner from Great Marlborough Street." I handed the warrant to the turnkey and he read it.

"Name?" he growled at the prisoner.

"George Platt," said the young cracksman.

The turnkey opened the door wider and stood to one side. "Come in, Platt, and stand over there." He pointed and then started to close the door again. I put my hand against it.

"And Mr Vickery has asked to see me," I said.

The turnkey frowned a little and then his face cleared. "Plank, you said?" I nodded. "That's right. In you come, constable. You can wait in the gatehouse while I deal with him." He jerked his head at Platt, who was gazing about him and looking none too pleased at what he saw. "I'll find out where Mr Vickery is and we'll take you to him."

♦

John Vickery was in the chapel, and the turnkey led me there through a long gallery, with doors to the cells ranged along both sides of it. Some cells were open, their occupants obviously engaged in activities elsewhere, while others were closed.

"Constable Plank," said Vickery, standing as we walked into the chapel and holding out his hand. "You find me in a moment of contemplation." He indicated that I should take a seat in the pew next to him. "Thank you, Hobbs," he said to the turnkey, who nodded and left us.

I looked about me. The chapel was indeed a peaceful place. It was perfectly square, with a high ceiling, and light flooded in through the large windows near the top of the tall walls. Vickery looked up as well.

"As the windows are so high," he said, pointing upwards, "they do not need to be barred. I think it is good for our prisoners to be reminded of windows without bars, of clear light. It gives them something to work towards." He looked at me. "And now to our business, constable. When you visited Coldbath some months ago, in the spring, you asked about George Fanshawe."

"I did," I said.

"I did not know it at the time, but it appears that Mr Fanshawe was rather unkind to our cook Bertha Longstowe when she worked for him." He paused and seemed to make a decision. "To be frank, constable, he assaulted her so cruelly that her injuries left her deaf."

"I know," I said.

"How?" asked the keeper. "Is that why you were asking about Fanshawe?"

"No, that was a coincidence," I said. "When we left your house that day, your daughter came after us and told us the whole story. She wanted us to know that George Fanshawe was a dangerous man – a brute."

Vickery sighed. "Others obviously thought so too," he said. He turned to face me. "It seems that Bertha has friends among the prisoners here. That is not unusual: some of them are here for a year or more, and of course London, for all its size, still has something of the village about it – even the turnkeys come to me from time to time to say that they've just put a cousin or a neighbour into a cell."

I thought of young Platt and his brother, and nodded.

Vickery continued. "Prisons are full of rumours, as you know. And word reached my ears yesterday that steps had been taken to make sure that George Fanshawe could never touch Bertha again. It was the first I had heard of any difficulty between the two of them and so I asked Bertha about it. Well, I wrote down my questions and we managed."

"When you say that word reached your ears…" I said.

"A whisper that had passed through many hands," he said. "No other names were mentioned – just Fanshawe and Bertha."

"Does Bertha know who might be the source of the rumour?" I asked.

"If she does, she isn't saying," he replied. "Anyway, I made my own enquiries and it seems that no-one has seen George Fanshawe for a while. And then I remembered that you had been asking about him, and I wondered whether you might know more."

I shook my head. "I know what you know: that Fanshawe has disappeared." I paused. "Well, it would explain his silence. And from what I know, he ran with a rough crowd – and a runner makes plenty of enemies. Hearing about Bertha's suffering may have been the last straw for someone who thought the world would be a better place without Mr Fanshawe. Did the rumour suggest what had happened, or where he ended up?"

"Forgive my coarseness, constable," said Vickery with a smile, "but the rumour was that he had gone where all turds belong."

"Dumped in a cesspit somewhere, then," I suggested.

"Aye," said the keeper. "And not much mourned, I imagine. I understand from Bertha that he was not a family man, preferring to enjoy the favours of many ladies."

"He had a brother," I said, "but I don't think he will miss George very much." And I thought of Jem, probably halfway to America by now, still running from a man who could never hurt him again.

CHAPTER THIRTY-EIGHT

Finding rogues

FRIDAY 19TH JUNE 1829

I was sitting in the back office reading the latest issue of the *Police Gazette* when Wilson opened the door and looked in at me. I assumed he was collecting me to walk home – he, Alice and George were to spend the evening with us – but he shook his head.

"Mr Conant has asked for us upstairs," he said.

"You and me?" I asked, standing and reaching for my coat.

"Everyone," replied Wilson, already on his way along the corridor.

And indeed, even Tom Neale was coming out from behind his counter as I reached the front office.

"What's this all about, Tom?" I asked.

"I'm no wiser than you," he said, holding the door open for me. I waited on the outside steps as he locked up behind us. Thin Billy was standing at the door of the staircase leading up to the magistrate's rooms and nodded as we passed.

In the magistrates' dining room were all the people Tom had been able to round up at – I glanced at the clock on the mantelpiece – a quarter to five. Apart from Mr Conant there was one other magistrate – Mr Dyer – and five constables, including Wilson and me. The gaoler George Cooper stood next to me, looking uneasy at being upstairs. And ranged in a row were the courtroom clerks, the two junior clerks flanking the senior, all three quiet and attentive in their neat black coats.

Mr Conant stood by his desk, holding a piece of paper. "I thought you would like to know, before you read about it in the newspapers, that today the Act for Improving the Police In and Near the Metropolis received Royal Assent. I know that most of you will have been following this development with close interest, since the Commons enquiry last year recommended the foundation of a police force for London. The new force – which I understand we are to call the Metropolitan Police – will come under the control of Mr Peel, as Home Secretary, and the new legislation provides for two commissioners."

"Mr Harmer was right," I said quietly to Wilson.

"The metropolitan police district," continued Conant, "is defined as..." he put on his spectacles and consulted the paper in his hand, "Westminster, and parts of Middlesex,

Surrey and Kent. The city will retain its own Watch." He took off his spectacles again and looked around the room. "Our days are numbered, gentlemen," he said.

"How many days exactly, Conant?" asked Mr Dyer. "Does it say when this new, what was it, Metropolitan Police will be formed?"

"I understand," replied Conant, "that the hope is to pass the Act into law within a month, and then to have the new force in place by the end of the year."

"Impossible!" barked Dyer.

"Perhaps," said Conant, but I could tell that he disagreed. "My father would be delighted." He gestured at the portrait of Nathaniel Conant that stared down at us from over the fireplace. "As some of you know, he was instrumental in persuading the government to set up our police offices nearly forty years ago, and ten years ago he gave evidence to a parliamentary committee, pointing out the benefits of a unified approach to law enforcement in London. Since his day London has grown quickly, and continues to do so, and we have all seen our workloads increase." The senior clerk nodded. "Of course," continued Conant, "not everything will change. The courtroom will remain here, as will its magistrates." He looked at me and smiled sadly. "But the constables will not. The magistrate's constable will be consigned to history, like the Charlie and the thief-taker."

Wilson cleared his throat and lifted his hand to catch Conant's attention.

"Yes, Constable Wilson?" asked the magistrate.

"Do you advise us – the constables – to join the new force, sir?" he asked. "Will we... fit in, do you think?"

"An excellent question, constable," replied Conant, "and one that has been much on my mind lately. It would be different for you, to belong to a much larger institution: the pay will be better, I imagine, but the rules will be stricter too. There will be more opportunities for advancement in a larger force, and perhaps a greater variety of work, both of which I know are important to you younger fellows. What I can promise is this: if any of you wishes to apply to join the new force, you will take with you my heartiest recommendation."

Wilson was subdued on the way home and made only the smallest protest when I steered him into the George and Dragon. Even the arrival of our ale did little to cheer him and he took a long drink and then stared miserably into his tankard.

"What is it, lad?" I asked.

He shrugged.

"If you go home with a face like that," I said, "you know Mrs Plank will notice. She'll not let you sit quietly, so you may as well talk about it now."

He didn't look up but he did smile. "It's this new police force," he said eventually. "I know you think I should sign up."

"I do," I said. "You heard Mr Conant: the pay will be good and you'll soon rise up the ranks."

Wilson looked at me. "The same's true for you, but you don't want to join."

"Think about it, lad," I said. "You're a whipper snapper, with a family to support. I'm nearly fifty years old and there's only me and Mrs Plank. I'm too set in my ways to work for a new master."

"I've worked with you since I started as a constable," said Wilson. "Maybe I'm too set in my ways as well."

"A complete change, then," I suggested. "You could become a jarvey, or open a shop, or take up barbering." I laughed at the horrified look on his face. "You're a constable to your marrow, Wilson – just as I am. Let them call you a 'police officer' if they want to, but as you once told me yourself, the job will be the same: you'll be finding rogues and bringing them to justice." I lifted my tankard and drained it. "And I'm not going anywhere, am I? I daresay this won't be the last drink we share in here."

◆

Martha sniffed as she helped me off with my coat but said nothing; she's not keen on taverns but as the daughter of a toper she can tell the difference between a quick drink and a skinful. Alice was sitting at the table with George on her knee and Wilson went over to them, squeezing Alice's shoulder and bending to kiss his son on the top of his head. George gurgled happily and held out his chubby fists. Wilson took the baby from Alice and lifted him high, nuzzling his tummy. George squealed and Alice laughed.

"A quick wash, if you please, gentlemen," said Martha, "and then we can eat."

♦

I did wonder whether Wilson might mention our news during the meal but even a new police force cannot get between a true trencherman and his plate. Once we had finished, Martha shooed the four of us into the sitting room. I took one of the armchairs and Wilson brought over an upright chair while Alice settled on the rug with George, lying him on his back and gently tickling his tummy. He wriggled for a minute and then closed his eyes and fell asleep; Alice leaned back against Wilson's legs.

Martha came in and held out a plate of Prince of Wales biscuits to Wilson. "Look what I found hidden in the cupboard," she said. "In case you're still peckish."

We each took one of the biscuits – Wilson eating his in two bites, Alice nibbling the edges of her to make it last – and Martha put the plate on the hearth before sitting in her own armchair.

"We had some news today," I said. Alice looked up at me, concern on her face. "Good news," I said quickly. "Mr Conant said that there is going to be a new police force. Instead of the police offices that we have now, there will be one police force for London. By the end of the year, he thought."

"So you're being put out to pasture at last, Samuel Plank," said Martha.

Alice looked alarmed. "Is that right?" she asked. "William too?"

Wilson put a reassuring hand on her shoulder. "I'm going to apply to join the new force," he said. "Mr Conant said he will give me a recommendation."

"They'd be fools to turn you down, William," said Martha. "He'd sooner die than admit it, but Sam thinks you're a fine constable. One of the best."

Wilson flushed and Alice looked proudly up at him. "So you are, Will," she said. "Shall we tell them our news now?" she asked him, and he nodded. "There's to be a baby," she said, putting her hand to her stomach. "A little brother or sister for Georgie."

♦

"Should I be worried about your acting abilities, Mrs Plank?" I said, sitting in bed and watching Martha's hands play over her hair as she searched for and removed the pins that secured her wayward curls.

"What nonsense are you talking now, Sam?" she asked, shaking her hair loose. It was flashed through with silver these days, but that only made her all the more precious to me.

I lifted up the bedcovers and she slid in next to me. "When Alice told us about the baby, no-one would have guessed that you already knew," I said. "With that talent for concealment, what else are you hiding from me?"

"My secret lover, you mean?" she asked.

"That's the fellow," I said, pulling her into the crook of my arm and kissing the top of her head. "You'll have to give him his marching orders, once we've closed up the police office and I'm here with you all the time. We'd get in each other's way, he and I, both wanting the best armchair."

Martha was quiet, but I could tell that she was thinking. She turned to look up at me. "What will you do, Sam? You're not one to sit at home all day."

"Wilson once suggested that they might need old codgers like me to train the new recruits," I said. "Some of them will come from the police offices and will know what they're about, but if it's to be a much larger force, they will have to take on lads who've never done anything like it before."

"Well, you've turned Wilson into a good constable – and a good man," said my wife.

"Flatterer," I said. "It won't happen for a while – setting up the new force will take months. There's still plenty for me to do before then."

Martha's eyes had been fluttering closed as she drifted off to sleep, but they opened again when I said this.

"What do you mean, Sam?" she asked seriously.

"George Fanshawe," I said.

"But he's dead," she protested.

"Almost certainly," I agreed, "and good riddance. But he's not the end of it, Mar. There's another man out there, more powerful, running his own force – his own army of criminals. I know who he is – I've known him for years. And I'm not going to leave him to a gang of raw recruits, no matter how fancy their name."

"Tomorrow, Sam," said Martha sleepily, reaching up to stroke my face. "He'll be there tomorrow."

Glossary

Bawd – pimp, procurer, someone who seeks clients for a prostitute (could be used for either gender, but male bawds were sometimes called "cock bawds" to make it clear)

Bird-wit – a foolish, unthinking person

Bethlem – Bethlem hospital (sometimes called Bedlam) was founded in London in 1247 and soon started to specialise in treating illnesses of the mind; it continues this work today, as Bethlem Royal Hospital in Bromley in Kent

Budget – wallet

Buffle-headed – stupid and dull, confused

Bye-blow – an illegitimate child

Cast up one's accounts – to vomit

Chaise – an enclosed, four-wheeled, small carriage seating up to three people (snugly) on one forward-facing seat – it is driven by a postillion mounted on one of the two horses

Charlie – before Sam's day, part of London's response to crime was a force of paid night-watchmen, instituted in the reign of Charles II and thus called Charlies – althhough as they were often elderly and frequently fell asleep on duty, they were not a serious deterrent force

Cork-brained – simple, foolish, unthinking

Cracksman – a house-breaker, a burglar

Crank – gin and water

Curricle – a light, open, two-wheeled carriage pulled by two horses side-by-side – a sports car of its day

Deep file – a person who has a long history of fraud is known as an old file, while someone who is both experienced at fraud and extremely cunning is a deep file, so an expert fraudster

Dropsy – the old medical word for an oedema (a swelling caused by fluid retention)

Guzzle guts – someone who is fond of their drink

Hackney coach – a vehicle for hire, with four wheels, two horses and six seats

Hazard – a game played with two dice and often seen in gambling houses – craps is a modern simplification of hazard

Helpmeet – a helpful companion or partner, particularly a spouse

In a maze – in a pickle, in a mess, in a lot of trouble

In the suds – in trouble, in a disagreeable situation

Jarvey – the driver of a hackney coach, see also *Hackney coach*

Ladybird – a woman of easy virtue, a prostitute

Lady of easy virtue – prostitute

Magpie – in a fraudulent scheme of any sort, a magpie spots the target (as the bird spies shiny objects) and then talks at them until they succumb to the fraud, so they are the ones with the sales patter

Mayhem – a serious type of assault, involving violently inflicting bodily injury on a person

Maze – see *In a maze*

Mrs Siddons – Sarah Siddons was the foremost actress of the Georgian era, reigning supreme in Drury Lane from about 1785 until her retirement from the stage in 1812

Nibbler – a pilferer, a petty thief

Nose – a criminal who informs or turns King's evidence in hope of a lighter sentence

Old file – a person who has a long history of fraud is known as an old file, see also *Deep file*

Old Lady – short for "the Old Lady of Threadneedle Street", a nickname for the Bank of England thanks to a James Gillray caricature published in 1797. At the time there was a financial crisis; the Bank had been forced to make large loans to the government to finance the war against France and the cartoon – titled "Political Ravishment, or the Old Lady of Threadneedle-Street in Danger!" – shows an elderly woman (representing the Bank) dressed in banknotes and sitting on a strong-box while Prime Minister William Pitt makes indecent advances to her to get access to the strong-box.

Poltroon – a coward, a rascal, a scoundrel, and a favourite nineteenth century insult

Postillion – the driver of a chaise, who sits on one of the two horses (the left one or the rear one, depending on how they are arranged), see also *Chaise*

Reticule – a lady's small bag

Rig – fraud or racket

Rookery – city slum area frequented by criminals and prostitutes

Rout – a crowded "standing and drinking" party, rather like a modern cocktail party

Sop – a bribe, short for "a sop for Cerberus", the multi-headed dog that guards the gates of the Underworld to prevent the dead from leaving

Square toes – an old man, as they are fond of wearing comfortable shoes with room around the toes

Stir Up Sunday – the unofficial start of the Christmas season was the Sunday before Advent (i.e. the fourth Sunday before Christmas) – on this day the family would gather to make the Christmas pudding, which would need to age before eating. The name comes not from stirring up the pudding, but because the opening words of the main prayer in the Book of Common Prayer for that day are "Stir up, we beseech thee, O Lord, the wills of thy faithful people...".

Suds – see *In the suds*

Thief-taker – in the late seventeenth century, concern about high levels of crime in London led the government to offer substantial rewards for apprehending and convicting those guilty of serious crimes such as highway robbery and coining. Individual victims of crime then started offering rewards for the return of their stolen goods. The thief-taker was born, using his knowledge of the criminal underworld to profit from the rewards that were widely advertised in the newspapers. The scope for abuse – such as sharing rewards with the criminals, framing innocent people or collecting protection money from criminals – was great.

Toper – a drunkard

Trencherman – a hearty eater, from the word *trencher*, which is a flat piece of wood on which a meal was served in mediaeval times

Thank you for reading this book. If you liked what you read, please would you leave a short review on the site where you purchased it, or recommend it to others? Reviews and recommendations are not only the highest compliment you can pay to an author; they also help other readers to make more informed choices about purchasing books.

ABOUT THE AUTHOR

Susan Grossey graduated from Cambridge University in 1987 and since then has made her living from crime. She advises financial institutions and others on money laundering – how to spot criminal money, and what to do about it. She has written many non-fiction books on the subject of money laundering, as well as contributing monthly articles to the leading trade magazine and maintaining a popular anti-money laundering blog.

Her first work of fiction was the inaugural book in the Sam Plank series, "Fatal Forgery". "The Man in the Canary Waistcoat" was her second novel, "Worm in the Blossom" her third, "Portraits of Pretence" her fourth, "Faith, Hope and Trickery" her fifth, and now "Heir Apparent" is her sixth. One more Sam Plank mystery is planned, to complete the series of seven.

She is also brewing a separate series of five novels, again set in the 1820s, but this time with a university constable in Cambridge at the heart of them. He might well be called Gregory.

48813288R00223

Printed in Poland
by Amazon Fulfillment
Poland Sp. z o.o., Wrocław